MICHA
NICI

SCARLET'S SECRET

Copyright © 2020 by Michael Nick

All rights reserved. No part of this book may be reproduced, scanned, or distributed in any printed or electronic form without permission. Please do not participate in or encourage piracy of copyrighted materials in violation of the author's rights.

Purchase only authorized editions.

Library of Congress Cataloging in Publication Data
Nick, Michael

1. Fiction – Suspense /Thriller
2. Fiction – Women's Fiction

ISBN: 9781655083990

Cover photo: iStock by Getty "Finger on Lips"
Story advisor: Michelle Nick
Story advisor and editor: Jennifer Clement

This book is a work of fiction. Names, characters, places, and incidents either are the product of the author's imagination or are used factiously, and any resemblance to actual persons, living or dead, business, companies, events, or locales is entirely coincidental.

To the love of my life Michelle, you make everything possible with your passion and love. This book is dedicated to you.

ONE

Greg and Carol Fletcher live in an old neighborhood in Queens. At this time of night, the street was dark and deserted. Not many of the streetlights were in working order because kids throw rocks at them for sport. Large oak trees were hanging over the street, making it even more ominous.

John Mancini had to park his Escalade in front of the neighbor's house. Because Greg had his pickup truck parked in front of his house, and his wife Carol parked her new Mustang in front of that.

Fletcher's house was a two-story brick, Tudor. Facing the street on the main floor was the den on the left and the living room on the right. The picture window in the living room had the curtains slightly open. On the second floor, the master bedroom window was on the left, and a spare bedroom on the right. All the windows on the second floor were dark. At this time at night, most of the houses in the neighborhood were dark too.

John pushed the button to turn off the ignition and made a point to turn off the headlights, so they didn't shine after the engine was shut down.

"Stay put," John said to his wife, Charlotte, "Go ahead and sleep; I'll only be a few minutes."

Charlotte was still annoyed that they had to drive out to queens at midnight after attending the theater in Manhattan. "Can you leave the car running, so I don't get cold, and I want to listen to the radio?" Charlotte asked.

"Yeah but keep the headlights off. I don't want to disturb their neighbors. Just go to sleep, I won't be long." John pushed the ignition button again to turn the SUV back on and checked to make sure he still had the lights off. He climbed out into the street and walked around the back of the vehicle. He paused for a moment, then continued walking up the sidewalk toward the house. John glanced through the living room curtains and then kept moving toward the front door. Standing on the front step, he reached for the doorknob and checked to see if it was unlocked. It was not. He pressed the doorbell, and the bedroom light came on upstairs, followed by the stairway light. A few moments later, Carol answered the door in her robe and invited John inside. Charlotte thought to herself, *Carol's up late, maybe I should go in and say hello.* She reached over and pushed the button to turn off the car and opened the door to climb out of the vehicle.

As Charlotte approached the house, she glanced through the curtain. "What the hell!" Charlotte said to no one in particular. She couldn't believe her eyes. Greg and Carol were on their knees with their hands raised above their heads, and John had a gun pointed at Greg's head. Charlotte could see Carol was sobbing and saying something. Then suddenly, the back of Greg's head exploded, and he fell backward. Blood and brain matter splattered all over Carol's face. "Oh, my God! Oh, my God!" Carol began to scream and cry harder. John calmly said something to her, and then he shot her in the middle of the chest. "Noooo, oh my God!" Carol's eyes grew large, and she grabbed her chest, her robe, and nightgown filled with blood. Stunned, Carol pulled her bloody hands in front of her face, and then she fell forward. John ignored her and turned to walk back toward the kitchen.

Shocked and horrified, Charlotte didn't know what to do. Her knees felt weak, and her body was shaking as she stood frozen in the moment. Then, she turned and ran back to the Escalade. Charlotte crawled into the front seat and started screaming and crying. "Oh, my God! What should I do? Holy shit!" Thankfully, John didn't come back to the car right away, so she had time to calm herself and think about what had just happened and what to do. About twenty minutes later, John calmly walked out the front door and down the sidewalk toward the car as if nothing happened. Charlotte immediately thought, o*h my God, did he see me out the window? Is he going to kill me next? What should I do?*

John climbed back into the SUV, not showing any sign of regret or remorse. He asked why the car wasn't running. Charlotte said, "I got too warm, and the radio was bugging me. It was easier to push the off button than to mess with all your controls." *Does he know? Did he see me outside? I'm so scared.*

John pushed the button to start the Escalade, put the shifter in drive, and slowly moved down Greg and Carol's street for about half a block with the lights still off.

"John, you need to turn the lights on," Charlotte said.

"Oh yeah, I forgot." *I doubt it.*

They drove in silence all the way home, just listening to the radio. Charlotte curled up in her seat and pretended to be asleep. Occasionally, she could hear John humming to a song he may have recognized on the radio. *Sick!*

Charlotte wanted to scream and cry out but held it back as best she could. Charlotte's mind kept bouncing between thoughts. *What the hell just happened? Did I have a bad dream? What should I do? Should I call the police? My God, who is this man? I don't know the man I'm married too! I thought I knew him. It can't be true, and I couldn't have just seen him kill our friends in cold blood.*

When they finally got home, John parked in their garage. They exited the Escalade and walked into the house. John casually mentioned he needed to run some errands early the next day. *Why did he tell me that? Is he going to go back to Carol's and hide the bodies? What should I do?*

As Charlotte headed toward the stairs, she turned and said, "I'm going to bed; be sure to turn on the alarm."

"Yeah, goodnight, babe. I'm going to check email quickly, and then I'll be up." He paused and then turned back toward Charlotte and said, "Oh, hey?"

Charlotte stopped on the bottom step, thinking he was going to tell her what he had done, or that he saw her outside and to keep her mouth shut.

"I enjoyed the play. Thanks for letting me tag along. I'll be up in a minute." He smiled and turned to walk toward his office while Charlotte slowly walked upstairs to the bathroom to wash her face with cold water. Every time she closed her eyes, all she could see was the image of Greg's head exploding and Carol's blood-splattered face with the expression of surprise when he shot her in the chest.

Charlotte looked in the mirror and began to cry again. Her hands were shaking, and she couldn't stop sobbing. *I can't believe I'm married to a killer. I can't believe I saw him kill Greg and Carol. I know, if John finds out what I saw, he'll kill me next. What should I do? Who can I tell what I saw? I can't call the police, he's here, and it's my word against his. Who is this man I married?*

TWO

Charlotte and John Mancini have been married just over a year. John owns a company that builds and maintains websites and e-commerce sites for major corporations. His company is a cover for his real job. He is an independent contractor or hitman for crime families around the country. Charlotte had no idea what John really does for a living. As one of the best hitmen in the world, John hides in plain sight. John is a handsome man. He's thirty years old and stands over six feet tall, with thick black hair combed to the side. His dark complexion sets off his intense emerald eyes. John works out every day, either at the gym lifting weights or running four or five miles around his neighborhood. He's almost always in pressed blue jeans, a crisp casual button-down Polo shirt, and a sport coat.

The hit he performed tonight was a last-minute request by a man named Big Tony Gambucci. Big Tony is the boss of the largest crime family in New York. He was adamant about John taking care of the Fletcher's tonight. Under normal circumstances, John would refuse to do any job at the spur of the moment. Big Tony, however, is very persuasive, and John finally agreed after talking with him from the theater.

John and Charlotte were at the theater in Manhattan when the call came in. It was intermission, and they were up by the bar ordering drinks. Charlotte overheard John say to someone named Tony on the phone, "He couldn't do it tonight because he was with his wife." This Tony person was persistent, and John finally acquiesced.

John was pacing back and forth in his home office, getting ready to dial Big Tony's number. It was essential to keep him informed of how the hit went down. Unlike most organized crime bosses, Big Tony likes details. He wants to know everything about a job after it was done.

"Yeah?" Tony answered.

"Ton? It's done."

"It's done?"

"Yeah, I made it look like a robbery. I trashed the place and took Fletcher's wallet, some jewelry, and all the money I could find in the house."

"Good, was he getting ready to run?"

"Probably, his truck and his old lady's car were parked on the street, not in their garage. They had some luggage out in their bedroom, but nothing in it yet."

"How much money did you find?"

"A couple of grand, how much did he skim?"

"Too much, keep the money, buy your old lady something nice. Did he deny he stole from me?"

"It didn't come up in the conversation. In fact, the asshole kept asking me why I was there to kill him."

"What did you tell him?"

"What I tell everyone. You pissed off the wrong guy, and that guy paid me to kill you."

"No, shit?"

"Yeah, it's not like he's Mother Theresa," John said.

"I guess that's how you sleep at night, John."

"I sleep fine, Tony. Somebody has to remove the scum from the earth. Why not me? Capitalism at its best, right? I get paid to clean up messes."

"Okay, John, look the world's a better place without that piece of shit. Nobody skims from me and gets away with it. Nobody! Thanks for doing this for me tonight. Did your old lady see or hear anything?"

"No, she pretty much slept in the car. I turned the heat up and put on some soft music. I don't think she had a clue."

"Good, the bastard was going to run, I needed this done right away. Thanks, I know you don't work this way."

"Yeah, it was tricky. In the end, Charlotte will just think it was a robbery gone bad when I tell her about it tomorrow night."

"Good. Also, I already transferred the money to your offshore account."

"Great, thanks, Tony." The line went dead.

John sat down at his desk and reflected on the dozens of people he's killed over the years. He believed he was doing the public a service by killing people for crime families. John lived by his own personal code that included the fact that he only killed people who deserved it. Carol was merely collateral damage; she married the wrong guy and, by association, deserved what she got. The guy she married screwed up and got himself killed for it. It didn't bother John in the least that he killed an innocent woman. He believed everyone he's killed made the world a better place.

THREE

Charlotte was still in the bathroom when John came up to bed. She rewashed her face with cold water and tried to calm herself. *How was it that he went about his business acting as if nothing happened? Who is this man? I'm so stupid that I didn't know.*

Charlotte put on a pair of pajamas, brushed her teeth and hair, and quietly walked back into the bedroom. John appeared to already be asleep. He had his back turned away from her side of the bed. She crawled in under the sheets next to a man she didn't know, next to a cold-blooded killer. *How does this man sleep at night?*

The next morning, after a restless night of little or no sleep, Charlotte woke up and John was gone. For a moment, she thought she dreamt the whole ordeal from last night. But reality set in and she knew it wasn't so, Charlotte saw her husband murder two people in cold blood, and not blink an eye. *The fact is, he has no conscience.*

Charlotte felt she had to pull herself together and go to work. She crawled out of bed and headed to the bathroom to take a hot shower. The warm, steaming water felt good against her face and body. She was hoping to wash away all the fear from the night before. It didn't work. When she turned off the water, she heard John in the bedroom talking on the phone. His conversation sounded like any other morning, soft- spoken and calm. He didn't act or sound like a man who killed two people the night before. It was just business as usual for John. *How does he do it? Is he a psychopath?*

Charlotte stayed in the bathroom and listened to John trying to convince the person on the other end of the line that he had the resources to do their project. It sounded like a job to program a new website or something.

After a couple of minutes, the room went silent. John must have gotten what he needed and left. Charlotte opened the door and peeked around the corner to make sure she was alone, and quietly walked to the closet naked to get dressed. Her plan was to avoid talking to John or seeing him this morning. She thought if she could get dressed and yell goodbye on her way out the door, she could avoid any contact with him at all this morning. Charlotte quickly slipped on some underwear, a pair of jeans, and a light sweater. She grabbed a pair of shoes to carry downstairs and used a hair tie to put her wet hair into a ponytail. Her plan seemed to work. Charlotte quietly walked down the stairs and yelled, "Bye, honey, I'm running late."

She heard John yell back, "Bye. Love you!"

She thought to herself, *seriously? How can you love someone if you have it in you to take a life? Hell, what did Carol do to deserve getting killed like that?* She backed out of the garage as quickly as she could without screeching the tires.

Charlotte didn't want to go to work but had nowhere else to go. She worked in a flower shop putting together centerpieces for corporate events. Her job was mostly calming and therapeutic, but today will no doubt be different. Charlotte considered herself an artist. For major events where the company needed something special, Charlotte would sketch out a design before produceing it. She believed it was fulfilling to see the client's reaction when a drawing came to life. She drove to the parking lot of the strip mall where the store was located and parked her car out front. Before going to work, Charlotte stopped off at the coffee shop next to the store.

"Hi Mary, can I have a large extra-strong cup to go?"

"Sure, Charlotte, bagel too? Rough night?"

"No, thanks, and you have no idea."

"What's up? Anything I can do?" *I wish.*

"No, just a personal thing with John. I'm fine. I just need coffee, thank you."

"Coming right up. Be sure to tell that husband of yours hello for me. He's so nice when he comes in." *If you only knew, he's really a cold-blooded killer.*

Charlotte paid for the coffee and walked to the flower shop to start working on an upcoming event at the Met. The owners of the flower shop, Conner, and Mark were already hard at work, sorting a shipment of flowers. After saying hello, Charlotte walked to the back of the store and started to review her sketches of the centerpieces, she needed to create today. After reviewing her drawings, she determined what flowers and foliage were necessary to build the centerpieces for the tables.

Charlotte was meticulous when it came to centerpiece design. After drawing a picture, Charlotte selected the best flowers and then arranged for them to fit the occasion. She would tell people it was the OCD in her. It was essential to have the right flower for the occasion, arranged in a way that made people feel something when they look at it for the first time. She wanted her designs to come alive and drive emotions.

Charlotte tried to focus on the task at hand but couldn't. The image of Greg's head exploding, and the look on Carol's blood-stained face kept creeping into her head. Charlotte didn't realize tears were seeping from her eyes. She finally stopped staring at the sketches, and whispered to herself, "I need to talk to someone, but who? Should I call the police, the FBI, or just call 911? I don't know what to do." *Hold it together, Charlotte.*

The coffee gave her a jolt and maybe even some clarity and courage. At noon Charlotte walked to the front of the store and told Conner she didn't feel well and was going home. She climbed back into her car and programmed Google Maps on her cell phone to find the FBI office in New York City.

FOUR

Charlotte drove in a daze to the FBI office. Her mind wandered back and forth from Carol's face covered in blood and brain matter to Greg's head exploding. Fear and anxiety overwhelmed Charlotte, and her eyes once again filled with tears. *How could I not know, how could I not see it? John couldn't be that person. Am I his next victim? Is he going to kill me?*

It took about forty-five minutes to get into lower Manhattan. When she arrived, there was a parking lot that had openings right up the block from the FBI office. Once Charlotte parked, she sat in the car for a while and continued crying. She looked at herself in the rearview mirror, and her mind wandered. *Am I really doing this? Suck it up, Charlotte; you need to talk to someone. Your friends died in front of you.* Finally, she wiped her eyes, put on a little makeup, and walked up the street to the FBI office.

When Charlotte entered the lobby, there were two receptionists at the information desk. The one on the left was on the phone, and the one on the right smiled and asked if she could help.

"Hi, can you direct me to someone in the FBI who handles Queens?" Charlotte asked.

"May I ask what's this about?"

"A murder, well actually two murders. I witnessed them last night." Looking around the lobby to see if anyone else was listening, she thought, *I can't believe I said that out loud. Stop shaking, Charlotte, you can do this. You owe it to Carol and Greg. When Charlotte noticed her hands shaking,* she pulled them below the counter and out of sight, so the receptionist couldn't see them.

The receptionist said, "One moment, please." Then she punched in a couple of numbers on her phone board and relayed the message to someone at the other end of the line.

"Miss, agent Patterson will be right with you. Please take a seat over there." Pointing to a seating area across from the receptionist's desk by the windows facing lower Manhattan.

Charlotte walked over to the seating area, but couldn't sit still, so she rose from the seat and started pacing around the chairs until a man approached. He was about thirty-five years old, tall, six-five or more, his dark hair was short and perfectly styled, bright white teeth, brown eyes, no facial hair, and he walked with a swagger. Like most agents in the FBI, he wore a dark suit and tie. The bulge in his jacket indicated he had a gun in a shoulder holster.

The man displayed his badge and identification, then reached out to shake Charlotte's hand and said, "Hi, I'm Special Agent Vincent Patterson, what's your name?" Reaching out to shake his hand, she said, "I'm Charlotte, um Charlotte Smith." Who knows why she lied, but at this point, she felt it was necessary?

"Hi Charlotte Smith, may I call you Charlotte?"

"Um, yes, of course."

Vincent knew right away she was lying about her last

name but didn't care for now. He wanted to know about the murders she was referring too. He was immediately struck by how beautiful Charlotte was. She stood five feet seven inches tall, blonde hair pulled back into a ponytail, bright blue eyes, perfect skin, perfect white teeth, and a thin athletic build. By every measure, a woman that could make a million dollars modeling in Paris. He said, "good, you can call me Vincent. What brings you to the FBI today? Nancy said it was something about a couple of murders in Queens?"

Again, Charlotte looked around to see if anyone was listening and said, "yes, can we talk somewhere more private? I'm not comfortable talking here in the lobby."

"Sure, come this way I have a conference room we can use upstairs."

Charlotte nodded and said, "thank you."

They walked to the elevator, where Vincent slid an ID card through a reader inside the elevator and pressed the button for the second floor. When they arrived, it was like most large office environments with private offices and conference rooms along the outside walls by the windows. There was a large bullpen in the middle with desks and cubicles and a lot of people in suits talking on their phones and typing into computer screens. Vincent led the way to a small conference room with a glass door and windows facing the Freedom Tower. When Charlotte entered the room, she noticed a round conference table with four chairs and nothing else.

"Please have a seat, would you like some coffee, soda, or water?"

"No thank you, I've had enough coffee for one day. I already drank a large cup, extra strong this morning when I went to work. I'm rambling, aren't I?"

"That's okay; it's a little intimidating talking to the FBI. So, how can I help you, Charlotte Smith?" Vincent put emphasis on the name Smith.

"Well, I have to tell you I lied about my last name."

"What it's not Smith?" Vincent asked lightheartedly.

"Um, no, it's not Smith," Charlotte said.

"Yeah, I figured that out, what is it?"

"It's Mancini. My real name is Charlotte Mancini."

Vincent grinned, and said, "well, hello again, Ms. Charlotte Mancini. I'm still Special Agent Vincent Patterson, and as I said before, please call me Vincent."

"I will." *He was right! It is intimidating to talk to the FBI.*

"So how can I help you?"

"I saw my husband kill two people last night."

"Where?"

"Queens."

"Why didn't you call the police?" *I keep asking myself that question too, why didn't I call the police?* "I don't know. I guess I was in shock when it happened, and I didn't know what to do. I couldn't call from home, he was there, and I didn't want to call from work. Hell, I'm probably still in shock. I don't know, I'm so confused, and I'm scared he's going to kill me next. I got to thinking about what to do, and I just decided at the spur of the moment to leave work and come here. I'm rambling once again, aren't I?"

"That's okay. Let me see if I can help you. Take a step back, please start at the beginning and tell me exactly what happened."

"Okay. We went to the theater last night here in the City. John, that's my husband, John got a phone call at intermission. I think from someone named Tony. He kept saying he couldn't take care of something tonight because we were at the theater and I was with him. Then as intermission ended, he said something like, I'll handle it. We got our drinks and were heading back into the theater when he got another call and told me to go back to the seats and that he would be there in a few minutes. He then turned around and walked back toward the lobby doors."

"Did he return after a few minutes?"

"Yes, it was probably ten or fifteen minutes later."

"Okay, what happened next?"

"Well, when the play ended, we got in John's car, and he said we needed to stop at Greg and Carol's to pick something up."

"Greg and Carol? Who are they to you? Do you know these people?"

"Yes, the Fletcher's, that's who he killed. I would say they were casual friends of ours. We've been to their house for a few parties, and we went out to dinner with them a couple of times. I sincerely liked Carol."

"Okay, then what happened?"

"We drove to Queens and pulled up by their house on the street." *This is crazy, am I telling the FBI I saw my husband kill our friends?*

"What do you mean by pulled up by? Didn't you park in front of the house or in their driveway?"

"We couldn't, Greg parked his truck in front of the house, and Carol had her brand-new Mustang in front of that. I found it odd she didn't park her brand-new car in her garage. So, we had to park in front of the neighbor's house."

"Do you know if they were awake, or if they happened to look out and see your vehicle parked out there?"

"I don't think so. It was pretty dark outside; the neighbor's house was dark too; in fact, most of the houses on the block were dark. It was late, close to midnight."

"Okay, what happened next?"

"Well, John got out of the car and told me to stay put. He turned the motor off and double-checked to make sure the lights didn't stay on. You know on some vehicles they stay on after you turn off the ignition?"

Vincent nodded. Charlotte continued, "He said he didn't want to disturb the neighbors with our lights. But then I asked him to turn the car back on so I wouldn't get cold and could listen to the radio. He pushed the button to restart the car and got out. Then he walked behind the car, paused for a moment, looked down, and walked up the sidewalk that led to their front door."

"Paused? What did he do when he paused?"

"I don't know, I turned around to look but didn't see

anything. He just stopped behind the car, looked down for a few seconds, and then kept walking toward the house."

"Okay, so he gets out of the vehicle, walks behind it and pauses, correct? What happened next?"

"Yes. I watched John walk up to the house and first look through the living room curtains. They were open a little bit. Then he kept walking up to the front step and checked the door to see if it was locked before he pushed the doorbell. When he did, all sorts of lights came on inside, and I saw Carol answer the door in her robe. They talked for a second or two, and then she stepped back and let him inside the house."

"Do you know why he checked the door before he pushed the doorbell?"

"No, I thought it was odd too, but then I assumed he talked to Greg from the theater, and Greg told him to walk in, the door would be open. But I don't know."

"Now, are you sure it was Carol who answered the door?"

"Absolutely, she was in a pink fuzzy robe, I could see it from the car."

"Okay, what happened next?"

"Because she answered, I thought as long as she's up, I should go in and say hello."

"Do you know what time this happened?"

"Yes, it was twelve, oh eight. I know this because I looked at the clock when Carol answered the door and thought to myself, I guess she's awake now."

"Good, okay, please continue."

"I pushed the button to turn off the engine and got out on the sidewalk. I walked up toward their front door and peeked in through the curtains. They were open a little bit, just enough to see what was happening in the living room."

"What did you see?" Vincent asked.

"Oh my God, I saw Greg and Carol on their knees with their hands above their heads. John was calmly talking to them and pointing a big gun at Greg. The next thing I know, Greg's head explodes, and he falls backward. Carol is covered in blood-splattered from Greg and is screaming and crying. Then John just shot her in the chest. She grabbed her chest, then looked at her hands, and fell forward on her face. The look on her face and the shock in her eyes will haunt me forever. Her face was covered in blood from Greg, and she looked like she saw a ghost. Her eyes got big, and her chest started bleeding, then she just fell forward." *I think I'm going to be sick.*

"What did you do?"

"I froze, I—I started crying, and then I ran back to the car. Honestly, I didn't know what to do. I was so shocked, I just cried." As Charlotte told her story to Vincent about what she had seen, tears streamed down her cheeks.

Handing her a tissue, Vincent asked, "What happened next?"

"Nothing, I sat in the car and cried until I saw John come out of the house. He walked down the sidewalk about fifteen or twenty minutes later, as if nothing happened. I couldn't believe it. He was calm and humming to the music on the way home."

"So, obviously, he didn't see you out there, right?"

"Well, I don't know. Probably not, or he would have killed me too. But I don't know for sure."

"What did you do when he got back in the vehicle? Did you say anything?"

"No, no way, I was mortified. I was afraid he was going to kill me next. I wiped away my tears, blew my nose, and tried hard not to give away my horror. I pretended I was sleeping on the way home, so I didn't have to face him or talk to him."

"What happened when you got home?"

"I went upstairs to our bathroom, and John went to the den to check his email. At least that was what he told me. When I got up this morning, he was already working downstairs in his office. John works from home. He owns his own company."

"Are you telling me you've never suspected him of doing anything like this before?"

"Oh my God, no. No fucking way. Oops sorry. I'm just so nervous and scared. No, he's so easy going, soft-spoken and quiet, usually. There's no way I would believe he could do this."

"How long have you been married?"

"A year and a half. We dated for a while before that."

"How did you meet?"

"I work in a flower shop, and John came in to buy flowers for a funeral. That's not ironic, is it? *Now I wonder if it was for someone he just killed.* We got to talking, and he asked me out for coffee at the diner next door to the flower shop. We ended up talking for a long time. After coffee, he asked me out on a date. I thought what a nice guy, he was good looking, smart, owns his own company, why not go out with him? And the rest is history. I guess little did I know."

"Okay, please wait here, I need to do some homework. I'll be right back."

FIVE

With her head buried in her hands, Charlotte sat in the conference room in a state of shock. It felt good to tell someone what she saw. Although sharing the story out loud made her realize she just ratted out her husband for murder. *My life is over, he's going to come after me and kill me.*

Vincent returned about a half-hour later and said, "Charlotte, I just checked with the NYPD to see if they had any homicides reported in Queens last night. It appears your story checks out. Greg and Carol Fletcher of 9001 109th Street in Queens, found in their home this morning with one gunshot wound each." Reading from a sheet of paper, Vincent continued, "It says that Greg was shot in the head and Carol in the chest, just like you said. The mail carrier looked in the window this morning when she delivered the mail and saw them on the floor with blood all around and called the police. The police have it as a robbery gone bad. The house was ransacked, and all the jewelry boxes were emptied. They didn't find a wallet on either victim."

Tears streaming down her face, Charlotte said, "oh, my dear God, those poor people. I don't believe this is happening. What am I going to do? I can't go home. He's going to know it was me who told you. He's going to kill me. There wasn't anyone else around."

"Do you remember anything else?"

"I don't know. I told you what I know. I told you what I

saw. I don't' want to see it anymore. Carol's face with blood and brain splatter all over it was horrifying enough."

"Charlotte, everything you can remember is essential; even the smallest detail that may seem insignificant can help us. Do you remember the gun? The gun probably had a silencer on it. Did you hear the gunshots? Did you notice anything in his belt in the small of his back? Or perhaps, something under his coat earlier in the night?"

"No, I didn't hear the gunshots. And, I know John didn't have a gun at home, or when we left for dinner. As I said before, I've never seen a gun in our house. I don't think he had it at dinner or the start of the play. I had my arm around his waist on the way into the theater. I didn't feel anything in his belt."

"What did John do after he shot Greg and Carol?"

"He just turned away from Carol—oh yeah, he put the gun down on the coffee table and took off the rubber gloves, and then, he walked away."

"Rubber gloves? You didn't mention he was wearing rubber gloves earlier. What did he do with the gloves when he took them off? Where are they now? Did you see what he did with them?"

"I saw him take them off and put them in his coat pocket. They were blue, you know the kind they wear in a doctor's office. That was the last thing I saw, and then I ran back to the car."

"Do you think they're still in his suit coat pocket?"

"I don't know; I'm not going home to check. When John finds out I talked to the FBI, I'm as good as dead." *He's going to kill me, just like Carol.*

"Did you see what he did with the gun after he shot them? You mentioned he set it down on the coffee table. There was no mention of it in the police report. Do you have any idea if he had it when he returned to the car?"

"I don't know; I didn't pay that close attention, I was so scared, and I didn't want to talk to him, I just pretended to be asleep."

"Anything else?"

"John drives an Escalade; doesn't it have GPS or something that you can look at? Won't it tell you we were there at that address in Queens at the time of the murders?"

"Yes, of course, and we'll do that with your permission. But dumping the GPS memory will take a little time because we still need a judge's order, even with your permission. The car is likely registered in John's name, not yours. Also, car companies are hesitant to give up private data without a court order. Remember, all it will tell us is that you were in front of the neighbor's house last night around midnight. Charlotte, please think, is there any way we can go back to your house and look for his clothes, the gun, or his shoes? I'd love to check and see if he left the gloves in his coat pocket, or maybe he threw them in your garbage. They probably still have blood splattered on them. Blood is tough to get out of clothing too, and unless he washed the gloves, they should still have some spatter on them."

"I looked at his clothes in the light when we got home and didn't see any blood, but I guess that doesn't mean it wasn't there.

There's no way I can go home, especially alone. I can't face him again. I can't do it, Vincent. If he sees me now, he'll kill me."

"Charlotte, remember the local police are reporting it as a robbery gone wrong. No one has gone to your house and accused John of murder. The police don't know your husband was involved. So, for now, he thinks he got away with it. If we wait too long, though, all the evidence will be gone. Are you sure he doesn't leave the house during the day? For lunch, maybe?"

"Well, John usually goes to work out when he's finished with work. He goes to a gym near our house at around five-thirty for an hour or so. Maybe we can go to the house then, and check. I can pack some clothes and makeup too. But there's no way I'm staying in that house tonight. You have to come with me and protect me from him in case he comes home and catches me there."

"Don't worry about it, Charlotte; I'll be there with you. We can go to your house together and look for the gloves and clothes and maybe find the gun he used. He may have thrown it all away in the garbage."

"Okay, but what am I going to do now, what's going to happen to me?"

"Well, we'll put you up tonight in a hotel or safe house. Don't worry; we'll keep you safe. But Charlotte, keep in mind, as soon as you don't go home tonight, he's going to know something's up and go looking for you. It's just a matter of time before he figures out you saw what he did last night. You must realize there is no turning back."

"I know, that's why I'm worried, you didn't see his face, he didn't show any emotion, he just shot them at point-blank range, and in cold blood, and walked away as if nothing happened."

"Look, Charlotte, right now it's a local police matter. I have a feeling this is going to end up in our lap as a murder for hire by an organized crime family. My guess is this was a mob hit ordered by someone from a local crime family."

"How is that possible? How could I not know he was a killer? Oh my God, what am I going to do?" *I can't believe this is happening to me, I'm so stupid.*

"Charlotte, first, I'll drive you to your house, and we'll look for his clothes and the gun. You can pack some things and then I'll take you to a safe place to stay tonight. I won't leave your side. Okay? Tomorrow, we'll figure out the rest and formulate a go-forward plan. I think some sleep in a safe place will do wonders for you."

"Okay." She paused and thought for a moment and then said, "Tell me, do you think John's a mobster?"

"It's possible. What bothers me is how cool he was. How deliberate. That usually means he's a professional. It sounds like he didn't hesitate when he shot them. I'm fairly certain this wasn't his first time to kill someone, that's for sure. What's so puzzling to me is that John was awfully careless doing it with you in the car. I would have thought he'd take you home and go back over there in the morning."

The thought of John killing someone in front of Charlotte

was just too much for her to handle. *How stupid of me, how could I not know who he really was?*

Vincent continued, "Charlotte, I would have to say this was a professional hit." Vincent handed her another tissue and said, "What's his mobile number so we can dump his phone? That'll help us determine who he was talking with from the theater."

Charlotte looked up John's numbers on her phone and wrote them down on a piece of paper. She gave Vincent both his office and cell phone numbers.

"Thank you. Based on what you've told me, it sounds like this was a spur of the moment hit. So, John was probably talking to the person who hired him. I'm also curious where he got the gun. My gut tells me the second phone call was to tell him to come and get it in the lobby or out in front of the theater. Someone had to have delivered it to him. We can pull the video from the street cameras and verify that too."

Right then, a woman knocked on the door and walked in. "Kimberly, can you please pull the video on—hold on. What play did you see?"

"Tootsie at the Marquis Theater."

"Tootsie at the Marquis, pull the video from out in front of the theater from 9:00 to 11:00 last night, please." Vincent then turned back to Charlotte, "Now, Charlotte, are you sure we can get in and out of the house while John is at the gym or running?"

"Yes, I think so. John usually goes to work out like clockwork, right after he's done working for the day."

"Let's hope he doesn't change his routine. At this point, we don't want to cross paths with him. We certainly don't want John to know we're on to him yet."

With her voice trembling, Charlotte said, "I don't ever want to see him again." *He's a rat bastard.*

"Charlotte, it's understandable that you're scared and upset. You've experienced something very traumatic. Believe me when I tell you, you're safe now, nobody knows you're here. It's only three o'clock, so we have a few hours before we have to leave. Do you need anything to eat or drink? Water or coffee, a soda, maybe?" *God no, I'm nauseous.*

"Could I have some paper and a pencil, please? I'm too nervous to eat or drink anything."

"Sure, now sit tight." Vincent left the room, and Charlotte was left alone with only her thoughts. The longer she sat, the angrier she became. *The fact was John is a cold-blooded killer, and now he had dragged me into his web of deceit. That son of a bitch!*

SIX

$\mathbf{A}$ little while later, Vincent returned with a legal pad, a pen, and a pencil. "Can John see where you are with an App on his phone like Find My Phone?" Vincent asked.

"I don't know. John's very computer savvy. I'm sure he thinks I'm at work right now. He wouldn't know I left work early to come here."

"Please unlock your phone and hand it to me. I'm going to have our tech guys make it look like you're still at work. Write down the address of your flower shop, and I'll take care of the rest."

Vincent took the phone and the paper with the address to the flower shop and left the room. Charlotte's thoughts turned to what was going to happen to her life now. *Will I have to testify in court? Will John come after me, or hire someone to kill me? Will John go to jail forever? What if he gets out and comes after me? Will I be on the run forever?*

Vincent returned with a bottle of water, and said, "alright, you're all set. Here are some water and your phone, which for all intents and purposes, is disabled. All your calls will go directly to voicemail, you'll not be able to call out on it either. If John tries to locate you with the Find my Phone App, it will say you're at work. I'm letting you hold onto your phone for now because you may want to write down what other information you have that you feel is important to you before we take it for good. Also, you may consider sending the pictures you want to keep to a program in the cloud. If you need help with that, our tech guys can do it for you."

"Um, okay," Charlotte said.

Kimberly knocked on the door again, entered the room, and handed Vincent some papers. "This is the last ninety days. But look at last night at 9:15 and 1:20, he spoke to a number we've been monitoring. As I thought, it was Gambucci," Kimberly said.

"Thank you, Kimberly." Turning toward Charlotte, Vincent asked, "Do you have any questions?"

"I don't know. I'm terrified, confused, and a little pissed off right now. My life is over, isn't it? I've lost my husband, and I'm going to lose my home and my friends. I'm not sure this was all worth it, Vincent. I—I don't know what to say."

"Charlotte, I realize how difficult this is on you. Maybe you can look at this as an opportunity to start a new life. A sort of do-over."

"I don't want a do-over, I like my life."

"Look, John's a bad guy. He appears to be a paid killer. The life you were living wasn't sustainable, and it wasn't real. You do see that, right? Sooner or later, you would have found out, and then what? Does he kill you? He might have been caught or killed himself. Either way, you're left with nothing. Also, you could have been charged as an accessory. This way, we get to put a bad guy away and provide you with a new life. A new opportunity to build the life you want. The one you deserve."

"If John goes to prison, do I still have to go into witness protection?"

"Probably, it appears he's working for Tony Gambucci. Gambucci is one of the most notorious mobsters of our time. If John is working for him, your life is likely in danger too."

"How does it work? Will I be able to get my stuff from my house?"

"Well, we're going there today, and you can pack as much as you want for now. Once you're relocated, the FBI will seize your house, cars, and bank accounts. In a few months, we'll send you whatever you want from the seizure. The bank accounts will be held in a trust account, and a check will be forwarded to you in about three months. We'll need a judge to determine whether you get all the money, or some of it will go to John."

"Where will I go?"

"I don't know, I'm sorry that decision won't be made for a little while, but until then, you'll be safe, I promise."

"I'm not so sure of that."

"You'll be safe; I'll make sure of it. Now, Charlotte, I have some details I need to take care of before we leave. You have your pad of paper and a pen; I suggest you write down everything you can remember. Start at the beginning. Close your eyes and focus. Every detail can be important. You never know what little detail will make a difference at trial. It will also help when you have to repeat your story several times in the next few days. Writing it down should help give you some clarity too. And don't forget to get what you want off your phone and move your pictures up to the cloud before we take it from you permanently."

As tears fell onto the sheet of paper, Charlotte sat in the

conference room alone and sketched an abstract picture of a face with a single tear on its cheek. The sketch resembled drawings by Picasso from his blue period. For Charlotte, drawing was a calming exercise; it forced her to focus on something other than her troubles. Charlotte's mind wandered to when she was a little girl, she would sketch pictures when life became difficult, the drawings were a way to express what she was feeling. It became an escape, a method for her to say she was scared or depressed, without having to say it out loud. When she completed her drawing, she flipped the page and tried to remember as much as she could about last night. The more she thought about it, the angrier she became. *How stupid am I that I didn't know my husband was a killer? He was always so sweet and gentle. He had never shown any sign of violence.* Charlotte wrote down what she could remember and then returned to her drawing.

SEVEN

Vincent returned to the conference room and said, "Charlotte, are you ready to go?" Looking down at the paper, he said, "that's an interesting drawing."

"It calms my nerves to draw. As for am I ready to go? No, but we have to go, don't we?"

"Well, yes, if you want to put this guy away for killing your friends."

They drove mostly in silence the entire way to Charlotte's house on the upper east side. They arrived at 5:15 and parked at the end of the block. They waited in complete silence and watched until 5:45 when the garage door rose.

"We probably have an hour before he gets back," Charlotte said.

As soon as John's Escalade was out of sight, Vincent said, "okay, let's go."

Vincent started his SUV and pulled up in front of the house and parked on the street. Charlotte grabbed her keys out of her purse as Vincent exited the vehicle and walked up to the front door. When she unlocked and opened the door, the alarm began to blare. Charlotte quickly punched in her code to disarm the alarm, and it stopped the siren instantly.

Charlotte suddenly became melancholy, feeling like she was going to miss this house. She knew she would never live here again. With teary eyes, Charlotte walked upstairs to the bedroom.

I wonder if John goes to jail and Gambucci goes to jail, can I come back and live in my house? I love this house. What would it take to do that?

Vincent said he was going to go out back and check the garbage cans. Charlotte first went to the closet and grabbed a large suitcase, then she returned to the closet and looked for the jacket John wore last night. It wasn't there among his other sport coats. Moving back and forth from the closet to her suitcase, Charlotte was having difficulty breathing. She didn't realize she was holding her breath all this time. She stopped packing, stood still for a moment, and took several deep breaths to calm her nerves. *You can do this, Charlotte.* She packed some clothes, underwear, jewelry, and everything else she could think of that would fit in the suitcase. Then she looked in the hamper for his clothes from last night; they weren't there either. *He must've taken them to the dry cleaners early this morning, that was the errand he had to do.*

After stuffing her suitcase full, she dragged the heavy bag down the stairs and left it in front of the door. Charlotte walked out to the kitchen and saw Vincent standing next to the island with a grin on his face.

"Look what I found?" he said, holding up a pair of latex gloves inside of a plastic bag that had the word "Evidence" written on it.

"In the garbage?" Charlotte asked.

"Yes, they were in a bag in the garbage outside. I wish I found the gun out there too."

"Did you find anything else?" Charlotte asked.

"No, I didn't, did you find anything upstairs?"

"No, I looked at his sportscoats, and I checked the dirty clothes hamper, I didn't find anything with blood on it." When they turned to leave, Charlotte noticed the green bag John used from the dry cleaner sitting on the dining room table. Pointing at the bag, Charlotte said, "Vincent, that bag on the table is John's dry cleaning. He must have forgotten it when he left for the gym. I bet his clothes from last night are in there."

"Let's take a look." Vincent then proceeded to open the top of the bag and pour the contents on the table. A couple of shirts, slacks, and a sport coat fell out. One of the shirts and the pants had a small amount of blood splatter on them. The sport coat looked clean. Also, a little black leather bag tumbled out. Vincent carefully picked up the clothes and placed them in separate evidence bags, and then opened the leather bag to see what was inside. He peered inside the bag and then turned it over onto the table. The bag was filled with jewelry and a couple of thousand dollars in hundred-dollar bills. Vincent carefully scooped everything back into the leather bag and placed it into an evidence bag too.

They walked out the front door with their newly found treasure of evidence. Vincent loaded up the back with the suitcase and the evidence bags. When they climbed back into the vehicle, Charlotte collapsed into the front seat and started to hyperventilate.

"Take deep breaths, relax Charlotte. It'll all be okay. You're safe now," Vincent said.

"I'm so scared; I think I'm going to be sick."

"It's alright; I can wait."

"No! We have to go. Go! Go! Go! Before he remembers he left the dry-cleaning bag on the table. He might come back to get it."

"Well, he was awfully careless by leaving all that evidence in a bag on your table. Also, the fact that he just threw the gloves in the garbage proves to me he didn't suspect you saw anything. He didn't cover his tracks very well for a professional."

Charlotte sat quietly and just wanted to go to sleep and wake up when this nightmare was over. "Where are we going, Vincent?"

"I'm taking you to a safe house in the Bronx where I have a female agent that will stay with you tonight. I'll have someone take all this evidence to the FBI lab and test it, and then tomorrow we'll figure out what our next steps will be. In the meantime, I'll call the US Attorney and fill him in on our progress. You're going to have to meet with him in the next day or so to tell your story. Charlotte, I promise you, I'll keep you safe."

EIGHT

Vincent drove for about an hour through the rush hour traffic, while Charlotte reflected on what was going on. He finally pulled up to a little house in a quiet neighborhood in the Bronx. It looked like any other middle-class neighborhood with trees, and kids riding their bikes up and down the street, and people grilling out in their driveways. All the houses on the block looked similar and were set on small lots remarkably close to each other. They were ranch-style homes with a small porch in front, small yards in front, and detached garages. If you wanted, you could reach out the window and touch the neighbor's house. The safe house had white siding, yellow shutters, and a solid wood front door. Vincent pulled the SUV up to the garage but left the car parked in the driveway.

They both climbed down from the SUV and headed toward the front of the house. As they approached the porch, a woman opened the door and said, "Hi, Charlotte, I'm Special Agent Michelle Taylor, it's nice to meet you. Please don't stand out there, come into the house, and I'll show you to your room." She moved aside to allow Charlotte to enter the house.

Michelle was about twenty-nine, five foot five, athletic build, brown eyes, with shoulder-length blonde hair up in a ponytail, and dressed in a dark blue suit, white blouse, and black closed-toe flats. She didn't have a wedding ring on, but she was wearing small diamond stud earrings and a simple diamond pendant around her neck. She looked like she could handle herself with no problem. "Charlotte, I'll be staying with you throughout this entire ordeal. It's my only job to keep you safe." *First impression, badass!*

"Thank you, Agent Taylor."

"Please, call me Michelle."

They walked through the living room, and Michelle pointed out where the kitchen was located. Then they turned and walked down a hallway with several doors on the left side, stopping at the first one. Michelle opened the door and showed Charlotte the room. She said, "this is your room; I hope it's comfortable for you."

It was nicely decorated with beige curtains, a queen-size bed, a colorful comforter, a small flat-screen TV, a couple of nightstands with lamps, and a dresser. The carpeting looked new, and the room smelled clean and fresh. Vincent brought Charlotte's suitcase in and set it on one side of the bed. After Michelle and Vincent left, Charlotte laid down on the other side of the suitcase on top of the comforter, closed her eyes for what she thought was a minute and fell asleep.

When Charlotte woke up, she recalled that her dreams took her back to her wedding day in San Diego. She remembered crying when John got emotional, saying his vows. What stood out though was the fact the Fletcher's were at the wedding too. John seemed nervous, he looked out of sorts. *John's never nervous, he's always in control.* This stuck in her memory for some reason.

Charlotte grabbed her cell phone off the nightstand to see

what time it was. She slept for a couple of hours. There were over twenty missed calls from John and a dozen voicemails. It was after eight at night, and she realized she hadn't eaten all day. Charlotte's stomach was rumbling and still upset; she followed the smell of pizza to the kitchen where Michelle and Vincent were sitting at a round metal table.

Vincent looked up and said, "How was your nap?"

"Good, I think. My phone has blown up with calls from John. I guess he knows something's up. My suitcase was obviously gone, my closet was cleaned out, and his dry-cleaning bag was missing. I'm sure by now he's beside himself with rage. Should I listen to the voicemails, or do you guys want too?"

"No, not unless you want to hear a hitman threaten you," Michelle said.

Vincent then interjected, "there's pizza and wings on the counter if you're hungry. Do you want a beer or some wine?"

"Wine sounds good, and I'll pick at a piece of pizza. Thank you." They talked about flowers, clothes, and the dress code at the FBI for women. To ease the tension in the room, Michelle shared a funny story about her dog, Duke. Before Michelle became a Special Agent in New York, she worked in the canine unit for the FBI at Quantico.

"Duke is trained to identify danger in a building before law enforcement enters, it's called patrol. He can sniff for bombs, and he'll determine whether someone is inside a building. But he won't do anything until he's told unless his or my life is in danger. So, a few years ago, I was called in to have Duke check out a building. The FBI thought organized crime figures were hiding women being brought from other countries and sold in a sick auction to enslave them. I told Duke to enter the building and let us know if anyone is inside. Duke went running into the building, and after about five minutes, the door burst open. This little Asian man came running out, screaming something in Korean. His pants were half off, and he peed himself. He must have been in the bathroom when Duke located him. It was so funny, and the easiest bust we've ever made in the canine unit."

Everyone avoided talking about the current situation. Vincent and Michelle realized the amount of stress Charlotte was feeling. After a few glasses of wine, Charlotte wound down and started to relax. She returned to her room, took a shower, and brushed her teeth. *I wonder if it will ever get better. I'm going to lose my husband, my home, and maybe my life.* She sat up on the bed and pulled out her sketch pad. A single tear dropped on the paper and stained it where she drew a picture of black orchids wilting in a vase. Then, surprisingly, Charlotte drifted off to sleep.

NINE

After a restless night of sleep, nightmares, and crying, Charlotte finally rolled out of bed at six-thirty the next morning. She put on the same pair of jeans from the day before, and an I love NY sweatshirt from her suitcase. Charlotte walked into the kitchen, and both Vincent and Michelle hadn't moved from the night before.

"Did you two stay in those spots all night?"

"No, Michelle slept in the back bedroom for a few hours while I kept watch, and I took the couch and caught a few hours of sleep while she kept watch. Why don't you have some coffee and a bagel, and we'll fill you in on what's happening today."

"Thank you, a bagel sounds good, and coffee sounds even better."

Michelle smiled, then winked, and said, "help yourself to the coffee; it's strong, Vincent made it."

Vincent, oblivious to the dig, began, "Charlotte, Michelle is assigned to you for the life of this case. She'll be by your side going forward through the trial. Whenever you step foot in the State of New York, Michelle will be there to protect you. I'll be her backup. Usually, we use the US Marshal service for witness protection, but in this case, because Tony Gambucci is such a high-value target, the FBI prefers to use its own resources. We feel it's important for now to keep this information and your existence as close to the vest as we can. Tony is immensely powerful and has friends and contacts all over the world. Okay, so far?"

Charlotte nodded and said, "Yes."

Vincent continued, "today, we're going to meet with the US Attorney in his offices in Lower Manhattan and tell him what you saw and heard. I've already confirmed John left the theater at intermission and met a man named Benny Molinaro out front. We got a copy of the tape from the street, and you can see Mr. Molinaro clearly handing John a Macy's bag and walking away. John took the bag and walked back into the theater. We've contacted the theater and have officers combing through the garbage trying to locate the Macy's bag. We also confirmed the blood on the sport coat, shirt, pants, and gloves belong to Greg and Carol Fletcher. Finally, we notified the NYPD that the FBI will be taking over the case under an Organized Crime directive from the DOJ and the US Attorney's office. They're sending over their files, and the autopsy reports this morning."

"Wow, that's crazy how fast you work," Charlotte responded.

Vincent replied, "Yes, we have a pretty significant organization here in New York. We also pulled the GPS from your husband's vehicle. We confirmed it was, in fact, in Queens near the Fletcher's address at midnight for thirty-three minutes. It would be nice if we could find the gun, but the jewelry will help put him inside the house if we can prove it was Carol's. We're checking with relatives to find out if they recognize any of it. Finally, the money we found in the bag will be checked for Mr. Fletcher's fingerprints. If we find his prints on the money, that'll put John inside Fletcher's house too. Do you have any questions so far?"

"Not about anything you've said. I'm simply curious how long I'll be here in this house?"

"We're not sure you'll probably stay here until we relocate you. But you must understand, you can't contact anyone you know, or reach out to family, nothing. I'm sorry to say; you're now on your own." Michelle continued, "Charlotte, this is going to be exceedingly difficult on you for a while, but I'm here to help you through it. I won't leave your side."

"I get that, I'm not so worried about calling anyone, but I'm really terrified John will find me here and come to kill me. If he really is a hitman, he'll find a way to kill me."

"Nobody knows where you are except Vincent and me. I assure you; he won't find you here. That reminds me, I'll need your phone now for good. We'll listen to all his messages and determine the threat level. I hope you got what you need off it," Michelle said.

"I'm fine, my parents died in a car accident years ago, and I don't have any siblings. The family I do have, I don't speak to them much, and they don't live near here. I have a few close friends, but most of my friends are John's friends too. I'm sure he called every one of them by now trying to find me."

"Okay, then. I think we're good to go. Please drink up and go get ready, we need to leave shortly to be in the City by nine to meet the US Attorney," Michelle said.

Charlotte returned to her room, showered, brushed her

teeth and hair, and put on clean slacks, a blouse, closed-toe shoes, and a scarf. She looked in the mirror on the way out the door and said to herself out loud, "Ugh, nothing can fix this." She was referring to the puffiness and bags under her eyes.

TEN

They climbed into the SUV, Michelle in the front passenger seat, Vincent driving, and Charlotte in the back behind Michelle. It took forty-five minutes to arrive at the underground garage in lower Manhattan. Once they were parked, Charlotte quickly jumped out of the SUV and started walking toward the elevators.

Michelle said in a somewhat stern voice, "Charlotte, please don't walk ahead of me. Wait for me; I'll either be at your side or ahead of you clearing the way, alright?"

"Oh, okay, I didn't know, sorry," Charlotte replied.

"No worries, it'll take some getting used to, then it'll become second nature after a while."

They stepped into the elevator, and Michelle pressed the button for the eleventh floor. The elevator never stopped before reaching its destination. When the doors opened, there was a young man in a blue suit waiting to escort them to the US Attorney's office. He introduced himself as Jeff and said he'd take them back to see Mr. Ellis. They walked nearly the entire length of the building to an enormous corner office. The plaque on the door said Mr. Randolf Ellis, Esq. US Attorney Southern District Organized Crime Group. When they entered the office, the first thing Charlotte noticed was the incredible view of New York City. It was almost a panoramic view of Manhattan.

About half the room was taken up by a beautiful cherry

wood desk. On the desk, there was a phone with several buttons, a computer monitor, and file folders piled up about a foot or two. He had beautiful paintings on the walls of places around New York City and a picture of himself and President Reagan shaking hands. On the wall above his credenza was a law diploma from NYU. Just below the degree on a pedestal was a statue of Lady Justice, complete with the blindfold and the scales of justice. Charlotte immediately noticed an old baseball in a glass case on his desk. She quickly walked over to the ball to see who signed it. It was Mickey Mantle.

"Do you like baseball?" Ellis asked.

"Yeah, the Yankees. Where'd you get the ball?"

"Oh, well, my old man was Mickey's lawyer toward the end of his career. So, when I was a kid, he got Mick to sign the ball personally to me. See how he wrote to *Randy, hit em long and hit em straight, Mickey Mantle #7*?"

"That's so cool," Charlotte remarked.

"Yeah, it's one of my prized possessions. My wife hates it and doesn't want it in the house, so I keep it here to impress people."

Randolf Ellis, Esq. is fifty years old, a thin build, six-two, with jet black hair and noticeably light skin. He was wearing an expensive gray pinstripe suit, custom shirt, and black leather shoes. He directed the small group to a round table in the corner and offered everyone coffee. Jeff left and returned with four steaming mugs on a serving tray with cream and sugar in a separate bowl.

"Okay now that we're settled in, I'm Randy Ellis, the US Attorney for this district. I mostly handle organized crime cases. It's a pleasure to meet you, Charlotte."

"It's nice to meet you too," Charlotte said.

"First of all, I want to thank you for your courage. It's not going to be easy on you from this point forward. There will be relocation, loss of family and friends, depositions, the trial, and finally, witness protection. You are pretty much starting your life over. There'll be a lot asked of you, young lady. Also, when you testify, the defense will make you out to be an unreliable witness. The defense attorney will be ruthless. But hang in there we'll spend time to prepare you and protect you. I know you'll have many questions. We'll answer them all as you go through the process. If you have any questions I can answer now, please ask away."

"Right now, I'm just worried John will find me and come to kill me."

"Let me assure you, Charlotte; you're safe. Michelle here will be at your side protecting you from now on, and I don't see Vincent going anywhere anytime soon. Now, can you please walk me through what happened a couple of nights ago. Please go slow and try to remember every detail. Everything is important. I'm going to record your statement, so if you need to correct anything from your earlier statement to Agent Patterson, please feel free to do so now."

Charlotte told her story again in the same order she did before for Vincent. Ellis took down some notes and asked a few questions along the way. When she got to the part about how Vincent took her home to retrieve the gloves and clothes, he wanted to know more details from Vincent. Ellis asked about the DNA testing and the chain of custody for the shirt, gloves, slacks, and bag of money and jewelry. He asked about the video of Benny Molinaro from the street, and the ballistics on the bullets. He also questioned Vincent on the GPS information from John's SUV. Vincent responded with all the right answers, and Ellis took detailed notes.

"The blood on John's clothes was Greg and Carol Fletcher's. The Jewelry they found was confirmed to be Carol's. And it looks like the SUV was in front of their neighbor's house at midnight. We also pulled the video in front of the Marques, and it showed Big Tony's nephew, handing John, a Macy's bag. Finally, the FBI acquired the Macy's bag from the theater garbage cans, and it's being tested for DNA, prints, and gun oil."

While Vincent and Ellis were talking, Charlotte's mind wandered. *Each time I tell the story, I get angrier. I trusted this man, and he screwed me. He didn't have to marry me, and he didn't have to ruin my life. What a bastard!*

Finally, Vincent and Ellis discussed the phone records. There were two calls to and from Big Tony and John's cell phone that night, and two calls from Big Tony to Benny, and finally, one text from Benny to John right around the time of intermission at Tootsie.

"Charlotte, let me put your mind at ease. I want you to

know John was arrested last night at your home at around midnight. We filed murder and racketeering charges in federal court. We used something called RICO statutes. For now, he's being held on Rikers Island. Once John is convicted, we'll send him to a federal prison out of state."

"What's a RICO statute?" she asked.

Ellis said, "Racketeer Influenced and Corrupt Organizations Act. We use it mostly to prosecute organized crime cases. It gives us some latitude around organized crime. If you're deemed to be part of an organized crime family, we can come after you under RICO. More importantly, we're also charging Tony Gambucci for hiring John to commit the murders. His case will be a bit more challenging because nothing seems to stick to this guy. He has great lawyers and plenty of them. All we have on Tony right now is the phone calls between him and John, and the call to his nephew. We also have your testimony as to what you heard John talk about on the phone when you were with him at the theater. And the fact, John said his name several times out loud. We'll hopefully be able to tie fingerprints from the Macy's bag to Benny, and that will give us another connection back to Big Tony. What we're diligently trying to do is to flip your husband John, to testify against Tony."

"Wait, did you say *my* testimony against a crime boss? You mean you want me to testify against a New York crime boss?" Charlotte asked. *Are you out of your mind?*

"Charlotte, we learned from informants last night that Big Tony has put a contract out on your life. He's offering fifty thousand dollars to kill you. That's a lot of money, so he's serious about you not testifying at his or John's trial. If you choose not to testify, the contract will still be active, and you're going to be in danger forever. If you do testify and we finally get Tony Gambucci on hiring a hit, you should be safe from him. You see, we need your testimony to help put him away."

"There's no way, are you crazy? I'm not testifying against a crime boss." Charlotte could feel fear throughout her entire body. She started to sweat, her hands were shaking, and her mouth got very dry.

Ellis said, "well, young lady, the conditions of your relocation and the protection services of the FBI depend upon you giving testimony at the trial." Ellis paused and looked Charlotte in the eye and said, "look, Charlotte; it'll be easy. I'll guide you all the way. All you need to do is repeat what you heard John say at the theater. That's it! With that, you're fully protected by this office and the Federal Bureau of Investigation."

"That's what you guys always tell witnesses. Don't worry; we got your back. That's bull shit, and you know it! Look, I'm already scared of John coming to kill me, and now you're telling me there's a contract out on my life, and the New York mob is after me too? My life is over." *I'm dead. John, what have you done to me?*

"Charlotte, just to be cautious, I've asked that the US Marshal's service to join the FBI in protecting you at the safe house. The Marshals will be used in addition to Michelle and Vincent."

"U.S. Marshal's protecting me? Are you kidding? Mr. Ellis, these people are crazy. I read the news, and I saw John murder two people he knew in cold blood and not blink an eye. These people are heartless, and they have no morals. Marshals can't protect me. John will figure out where I am, he's a computer nerd. And this Big Tony character, I've never heard of him before, but it sounds like he's crazy too, and now *he* wants me dead?" *I'm dead.*

"First of all, John is being held on Riker's, and right now, only Vincent and Michelle know where you're staying. Once you're back at the safe house, we'll notify the US Marshal's office to send out more agents to protect you. We've recently purchased the house next door to your safe house as a precaution. That's where we'll send the Marshals. They'll be informed once you are back and safely tucked away with both Michelle and Vincent if that's okay with you?"

Looking back and forth between Vincent and Michelle, Charlotte said, "Yes, of course, I feel safer with both Michelle and Vincent around. But I don't know about testifying against the New York mob."

"I hate to put it this way, young lady, but you really don't have many choices."

The room became quiet. Charlotte looked out the window at the freedom tower and thought to herself. *I don't believe this is happening to me, what am I going to do? If I testify, I get protection; if not, I'm on my own. If John doesn't kill me, the mob will. How didn't I see this? What's wrong with me? What if I testify and stay in New York? What if I don't testify and move away on my own. I have a car and a bank account. God damn you, John!* Suddenly her mind wandered once again to her wedding day. *John was gone the entire day, he looked crumpled and nervous and sweating for the ceremony. Did he use our wedding as cover to kill someone? Is that why he insisted we go to San Diego to get married?*

Charlotte slowly looked up with tears streaming down her cheeks. She glanced at Vincent and then Michelle. Then, she looked Ellis in the eyes and blurted out, "Okay, I'll testify."

"Alright, I'll also start the paperwork for witness protection. We're going to fast track this through a special FBI organized crime budget. Is there somewhere you want to live?"

"We always talked about living in Scottsdale, Arizona!"

"Does John know this?"

"Yeah, of course, it was our dream to live out west together."

"Well, that's the first place he'll look for you. How do you feel about Wisconsin?"

"Really? The cheeseball State?"

"That's cheese head State, and they have a baseball team in Milwaukee, an excellent one at that. Charlotte, the least likely place they'll look for you, is Wisconsin. We have a home ready to go that didn't quite work out for someone else. We've thought of every detail; we have a house where utilities are already set up, a car, credit history, and even a bank account. We can transfer the title to your new name and have you there in a matter of days. You're going to a small town outside of Milwaukee called Jackson, Wisconsin. The population is only three thousand, and it sets right in the heart of the Kettle Moraine Forest. You'll love it."

"Kettle Moraine Forest? Population three thousand, are you kidding me? I'm a New Yorker, I can't live in a small town in the middle of nowhere."

"I'm sorry, but given the circumstances surrounding this case, I don't think we can put anything else together quickly enough to get you out of here in a week. New York is too dangerous, and it will be impossible to hide you locally. Gambucci has too many friends all over the City."

ELEVEN

Vincent, Michelle, and Charlotte left the US Attorney's office and headed back to the safe house. They stopped at a drive-through for a quick burger and fries and then drove straight to the Bronx. *You guys know an occasional salad wouldn't kill you?* This time when Vincent pulled up to the safe house, he parked the SUV inside the garage. Michelle took the lead and quickly checked out the yard and went into the house to check it out. She returned to the garage a few moments later and said it was clear. Charlotte followed behind Michelle, and when she got inside the house, she went straight to her room and laid down.

While lying on the bed, she couldn't stop thinking about how she should have just kept her mouth shut and ignored the situation. Maybe divorce John and move on with her life, just forget what she saw. *Why in the world would I throw it all away? What was I thinking?*

Charlotte sat up on the bed and crossed her legs underneath her body. Then she pulled out her sketch pad and started drawing a new design. She drew a picture of a girl standing outside in a yard facing a large picture window. Beneath the window was a flower bed with rose bushes. By the look on the girl's face, you could tell she was confused.

Her eyes were drawn to the roses. This made Charlotte smile, recalling something Matisse once said, *roses are the hardest flower to draw because everyone draws them.*

After a little while, she drifted off to sleep and woke up a few hours later. She reached over on the nightstand and grabbed the remote to turn on the TV. A few moments into the local news, John's face appeared on the screen next to the face of Tony Gambucci. The newscaster talked about how John was being charged with the double murder of Greg and Carol Fletcher. She continued, "how can our government be willing to let a hitman go free, just to convict Gambucci?" *Is John going free?*

The newscaster said, "John Mancini, the hitman, killed at least two dozen people if not more over the past decade." *How was that possible, how stupid am I?* The newscaster continued, "and Tony Gambucci, the crime boss, ordered dozens of murders over the same period." The logic was to go after the head of the snake. Charlotte thought *this could be a good thing, right? Maybe I won't have to testify if John testifies instead of me.* She was sick to her stomach, hearing this.

TWELVE

Charlotte stood in front of the TV in a trance. An unexpected knock at the door brought her out of her daze. It was Michelle. She walked over and opened the door. "Come in."

"Hi, we wanted to know if barbecue ribs are okay for dinner. I know a great place around the corner."

"Um, right now, I'm sick to my stomach, but in general sure, I like barbeque."

"Great, we'll eat around six-thirty. Do you need anything?"

"No, I'm good. It would be nice to have my hair products. Damned if I didn't forget to grab them."

"I know how it is; I'm sorry you have to use what they give us here for now. You shouldn't be here too long; it's too risky to keep you in New York. The higher-ups want you sent to Wisconsin and out of the State as soon as possible. There are concerns regarding the contract that Big Tony had put out on you, and now if John goes free, we fear he'll be looking for you too."

"Do you think John will go free?"

"Well, he may make bail, but eventually he'll probably do a little time. You must realize he's going to help the Federal Government take down one of the most notorious crime bosses of our time. Big Tony is responsible for more than a hundred murders: child prostitution rings on several continents, drugs, and tons of extortion cases. He came from Italy years ago and set up shop in New York City. He wiped out most of the other families and took over the entire city. We believe he still has ties to organized crime throughout Europe, South America, and Canada. Charlotte, this is, without a doubt, the highest profile target the FBI has had in at least a couple of decades. He's at the top of the FBI wish list. We've never been able to make anything stick to this guy. John is the most promise we've ever had. He literally knows where the bodies are buried."

Suddenly, the house shook from an explosion, and the windows in the bedroom blew right out. There was glass all over the room. Charlotte was flung off her feet and onto the bed, "What the hell was that?" she screamed.

Michelle was thrown up against the wall and landed on the floor on her butt. "I think the house next door just blew up! Dammit, they found you, but they got the wrong house. They got the address we gave to the US Marshals."

Michelle rose to her feet and drew her gun. She yelled to Charlotte, "Get in the bathroom now! Lock the door and lay down in the tub, and don't move until Vincent or I come back to get you. Do you understand?"

Shaking her head, Charlotte said, "I—I—I do." Charlotte tried but couldn't get anything else out of my mouth. Her ears were ringing and plugged like when you get off an airplane. Charlotte crawled into the tub as Michelle had instructed her too. She closed her eyes and buried her face in her hands. *Charlotte's mind again flashed back to her wedding day. The image was vivid now, John's tuxedo was crumpled and had dirt on it. He was sweating profusely and nervous. John never sweats, he was always calm, relaxed, and in control. I know he was there to kill someone. Son of Bitch if he didn't use my wedding as cover to do a job. What a lying bastard.*

Moments later, she heard knocking on the bathroom door. "Charlotte, it's Vincent come on out we need to get you out of here, now!"

Charlotte quickly crawled out of the tub and unlocked the door to peek out and see if it was, in fact, Vincent. With the ringing in her ears, she could vaguely hear what Vincent was saying. Charlotte yelled aloud, "Yeah, I'm fine. My ears are ringing, but I'm not hurt."

Vincent had his gun drawn, and then grabbed the suitcase with his other hand and yelled, "the ringing will go away in a while, we need to get going. Come on." He pushed her through the doorway and down the hall, out the back door and into the garage.

Charlotte moved quickly and climbed into the back seat. Michelle was in the driver's seat this time, with her weapon drawn. Vincent placed the suitcase in the rear of the vehicle and told Charlotte to lie down in the back and stay down. Weak from fear, somewhat deaf from the blast, and shaking, she laid on the floor of the SUV, covered her head with her hands, and once again, quickly flashed back to her wedding day. Fletcher's were there, they *knew what was going on too. How could I have been so naïve? Did Carol know also? Am I the only stupid one here?* Finally, Charlotte snapped out of it and yelled, "Where are we going?"

"A hotel far away from here. And then to the airport in the

morning. We need to get you out of New York City, now!"

Michelle quickly backed the SUV out of the garage. She drove like their lives depended upon it. Charlotte laid still on the floor in the back of the SUV. Sad and depressed that her life had taken such a turn. Life will never be the same, Charlotte will never be the same.

THIRTEEN

The house next door was demolished, all that was left was smoke and rubble. They traveled to interstate 95 and drove south for about two hours. After 20 minutes on the highway, Michelle told Charlotte she could sit up. "What the hell just happened?" Charlotte asked.

"Big Tony must have found out where we were hiding you from someone in the US Marshals office. He somehow arranged the place to explode. Probably a gas explosion if I had to guess," Vincent said.

"I told you guys, there's no way you can protect me; these people are crazy. Are you sure you want to be assigned to protect me? My life is over, he'll find me, I know it."

Michelle interrupted, "Charlotte, listen to me, you're safe. We took every precaution by not telling anyone the exact address where you were staying. I promise to keep you safe."

"I know that and thank you for protecting me. But I don't see how you can protect me forever. They'll find me, you said it, Big Tony has people all over the world." *My life is over, I know it. Shoot me now and save them the trouble later. It will be a mercy killing.*

After driving for another hour, they decided to stop at a roadside diner for dinner. Michelle ordered a burger and fries, while Charlotte picked at a salad. Vincent, however, ordered a steak, baked potato, and dessert.

"How can you eat at a time like this? Especially a bloody steak?" Charlotte asked.

"I like steak, and we're safe, aren't we? It's a good thing they had the wrong address." *Charlotte looked at the steak and wanted to vomit.*

"We gave the Marshal Service the address next door on purpose. It looks like Big Tony had his hooks in someone there too. No doubt, there will be an investigation on who knew what and when. I promise you; someone is going down for this screw-up," Michelle said.

When they finished eating, Vincent retrieved the SUV and pulled up to the door of the restaurant. Michelle cleared the way, and Charlotte followed her and climbed into the back seat.

They drove a few more minutes down 95. They then exited onto 295, finally stopping at a hotel in Cherry Hill just outside of Philadelphia. Not a fancy place, but adequate. One of those two-story hotels or maybe they're called motels where the doors all lead to the outside.

Vincent said, "We should be safe here for the night. Tomorrow we'll meet our jet at Northeast Philadelphia Airport and take you to the West Bend Airport."

FOURTEEN

Vincent rented three adjoining rooms. Michelle took the connecting room next to Charlotte, and Vincent took the room on the other side, boxing her in between the two agents. It was your typical motel room in that it smelled like Lysol and stale cigarettes. These places were the last to ban smoking in the rooms. The carpet was old and stained and probably held most of the smell, the TV's were small flat screens, and the clock on the side of the bed was bolted to the nightstand. The curtains were some color that Sherwin Williams would have difficulty identifying. The heater and air conditioner were single units coming out of the wall. In the bathroom, the tub/shower combination was cast iron. Surprisingly, the shower curtain was new. The sink was just that, a sink attached to the wall, with no vanity to set anything on. Finally, the towels were old, tattered, and rough on your skin. They had the name of the motel printed on one side. *Like someone would want to steal them.*

Charlotte had some trouble falling asleep on account of her ears still ringing a little, but mostly because she was afraid, the mob followed them from New York. Eventually, she fell into a deep sleep.

Michelle woke Charlotte up at five-thirty the next morning. *Don't these people ever sleep-in?* She quickly showered and brushed her teeth. When Charlotte was dressed and ready to go, she made herself a cup of hotel room coffee.

They left the room by six AM. It took approximately an hour to get to the private airport just outside of Philadelphia. Vincent drove right up to the airplane, and they boarded immediately.

Vincent and Michelle both boarded the plane, but Vincent just wanted to say goodbye. Michelle will be the only one joining Charlotte on this trip to Wisconsin. He put his giant arms around her and held her tight for a full minute. He whispered, "be safe" and told her to call him if she ever needed to talk. His personal number is programmed into the new phone she'll get from Michelle on the plane. *I'll miss Vincent.*

FIFTEEN

The G5 jet was fancy inside. It had twelve big comfortable leather seats and a couple of tables: small televisions and a small kitchen for drinks and meals. The pilot wasted no time taking off. As soon as Vincent deplaned, the flight attendant shut the door, and they sped down the runway and lifted off very quickly. The pilot announced that from takeoff to touchdown, the trip would take less than two hours at fifty-five thousand feet.

For the duration of the flight, Michelle explained in detail what was going to happen over the next few months. The plane was landing in a small town about an hour north of Milwaukee, Wisconsin, called West Bend. A car will be waiting for them, and they'll drive about fifteen or twenty minutes south to Jackson, to a house the FBI purchased for the witness relocation program. Charlotte was given a smartphone with both Michelle's and Vincent's number's pre-programmed into it. Also, a new Social Security number, a credit card, a new driver's license, and even a one-year membership to the local YMCA. Her new name is going to be Scarlet Maxwell. Michelle said, "it will be hard at first, but you'll get used to the name Scarlet in no time at all."

"It sounds like a stripper name. Why couldn't I pick something like Jessica? Victoria? You know I always liked the name Michelle, how about that?"

"Scarlet, we like to keep the names close to your current name. We find it is easier to adapt to the new life when your new name is close in sound to your existing name. Besides, Scarlet O'Hara is from Gone with the Wind. I think it's pretty."

"Well, okay then, Scarlet it is," Scarlet said.

It was a smooth flight from Philadelphia. When they landed in West Bend, the plane taxied up to one of the many hangers where there was a white Jeep Grand Cherokee parked and running. Michelle grabbed her bag from one of the other seats on the plane. While they deplaned, the pilot pulled Scarlet's (Charlotte's) bag from the underbelly and put it in the back of the waiting Jeep.

The pilot handed Michelle a card and said to call when she was ready to return to New York. Michelle nodded and said, "Thank you."

SIXTEEN

They climbed into the Jeep and drove down Highway 33 to the 41/45 freeway and turned south. About ten minutes later they exited at Highway 60 (or Main Street) in the town of Jackson. Following Google Maps on Michelle's phone, she drove ten more minutes until they reached a street called Rosewood Lane. It was the third house on the right. They pulled into the driveway next to the house.

The house was a two-story brick home with a small porch and a picture window facing the street. The front door had a round top, which gave the house character. Scarlet stayed in the Jeep while Michelle went inside to check it out. After a little while, she stuck her head out the front door and waved at Scarlet to come inside.

Scarlet walked into the house and noted at once that it smelled like a new home, with fresh paint and what looked like newly refinished hardwood floors. The living room was on the left, and it had green curtains and white shutters. There was a lovely sofa with pretty pillows, a big overstuffed chair, a couple of tables with lamps, and an ottoman in front of the couch. There was a good-sized flat-screen TV on a stand across from the sofa too. To the right, you could see the dining room. It had an oval-shaped cherry table with six chairs. The dining room also had lovely sheers and shutters on the windows. All the floors were hardwood with what looked like wool accent rugs scattered throughout. The kitchen was straight ahead with all new stainless-steel appliances.

The windows in the kitchen had curtains and shutters. Off to the left of the kitchen was a small three-quarter bathroom. On the other side of the kitchen and down two steps, there was a landing. To the right, it led to a side door and out to the fenced-in backyard. To the left, it led down a set of stairs to the basement. The garage was detached and off to the side of the yard.

They continued down the hall, where there was a set of stairs that led up to the second floor. Scarlet walked up the creaking steps, turned a corner, and reached a hallway. There were three painted four-panel solid wood doors, two on the right, and one on the left. Turning into the room on the right, she found the first small bedroom, with hardwood floors and a queen-sized bed, a small nightstand, and a dresser. There were dark blue curtains and shutters on the windows to block out the sun. Scarlet returned to the hallway and turned toward the next room and entered the master bedroom. It was much larger than the other rooms with the same hardwood floors, except this room had beautiful wool rugs on the side of the bed and in front of the bathroom door. Taking up most of the room was a king-size bed with a fluffy white comforter, nightstands on both sides, and pretty lamps. There were patterned curtains over these windows too.

The bathroom door was off to the right. Scarlet looked in and could see one of those old cast iron claw tubs and a separate shower, toilet, and vanity. The bathroom floor consisted of a beautiful large decorative tile. She walked back into the hall to check out the last door. It was another bathroom with a shower, no tub, a toilet, and what looked like a granite vanity. When Scarlet returned to the living room, Michelle was there with her suitcase.

"Cute place, isn't it? It has everything but the family dog," Michelle said.

"Yes, it's adorable," Scarlet said. "Very nicely decorated, and clean. What am I supposed to do here?"

"Well, whatever you want. We've opened a bank account for you at a local bank called Commercial Bank of the Midwest. And we've deposited $50,000 in an account with your new name on it. That should be enough to keep you going for a while. We have a Visa card for you with a $20,000 limit. You, of course, are responsible for any charges. We built a credit history for you, so you have established credit and don't have to worry about applying for other credit or credit cards. I'll leave you a file with all the information you need to know about your credit history. I have names, addresses, education, and so forth all in the file for you. I'm certain we've thought of everything. You'll probably need to memorize your address, social security number, and your new cell phone number."

"I'll try to remember them. Do I get to keep the Jeep outside, too, or do I need to go buy a car?"

"Yep, it's yours. It's paid for too, the title is in your paperwork, and it too is in your new name. You should not have any expenses except for utilities like gas, electric, and water. We've put all those in your new name, so you'll receive a monthly bill from the utility companies. We assumed you would want the internet and cable, too, so you'll receive a bill each month from Charter Cable. Your internet password is in the file, as well. I suggest you get the lay of the land and then find a job and start making friends. It looks like a nice little town. Scarlet, it's an opportunity for you to start over with an established credit history, work history, and some money in the bank. In a couple of months, you'll receive the rest of your clothes from your home in New York. As soon as John is convicted, we'll seize your house cars and bank accounts. Also, we'll make sure you get officially divorced from John too. Look, the bottom line is, we believe you'll be safe here."

"Do I have to return to New York to testify?"

"Most likely you'll have to corroborate John's story about Big Tony calling him at intermission. You may also have to testify you and Vincent found the gloves, jewelry, and his clothes in the bag on the dining room table. Someone will reach out to you when the trial begins. Ellis will want to prepare you to testify."

"Michelle, how long are you staying with me here?"

"Only a day or two, I want to make sure you're okay and settled in," Michelle said.

"Thank you, Michelle. I know it's going to take some time to get used to the new surroundings and the name Scarlet."

"You'll be fine, after a week or so, it'll become second nature."

"I hope you're right." Scarlet opened the refrigerator and said, "Wine?" Scarlet opened a bottle of white wine, and they discussed the witness protection program in greater detail.

Michelle explained how and when to contact either her or Vincent. Michelle reiterated the importance of staying off social media like Facebook and Instagram. They discussed getting a dog. Michelle kept talking about how special her dog was and how important he is to her life.

Scarlet said, "I love animals, and I'm just not sure I could handle being responsible for another life right now. I need to figure out my own life first."

"I completely understand," Michelle said.

SEVENTEEN

Michelle stayed with Scarlet for a few days. While she was in Jackson, they drove around and located the bank where the FBI deposited the fifty thousand dollars. They visited the local Piggly Wiggly grocery store and used Scarlet's new ATM card to stock up on some supplies.

On the second day of Michelle's visit, Scarlet drove to West Bend. West Bend is about five or six times the size of Jackson and sits on the edge of the Milwaukee River. They located a Walmart, a farm store called Fleet Farm, a movie theater with fancy reclining seats, several more grocery stores, banks, and several auto dealers. The airport they flew into was private, so it was necessary to drive the hour to Milwaukee to catch a commercial flight to anywhere. West Bend had an eclectic downtown area where the sidewalks were made up of small bricks and loaded with little boutique shops, bars, restaurants, and a recently refurbished theater. There was also an art museum that currently had on display 1920s art deco and fashion.

Michelle explained how the FBI had set up an entire background, including credit history, past employers that can be contacted for references, and even friends that would vouch for her if necessary. Of course, they were probably FBI agents posing as former employers and friends. The FBI also provided copies of a new resume. The past they created for Scarlet had her living and working in Westerville, Ohio. Scarlet attended Otterbein, and her degree was in Art & Design, with a minor in horticulture (which was true, except her actual degree was from NYU).

They discussed the need for a back story about how Scarlet ended up in Jackson in case it came up in conversation. They decided on her Grandmother, who lived in Jackson after remarrying a man from West Bend, recently passed away. Scarlet came to Jackson to settle her estate and liked it so much she stayed. She had a bad breakup a few months ago, and it gave her a chance to start over clean. It was essential to try and stay somewhat close to the truth.

EIGHTEEN

It had been more than five months since Scarlet moved to Wisconsin, and today she decided to look for a job. Her bank account dropped a little from buying food, tools, gardening supplies, paint, and of course, wine. However, the FBI sent her a check for sixty-five thousand dollars. It was money seized from her and John's bank accounts and the proceeds from the sale of her car. The FBI also managed to arrange for an annulment from John.

While sitting in her Jeep outside of the local Piggy Wiggly store in Jackson, Scarlet's cell phone buzzed. She didn't get a lot of phone calls, and the area code was 202, so she knew it was either Michelle or Vincent.

"Hello?"

"Hi Scarlet, it's Michelle."

"Hi Michelle, what's up?"

"Scarlet, how are things going?"

"Pretty good, I was thinking of finding a job. I need something more challenging to keep me busy."

"That sounds like a good plan. Work will not only keep you busy but help you meet people. Have you made any friends yet?"

"Not really, but that's okay, we'll see how the job hunt goes first."

"You know a dog would help you meet people too? You get out for walks, go to the park. You know my Duke is a dude magnet. Guys love girls with big dogs."

"That's funny, a dude magnet. Look, Michelle, I'll really give it some thought. I can't logically get a dog until I make some friends, and this court case is behind me. So, tell me, what's going on?"

"Well, the trial is moving forward, and we're going to need you back in New York for a couple of days. I'll meet you at the West Bend Airport at two o'clock tomorrow afternoon. Go to the same place you and I were dropped off and leave your keys with a man named Bob."

"Will John be there too?"

"Yes, but you'll likely be able to avoid him. He cut a deal with the prosecutor to serve three years in El Reno Federal prison in Oklahoma, in exchange for testimony against Big Tony. I would guess he'll likely get out in a year and a half or two for good behavior. That means you only have to testify once, this week against Tony Gambucci."

"Are you sure I'm going to be safe? There's no way John or anyone else can get to me is there?"

"Yes, you'll be safe, I'm betting my life on it too, Scarlet. I'll be by your side every moment you're here. I have your back. Besides, no one knows you're coming back except the Judge, Ellis, Vincent, and me. We kept the Marshal Service out of it this time."

"That's good to know," Scarlet said.

"Scarlet, I know there's still a contract on your life, however, if it makes you feel any better, there's a contract out on John too. The word is for John dead before the trial, the payout is a hundred thousand dollars, and after the trial, the payout is fifty thousand dollars. Believe me when I say, Big Tony is profoundly serious about killing John." *Good, I hope it happens.* "Your testimony will be used to corroborate what John tells the jury and that you and Vincent found the evidence against him at your home. John's testimony is the one that's going to bury Big Tony. John had already led prosecutors to several of the bodies Big Tony ordered hits on."

"Michelle, I feel so stupid. I'll never understand how John hid all of this from me for so long. I'll never trust a man again. Men suck!"

"He's good Scarlet; he's incredibly good. I watched his deposition, and he is a solid witness. He came across very charming and believable. I could see how he was able to keep all this from you. It's not your fault."

"I guess so. Well, I'll see you tomorrow at the airport." Scarlet skipped her trip inside Piggly Wiggly and drove back home to pack an overnight bag with some dress clothes and toiletries for her flight back to New York. *Ugh! I'm sick to my stomach.*

NINETEEN

The next day Scarlet made the short trip to the West Bend Airport and met Bob. He took the Jeep keys and moved it into an airplane hangar. He told her it would be safe there until she returned. Just then, the FBI G5 approached the airport and landed. It slowly taxied over to where Bob and Scarlet were standing. When the plane stopped, the door dropped open, and Michelle appeared at the top of the stairs.

"Hi Scarlet, are you ready to go?"

"Not really, I'm scared to death."

"Oh, don't worry, I have your back. Come on up; we need to get going. I'll fill you in on what's happening and what to expect on the way back to New York."

Scarlet boarded the airplane and took the same seat she had over five months ago when she moved to Jackson. They sat across from each other and discussed what was going to happen when they landed. Michelle said, "Vincent is picking us up at Teterboro airport in New Jersey and driving us to the US Attorney's office in lower Manhattan. You remember Mr. Ellis, don't you?"

Scarlet nodded.

"He'll brief you on what he'll ask when you're on the stand tomorrow. He'll then prepare you for what the defense attorney is likely going to ask you. Then we'll go to a nice hotel in downtown Manhattan, compliments of the federal government, have dinner in the room, get some sleep, and then head to the courthouse in the morning. After you testify, we'll go right back to Teterboro and put you on the plane back to West Bend."

The plane landed a couple of hours later, and as promised, Vincent was there waiting in his black Chevy Suburban. Like before, Michelle looked around the tarmac before she allowed Scarlet to deplane. Once it was safe, Michelle stuck her head back in the plane and told her, "it's time to go."

Vincent waved and said, "Hi, Scarlet, it's been a while."

"Hi Vincent, it's so nice to see you again." *It was comforting to see a familiar face, and I really missed Vincent.* Vincent gave Scarlet a big hug and said, "Hop in the back, and we'll get going. Are you hungry? Should we stop and get something to eat before we head to Ellis's office?"

"No, I'm good, I just want to get this over with," Scarlet said.

"As you wish," Vincent said as he climbed behind the wheel. Scarlet walked around the SUV and climbed into the back seat behind Michelle.

The drive into New York City with traffic took about forty minutes. They pulled up to the underground garage. The guard was different this time, but they didn't have any problems once Vincent flashed his FBI badge.

TWENTY

They boarded the elevator, and Michelle pushed the button for the fifteenth floor. Scarlet asked, "Why fifteen? We were on eleven before, right?"

Michelle explained, "It's just a precaution, Scarlet. It's a private floor we use from time to time. It's mostly for witnesses we don't want anyone in the office to see or know who we brought in. We believe It's important that nobody knows you're back in New York. It's for your protection. Ellis will meet us in a conference room up there."

The elevator stopped at fifteen, and they were met by an empty lobby with secured doors on the right and left. Vincent used an electronic key card to open the door on the left. When they entered the door, there was a long hallway with about a dozen additional doorways on both sides of the hall, all closed. They walked into the first door on the right. It was a small conference room with no windows and a solid door. Vincent flipped on the lights and directed Scarlet to a seat. Vincent and Michelle sat across from Scarlet, facing the door. The table was rectangular, and it had eight comfortable cloth chairs around it. There was also a projector hanging from the ceiling and a screen at the front of the room. A few minutes later, Mr. Ellis entered the room. He held a large stack of folders, a legal pad, and a leather briefcase. Ellis sat at the head of the table and placed his folders and legal pad down in front of him.

Ellis immediately turned to Vincent and asked, "Did you enter through the garage, and did anyone see you?"

"We did, and I don't think anyone except the guard saw us." Vincent slid the keycard across the table to Ellis.

Next, he turned to Scarlet and said, "good afternoon, Charlotte, how're you doing?"

A curious look crossed Scarlet's face, she hadn't heard the name Charlotte in a long time. "I'm scared to go anywhere near New York City. It's frightening after the last time I was here; remember, someone tried to blow me up."

"Well, Charlotte, this time, we took a lot of extra precautions. No one knows you're here except the people in this room and the judge."

"You know it seems odd to hear you call me Charlotte."

"Oh yes, my apologies. But when you get on the stand, we'll address you as Ms. Mancini or Charlotte. I will first ask you to state your name, and that's the name you must use to protect your witness protection identity. Do you understand?"

She nodded and said, "yes, of course."

"Before we get started, does anyone want coffee or something else to drink?" Everyone shook their heads no. Ellis continued. "Good. Today we're going to cover what I'm going to ask you tomorrow on the stand and what we believe the defense attorney will ask you. Charlotte, it's critical you keep your answers short and to the point. Don't try to explain anything unless the opposing attorney or I ask you to explain further. If you can answer yes or no, do it. Do you understand?"

"Yes. No. I get it." She was extremely nervous, her hands were sweating, and she was trembling.

"Listen to me, young lady, when I tell you, I will protect you when I can. I will object when the defense attorney crosses any lines. Otherwise, just be honest and answer with yes or no when you can."

"Okay."

"Now, Charlotte; this is especially important. Tony Gambucci has many resources and is extremely dangerous. The defense attorney, Mr. DeCarlo, is an exceptionally good attorney. He will try to trip you up, and if he finds any inconsistency from your deposition and your testimony, he'll pounce on you like a caged tiger. He has a copy of your deposition. That's the statement you gave to me that we recorded, the last time you were in my office. So, he already knows your story. Just stick to the facts. Okay?"

"I understand," Charlotte said.

"Please relax; I don't mean to scare you. What I'm trying to do is prepare you. Remember, keep it simple and be truthful. If you do that, you can't get into any trouble on the stand. If you don't understand a question, say you don't understand and leave it at that. He'll have to rephrase the question. Ok?"

Scarlet nodded. The entire afternoon was spent reviewing her original testimony. Ellis would ask questions in different ways, and Scarlet was expected to answer. He continued to try and drill into her how important it was to stick to the facts. It was a scary experience for Scarlet. She was terrified to take the stand.

TWENTY-ONE

They left the US Attorney's office and checked into a hotel nearby called Plaza Athenee. Vincent rented three rooms again, with two connecting for Michelle and Scarlet. Scarlet's room looked like something out of a Jane Austin novel. The furnishings were all colorful and full of flowers, the carpet was red, and the bed was made up like a dollhouse. It had a floral comforter, no less than ten pillows, and a white bed skirt. The bathroom was magnificent. There were separate shower and tub, dual vanity, fluffy towels, and all the toiletries you could ask for. There were small bottles of fancy shampoos and conditioners, along with bath salts for the tub, and French soaps.

After they checked-in, everyone went their separate ways for a couple of hours to freshen up. Scarlet pulled out a sketch pad and began to draw pictures of the beautiful flowers on the furniture and bedspread.

At six, they met in Vincent's room to order dinner from room service. The conversation was mostly focused on life in Wisconsin. Scarlet explained how she was going to look for a job when this was all over. She hadn't made any real friends yet but was looking forward to it. She said she was spending a lot of time decorating the house, painting, and drawing.

When they finished eating, everyone retired to their rooms. Scarlet laid on top of the comforter and listened to the TV in the background. She kept staring at the painting of Venice, Italy, on the ceiling until she finally dozed off to sleep, still in her clothes. *Oh my God, this bed is so comfortable.*

Scarlet's dreams were more nightmares than they were dreams. She had to re-live John shooting Greg in the head and seeing the look on Carol's face when her chest exploded with blood. There was so much blood on Carol's face and hands; the sight was disturbing. She must have wept throughout the night because when Scarlet woke up the next morning, her eyes were swollen and sore, and the pillow was wet from her tears.

The alarm clock buzzed at seven AM. Scarlet was already awake, lying in bed staring up and daydreaming of visiting the place the picture on the ceiling was painted from. After some coffee and a shower, she was ready to go by nine. Today, Scarlet wore her hair up and out of her face. She dressed in black slacks, a floral blouse, a jacket, and black pumps that made her look nearly six-feet tall.

TWENTY-TWO

Vincent took the elevator down to the garage to pick up the Suburban. At the same time, Michelle and Scarlet waited in their room. A text came through to Michelle to notify her that Vincent pulled the Suburban out front. The girls took the elevator down to the lobby, and Scarlet waited in the portico until Michelle looked around the street and summoned Scarlet that it was safe to climb into the vehicle.

They drove to One Federal Plaza in lower Manhattan and pulled into the underground garage. Once again, Vincent had to show his FBI credentials before they were allowed to use this garage. Vincent parked the SUV in a spot away from all the other cars. Once parked, they boarded the elevators, and Vincent pushed the button for the twelfth floor.

Michelle began explaining the procedure they must follow this morning. "We're going to wait in a conference room outside the courtroom until they're ready for you. Both Vincent and I will be there the entire time. When they're ready for you, we'll walk you to the door, and then leave you at the courtroom with a US Marshal to enter. I'm not allowed to enter the courtroom with you because *I'm* armed. Vincent is a witness, so he isn't allowed inside either. We'll both be right outside the courtroom door when you're done testifying. Do you understand?"

"Yes, of course," Scarlet said.

"After you're finished testifying, we'll go directly to the

airport and fly you home. Alright?"

"Great, I can't wait to get this over with. Do you know if John is in there?"

"No, he's not, he testified yesterday, so he's now on his way to Oklahoma. But I'll tell you this, Big Tony is at the defense table. Try not to make eye contact with him. He's big and scary and will likely try to throw you off your game and try to intimidate you by staring through you," Vincent said.

"Ok, I'll try not to look at him," Scarlet said. *How scary can he be?*

Michelle said, "Remember what Ellis told you, look at the Jury, not Big Tony."

They were only in the conference room for an hour when there was a knock at the door. The bailiff said, "We're ready for you, Ms. Mancini." Suddenly it was hard for Scarlet to breathe. Her nerves were getting the better of her. Under her breath, she said to herself, "Relax Scarlet, you're going to be okay. Damn, I need a drink."

TWENTY-THREE

As they approached the courtroom, the door opened slowly. Scarlet was met by a US Marshal who walked her to the stand. She kept looking at the crowd as she walked past each row. She was met at the witness stand by a bailiff. Scarlet stood in front of the seat and noticed her hand was shaking as she placed it on the bible and agreed to tell the truth. *Stay calm; you can do this, be strong; this bastard has ruined your life.*

The room was more substantial than Scarlet thought it would be. It was cold and very bright. The audience was filled with all sorts of people. She immediately recognized some were reporters because they had their pads out and were writing. A couple of artists were drawing the room. Scarlet thought, *I hope they sketch me pretty.* Some of the audience were spectators, and some were there to support Big Tony. His supporters looked just like gangsters in the movies. They wore pin-striped suits, with starched white shirts, fancy ties, pocket squares, well-shined shoes, pinky rings, and slicked-back hair. Just in front of the audience, there were two large tables. Mr. Ellis and what appeared to be a couple of other attorneys were at the table on the right. On the left, Big Tony and his attorneys were sitting and staring at her every move. In front of the lawyer's in the middle between the two tables was an elderly woman sitting at a small table with what looked to be a PC taking down everything said in the courtroom. The room was old, with a lot of dark wood walls, very worn solid wood floors, high ceilings, and artwork of courtrooms from the past. The Jury was off to the left of the witness stand, and the Judge was to the right.

Scarlet couldn't help herself; she had to look at Big Tony. The man was enormous. He was six-three, three hundred and fifty pounds with a dark complexion. His hair was jet black, probably dyed, and thinning on top. He had unusually large ears, dark bags under his eyes, and a prominent Italian nose. Big Tony wore a custom made dark blue pin-striped suit, white shirt, red power tie, with matching pocket square, and cuff links. He had a couple of flashy rings on his fingers too. Big Tony's eyes were very dark and scary. He stared intently at Scarlet like he wanted to burn a hole through her heart. *Vincent was right; Big Tony is very scary.*

TWENTY-FOUR

Scarlet sat down and immediately took a drink of water. Her nerves caused her mouth to dry up. She cleared her throat a few times and took another sip. Ellis rose from his seat and slowly walked toward the stand. "Good morning Ms. Mancini."

"Good morning."

"Please state your full name and relationship to the defendant."

"My name is Charlotte Marie Mancini, and my ex-husband worked for the defendant."

"Who is your ex-husband?"

"John Mancini."

"In what capacity did he work for the defendant?"

"John was…is a hitman; he kills people for the defendant."

"Objection, your honor, there's no way for Ms. Mancini to know if her husband worked directly for my client."

"Your honor, we will establish how Ms. Mancini came to this conclusion with my next question, may I have a little latitude, please?"

"Mr. Decarlo, I don't have a problem with the question. Asking a wife about her husband's employer, regardless of what he does, it makes perfect sense to me. You may not like the answer, but I think it should be fair game. Overruled!"

"Thank you, your honor. Now, Ms. Mancini, how do you know that your husband worked for the defendant?"

"I saw him kill two people." Scarlet lost focus for a moment, and suddenly her mind flashed back to their wedding day, *I know he was in San Diego to kill someone.*

"Objection, your honor. Mr. Ellis is laying crumbs disguised as facts, we need facts."

"Your honor, the fact is Ms. Mancini saw her husband kill two people. I'll tie the murders back to the defendant in just a moment, let her finish telling her story."

"I agree, allow her to finish the story. Overruled."

"Please explain."

"We were at the theater on Thursday night, March first, and John got a phone call from someone named Tony at intermission."

"Objection, it's hearsay." *Bastard won't let me finish a sentence. What an asshole.*

"But it's not your honor; Ms. Mancini was standing next to her husband when he took the phone call, she heard her husband clearly say the name Tony several times. She heard what she heard your honor, it is not hearsay. It's not like she is saying she heard the person on the other end of the phone say yeah, this is Tony Gambucci."

"Objection overruled. Please continue Ms. Mancini."

"Well, John kept telling this Tony person he couldn't do the job because I was with him. Finally, he gave in and said, Tony, I'll handle it. A few minutes later, another call came in, and he told me to go back to the seats, and he would be there shortly."

"How long was it before he returned to the seats?"

"I'd say fifteen minutes." *Calm down, you can do this. Focus.*

"Thank you; please continue, what happened next?"

"On the way home, John told me we were going to stop at our friend's house in Queens. We pulled up in front of the neighbor's house, and he walked up to the front door. At first, he tried to open the door, and when it didn't open, I could see him press the doorbell and knock. I saw that my friend Carol answered, and then let him inside. So, I decided to go up to the house and say hello. On my way to the front door, I stopped for a moment and looked through the curtains in the living room window. I saw Greg and Carol on their knees with their hands in the air." Scarlet's chin dropped to her chest; tears began to flow down her cheeks. Her voice slightly cracked.

"I know this is difficult, Ms. Mancini, please tell us what happened next," Ellis asked.

"Then, then John just shot them. He shot Greg in the head and Carol in the Chest." *Oh my God, I am so nauseous.* Again, Scarlet put her head down and cried.

"Do you need a moment?"

She looked up with red swollen eyes and tears streaming down her face, and said, "No, I'm okay."

"What did you do next?"

"Well, at first, I froze and let out a scream and started crying, then I ran back to the car." Still visibly upset and with tears streaming down her cheeks, Ellis handed Scarlet a box of tissue. Scarlet said, "I can see it like it happened yesterday; it was so scary."

"Ms. Mancini, we can pause, are you sure you don't need a moment?"

"No, I'm sorry, I didn't realize…no I'm fine."

"Ok, did John Mancini, your ex-husband know you saw him kill these people?"

"No, he didn't. He never said anything; he just hummed to the music on the radio all the way home."

"What did you do on the way home?"

"I pretended to be asleep."

"Okay, what happened next?"

"We got home, and I went up to our bedroom, and John went to his den. He said he was going to check his email. The next day I went to the FBI office and told them what I saw."

"Please tell the court how you came about the blood-stained clothes and Mrs. Fletcher's jewelry found in your home."

"Special Agent Patterson from the FBI drove me to my house on March second, that was the next day. He joined me in the house and searched the garbage cans in my backyard. He found a pair of latex gloves with blood on them. While he was out back checking the garbage cans, I went up to my bedroom to look for any clothes John may have put in the hamper and to pack a bag. Before we left the house, I noticed a dry-cleaning bag on the dining room table. Agent Patterson dumped out the bag with the clothes and jewelry onto the table. We looked at the clothes, and they had blood splattered on them. We also found a leather bag inside that was filled with jewelry and a bunch of money."

"It wasn't your jewelry, correct?"

"Correct, it was not."

"Do you know whose jewelry it was?"

"I believe it was my friend, Carols. The one that John killed."

"Thank you, Ms. Mancini." Ellis turned to the defense table and said, "Your witness."

Whew, one down one to go. Scarlet could feel herself sweating through her jacket. Her mouth was dry, so she turned and asked the Judge for more water.

"Good morning Ms. Mancini. My name is Mr. DeCarlo; I'm the attorney for Mr. Gambucci. Thank you for returning to New York to testify. Please tell me, have you ever met Mr. Gambucci before today?"

"No." *Keep it simple, yes, or no when possible.*

"Did Mr. Mancini ever mention the name Gambucci to you?"

"No. But he did say, Tony—"

Interrupting, Decarlo said, "wait, that's not what I asked you, Ms. Mancini. Please only answer the question that I ask of you, did he ever mention the name Gambucci?"

"No."

"Let me make sure I understand your testimony for the Jury. You're saying you never met Mr. Gambucci. You don't know Mr. Gambucci. Your husband never mentioned Mr. Gambucci's name or doing work for Mr. Gambucci. And you have never heard of Mr. Gambucci until Agent Patterson said his name to you? Correct?"

"That is correct the way you stated it," Scarlet responded.

"So, your testimony earlier that your husband works for Mr. Gambucci doesn't make sense, does it? How could you not know the name of your own husband's employer?"

"Is that a question? It seems like he killed two people for Mr. Gambucci, I would say he works for him."

"We call that hearsay. You don't know for sure that it was Mr. Gambucci that hired your husband, now do you?"

"Objection, whose testifying your honor?"

"Sustained, move on, Mr. Decarlo."

"Yes, your honor. Ms. Mancini, can you tell me where you're currently living?"

"No."

"Why not?"

"Because I'm in—"

Mr. Ellis quickly rose and said, "Objection, your Honor!"

"Withdrawn." *Bastard did that to throw me off.*

"Ms. Mancini, on the night of March first, you allegedly saw your husband kill two people. How did you know it was my client on the phone at intermission since he never mentioned the name Gambucci?"

"First of all, John said the name Tony several times, and the FBI told me they got John's phone records, and that's who he was speaking with."

"You mean to say the phone number your husband was

speaking with came from Mr. Gambucci's home. You can't possibly know who he was talking with unless you recognized the voice on the other side of the conversation and knew from experience what Mr. Gambucci's voice sounded like, correct?"

Ellis rose from his seat again and said, "Objection, your honor, Mr. DeCarlo, is testifying again by trying to put words in the witness's mouth."

The judge said, "Mr. DeCarlo, if you would like to testify, put your own name on the witness list. If not, you need to move on."

"Yes, your honor. Ms. Mancini, did you see Mr. Mancini leave the theater at intermission?"

"I don't understand the question."

"In your statement, you said after intermission, you walked back to your seat alone, and Mr. Mancini turned and walked back toward the lobby, correct?"

"Yes"

"Did you see him go to the lobby or leave the theater? Couldn't he have been just gone to the men's room?"

"I suppose."

"Ma'am, yes or no?"

"What was the question again?"

"Did you see your husband leave the theater?"

"No, I did not," Scarlet said.

DeCarlo turned and walked back to his table and picked up a note pad. Reading from the pad of paper, he looked up at Scarlet again, and read the next question. "Now, why did you wait until the next day to go to the authorities?"

"I don't know; I was afraid, I guess."

"Did you get out of bed the next day and just drive to the FBI office in New York City?"

"No, I woke up and brushed my teeth and showered."

There was laughter in the courtroom.

"Ms. Mancini, what else did you do that morning after the alleged incident?"

I should say I masturbated. That would throw him off. "I went to work until noon and then decided to drive to the FBI office."

"An epiphany of sorts? Why didn't you just call the Police, why drive all the way to the FBI office in downtown Manhattan? We all know parking in Manhattan can be difficult at best."

"Gosh, I hadn't thought of that. I honestly don't know. It just seemed like the right place to go. I'm pretty certain I was in shock and not really thinking straight. After all, I did just see my husband shoot two people."

"Please, once again, only answer the questions I ask. So, let's be clear. You allegedly witnessed your husband shooting two people. Then, you go home without saying a word to your husband or contacting the police. I assume you sleep in the same bed with the man you just saw allegedly commit a crime. Then, the next day you wake up, brush your teeth, and shower, and go to work. At noon, you have a sort of conscience of mind and decide to physically drive to the FBI offices in New York City to tell them what you think you saw. Is this correct?"

"Yes, except for the allegedly part, I definitely saw what John did." There was some laughter and stirring in the audience, and the judge banged his gavel and told everyone to quiet down.

"Ms. Mancini, have you ever seen your husband use a gun?"

"No."

"Do you have guns in your home?"

"No."

"Have you ever discussed having a gun in your home with your husband?"

"No"

"Do you even know if your husband knows how to handle a gun?"

"Apparently so. I saw John shoot two people with a gun," Scarlet said smugly — more audience laughter.

"Quiet in the courtroom, or I will clear it." The judge banged the gavel down once again.

"What did the gun look like that your husband allegedly used?"

"It was big, like long. I think you call it a noise suppressor or a silencer on the end of the barrel. Because I didn't hear a gunshot."

"You didn't hear a gunshot?"

"No, but I saw…" *Damn it! I opened the door for this asshole.*

"Please just answer yes or no, I don't need you to explain."

"No, I did not hear a gunshot," she repeated.

"So, it may not have been a gun after all. If there was no sound, maybe there was no gun."

"I'm certain I saw a gun," Scarlet retorted.

"I'm sorry I didn't ask a question. Tell me, Ms. Mancini, did you have a drink at the theater?"

"Yes."

"How many drinks did you have?"

"A couple or maybe three glasses of wine."

"What was it, Ms. Mancini, two, three, or four?"

"It was just three. I'm sure of that."

"Did you have any drinks at home before you left the house?"

"I did, I had one glass of wine while I was getting ready to go."

"Let me make sure I counted correctly, you had four glasses of wine that night?"

"I guess so."

"No, it sounds like a fact, correct?"

"Sure, yes." *Asshole is making me out to be a drunk.*

"Do you think you were, say a little tipsy or even drunk?

"I don't think so."

"You know, or you don't know, this is not about, I think so."

Ellis rose again and said, "Objection your Honor, counsel is badgering the witness."

The Judge then weighed in with, "Mr. Decarlo asked and answered, move on."

"Yes, your honor. Ms. Mancini, you had a drink at home and three at the theater. Did you have dinner out in the City?"

"We did."

"Did you have drinks at dinner?"

"Um, yes."

"More wine?"

"Well, I had a cocktail when we got to the restaurant, and a glass of wine with my dinner."

"You had a cocktail and wine. What sort of a cocktail?"

"A martini, with four olives." The audience laughed again.

"Quiet, please," the Judge weighed in.

"Ms. Mancini, how much do you weigh?"

"Um, about a hundred and five or ten pounds."

"And you're about five-six or five-seven?"

"Yes, about."

"So, you had a martini and five glasses of wine. That's about an entire bottle of wine. Do you think your mind might have played a trick or two on you? Is it possible that you imagined any part of your story? Remember, you never heard a gunshot."

"First of all, they were small glasses of wine over four or five hours. And no, I saw what I saw. I know John shot my friends in cold blood; I saw it. The police found them dead the next day, shot right where I said, in the head and the chest." Her bottom lip began to quiver, and her hands began to shake. Scarlet felt a cross between really pissed off, and scared. *This lawyer is a major asshole.*

"I'm sure you did, Ms. Mancini. But at a hundred and ten

pounds, and five foot seven inches tall, and all that alcohol—"

Ellis Rose again, "Objection, your honor, Mr. Decarlo, is testifying again." The Judge told the jury to ignore Mr. DeCarlo's last statement. And he warned him to stop testifying.

"Sorry your honor, I have just one more question for you, Ms. Mancini. Did you see Agent Patterson take a pair of latex gloves out of the garbage can at your house?"

"No, sir, I didn't, but I did see them when he brought them into my kitchen."

"All I am asking is if you saw Agent Patterson take the gloves from your garbage can."

"No, I did not."

"Thank you, Ms. Mancini. So, to sum up, your testimony for the jury, you had never heard the name Gambucci before Agent Patterson said it to you, correct? You drank a bottle of wine and a martini the night of the alleged shooting. You never heard a gunshot. And you did not see Agent Patterson take the gloves from your garbage cans. Finally, to the best of your knowledge, you don't and never have had a gun in your home; am I correct on all accounts?"

"Yes, except for the bottle of wine. The wine I had were in really small glasses," Scarlet angrily said.

"Thank you, Ms. Mancini, no more questions for this witness, your honor."

The Judge then turned to Scarlet and said, "Thank you for your time; you may step down Ms. Mancini."

Before she could get up, Ellis said, "Your Honor, we

would like to readdress this witness."

"One moment, please remain seated, Ms. Mancini. Go ahead, Mr. Ellis."

"Ms. Mancini, the last time you were here in New York City, the FBI kept you in a safe house, correct?"

"Yes."

"Did any significant event occur when you were staying as a guest of the FBI?"

Before Scarlet could answer, Mr. DeCarlo jumped up from his chair and yelled, "Objection! Relevance?"

Ellis immediately turned to the Judge and said, "Your honor, we want to merely point out that Ms. Mancini is the target of a contract killing ordered by Mr. Gambucci, and—"

DeCarlo interrupted, "what does that have to do with this trial and my client? It's all irrelevant and unrelated in this particular trial."

Ellis turned to face the defense attorney and began to say, "really, counselor—"

The Judge finally stepped in, "Enough, you two. I tend to agree with Mr. DeCarlo Sustained! The Jury will ignore the question asked by the prosecutor and all his bloviating that followed. Do you have anything else, Mr. Ellis?"

"No, your honor, thank you."

The judge turned to Scarlet and said, "Ms. Mancini, thank you for your testimony; you may step down."

Scarlet was sweating so severely her blouse had soaked through her jacket, and her slacks stuck to her butt. The Marshal walked Scarlet to the door and opened it. As soon as she stepped out, Vincent and Michelle were there to escort her to the elevator.

"How did it go," Vincent asked.

"I don't know. I'm soaking wet from sweating, I can tell you that, and apparently, I have a drinking problem." *Damn, I need a drink.*

"Let's get you to your plane. You'll be home in no time and out of harm's way. You can put this all behind you and move on."

"Hey Michelle, do they have wine on that airplane?" *Shit, maybe I do have a drinking problem...Hmm, nope, my problem is I need a drink.*

Michelle smiled and said, "I think so."

TWENTY-FIVE

After Scarlet's testimony, they boarded the elevator and pressed S2 for sublevel two. The elevator made a couple of stops for people to get on and off before it landed on S2. The air was stale in the parking garage, but it felt good to Scarlet to be out of the courtroom. She climbed into the back of the SUV and scooted to the middle of the seats. She asked Vincent to turn on the air conditioning full blast so she could cool down.

"Teterboro is only thirty minutes away, at this time of day. Sit tight, and you'll be home before you know it," Vincent said.

As they pulled away from One Federal Plaza onto Lafayette, the window to the right of Scarlet exploded. Glass filled the seat where she usually sat. Michelle pulled her weapon from its holster, turned to Scarlet, and yelled to get down on the floor. Vincent made a quick left hand turn down Worth Street and sped up. Michelle kept looking behind them for any sign of the shooter.

"Vincent yelled, Scarlet, are you hit, are you okay?"

"I don't think so. I think I'm okay."

"How the hell did anyone know she was in town?" Michelle said.

"The courtroom was full of Tony's friends. Any number of them could have made a phone call or sent a text," Scarlet said. *Oh my God, I can hear my heart pounding in my ears.*

Scanning his rearview mirror, Vincent said, "Well, I think we're safe now. It appears to have been a sniper on one of the buildings across from the courthouse. I don't see anyone back there trying to follow us."

Michelle said, "I'm calling it in right now." She pulled out her cell phone and proceeded to call her office and report the sniper.

Scarlet got up from the floor and brushed the glass off the seat. She realized that if she sat where she usually does, the bullet would have hit her right in the head. Shaking and nervous, she said, "thank God I moved to the middle of the seat."

Michelle made several more phone calls trying to determine if Scarlet had been compromised. There were no other reports of a sniper in front of the courthouse. They arrived at Teterboro airport, and Vincent pulled up next to the airplane. Michelle told Scarlet to stay put, and she jumped out and ran up the steps and disappeared inside the plane. A few moments later, she returned and opened the back door and said it's all clear. "Come on, let's get you on the plane and out of here."

"Look, Scarlet, I'm going to ride with you back home and check things out. We need to make sure you weren't compromised."

"Okay, why do you think I was compromised?"

"Well, we don't know for sure someone inside the courtroom made a call. We think it would be safer if I came back to Wisconsin with you to check out your vehicle and your house one more time. The FBI takes an assassination attempt very seriously, especially when it's one of our protected witnesses. We need to ensure this attempt on your life was a random shot in the dark at trying to pick you off with a sniper. Our concern is they picked you up from the airport and figured out where you came from."

"I don't understand how they could possibly know I'm living in Wisconsin."

"Look, Scarlet, Tony has eyes everywhere. I'm sure your picture was passed around New York, New Jersey, and probably to other parts of the US trying to find you. We just don't know. Vincent will work the sniper from here, and I'll accompany you back to Wisconsin."

TWENTY-SIX

On the flight back home, Scarlet asked Michelle about the contract that Gambucci had out on her; "Why try to kill me now? I already testified, silencing me now won't make any difference."

"Scarlet, these guys hold a grudge forever. I'm sure Gambucci blames you for all of this. If you hadn't reached out to Vincent in the first place, this trial would never have taken place."

"So, you think this contract will never go away?" Scarlet asked.

"I'm sorry, but yes, it's likely Gambucci, and his people will look for you no matter where you are. That's why I'm going back home with you. Remember, this gangster has his hand in crime all over the world. You really won't be safe anywhere. That's one of the reasons why I think you should get yourself a guard dog, stay off social media, and always be aware of your surroundings. You need someone to watch your back, Scarlet. If you haven't learned by now, you will, that life is different when you're in witness protection. You're no longer like everyone else. You must always be on guard. A dog will have your back even when you're not aware of what's going on around you."

When they landed at the West Bend Airport, Michelle told Scarlet to stay on the plane for a minute while she looked in the hanger and made sure the Jeep was safe. Michelle disappeared for about ten minutes. When she returned, she said, "it's all safe, no bombs on or under the Jeep."

"Holy crap, bombs? What are you talking about?"

"Well, we can't be too careful. I told you Gambucci has an exceedingly long reach. Let's go, I want to look around your house."

TWENTY-SEVEN

On the drive south to Jackson from the West Bend airport, Scarlet said, "Hey, Michelle, are you hungry? Can we stop for something to eat?"

Michelle nodded, "sure, I could eat."

Scarlet drove toward her house and stopped at a little place on the main street in Jackson called Jimmy's Family Italian Diner. "I run past this place every day, and I've wanted to try it for some time now. I didn't want to go in alone."

Scarlet parked the Jeep, and they walked into Jimmy's diner. On the door, there was a handwritten sign that read *"Best Bloody Mary's in Wisconsin."* As you enter the restaurant, you're met by a bar that extends from the front door left for about thirty feet. There were a few booths up by the windows in front of the bar. The register was right in front of the door, and to the right was a dining room filled with tables and booths. Behind the cash register was a swinging door that led to the kitchen, and there was another swinging door from the dining room into the kitchen. The dining room was dim, but the windows up front let in some additional sunshine, that gave it some ambiance.

The waitress behind the counter said, "Hi, welcome to Jimmy's, just sit anywhere, and I'll follow you with menus."

In the dining room, several of the booths in front of the restaurant were occupied. They walked past a dozen more tables in the middle of the place to sit at one in the back. Of course,

Michelle sat against the wall facing the front of the restaurant. The waitress handed both women a menu and another single page with daily specials typed on it.

"Hi, my name is Mallory. What can I getcha to drink?"

Mallory was about Scarlet's age, tall, leggy, and thin, bushy blonde hair up in a ponytail and deep-set blue eyes. She had sort of an accent like she was from Fargo or Canada. She wore a black skirt and a black polo-type shirt that said Jimmy's on the left breast, and black Nike tennis shoes.

Scarlet asked, "are the Bloody Mary's really the best in Wisconsin?"

"Well, Jimmy thinks so," Mallory said.

"I'll have a Bloody Mary then, Michelle, how about you, can you have a bloody?"

"No, thanks, I'll just have coffee, black please."

Mallory wrote down the order and said, "Ok, ladies, there are a few specials on that one-pager, and I'll be right back with your drinks."

When she returned, she had the biggest Bloody Mary they both had ever seen. It was loaded up with olives, pickles, sausage, melon, and a small glass of beer on the side. As if there wasn't enough alcohol in the Bloody Mary, it came with a beer on the side.

"What's the beer for? I didn't order that."

"You're not from around here, are you?" Mallory asked.

"Ah, no, how'd you know?"

"We call it a chaser; it comes with a Bloody Mary when

you order it pretty much anywhere in Wisconsin."

"Why?"

"Well, I'm no expert, but I hear there are several theories of why we give you a beer chaser. The one I like most is that a Bloody Mary is supposed to be a hangover cure, and the beer is supposed to help ease all day drinkers back into drinking beer all day. A lot of the old guys that come in here still pour their beer in their Bloody Mary as they drink it down. I'm not sure why nobody knows the real story? Look, enjoy the beer either way. Are you ready to order, or do you need a little more time?"

"I'm going to have the minestrone and a Caesar salad without anchovies, please," Scarlet said.

Michelle said, "I'll have a tomato and cucumber salad and the lunch portion of the shrimp scampi."

Looking at Michelle, Mallory said, "I'll put your orders in right away. Flag me down if you change your mind on the Bloody Mary."

The food at Jimmy's was good. The salad was excellent with plenty of crispy fresh lettuce, and the tomatoes were amazing. Michelle said the scampi was great, and the tomato salad was delicious and fresh. Scarlet noted how she wanted to come back sometime for breakfast. They ate their meals and paid the bill and left Mallory a good tip.

Before Scarlet walked to the Jeep, Michelle went through the same security routine as they did in New York. Michelle left first and looked around and then returned to get Scarlet. The drive to the house was only about ten minutes from the restaurant. They pulled up in front and paused, then Michelle said to park in the driveway. Scarlet stayed in the Jeep until Michelle walked through the entire house, garage, and backyard. It was all clear. She came back to the Jeep to retrieve Scarlet, and they walked together into the living room. They visited for a couple of hours and talked about how important it was to be aware of your surroundings.

Michelle made the point to Scarlet again that she needed to, "make sure no one is following you, it's important to know your surroundings. And remember to stay off social media sites like Facebook and limit your use of the internet." After a few hours, Michelle gave Scarlet a big hug and called for an Uber for a ride back to the West Bend Airport.

Scarlet poured a glass of red wine, walked upstairs, brushed her teeth and took a shower. She put on a soft pair of pajamas and crawled into bed, drank her wine, and worked on a sketch of a little girl picking pretty wildflowers in a field. Her mind wandered, and she thought to herself, *I miss my life in New York. I miss being married, not necessarily to John, but the idea of having a partner to keep me company has some appeal. I wonder if I'll ever have the chance to have children. I am definitely feeling lonely and really want someone to do things with and share my life with.* Scarlet put the sketchbook down, laid her head on her pillow, and slowly dozed off to sleep.

About a week later, Scarlet saw on the news that Big Tony was convicted of murder and racketeering under the RICO act, and his sentence could be up to fifty years. She thought, *Good, I wish John would have gotten the same.*

TWENTY-EIGHT

Scarlet's plan before she left for New York was to find a Job. Upon her return to Jackson, she applied at several flower shops in the area and one high-end grocery store called Sendiks. Several offers poured in from the florists around the area, but she decided to take the job in West Bend at Sendiks. The family that owned the stores was involved in the hiring process. Scarlet shared many of her drawings, and they complimented her on how beautiful they were. When they hired Scarlet, they asked if she was flexible enough to vary her hours based on the need. Scarlet's job was to design and build flower displays for holidays and centerpieces for corporate events and weddings. Several corporations have their headquarters in West Bend, and they keep the flower shop busy in-between weddings. The first few weeks proved to be thrilling to see some of her drawings come to life again as centerpieces for corporate events.

Usually, each day on her way to work, Scarlet stopped at Jimmy's to get a coffee. Sometimes she'd order a bagel and draw a picture while sitting in a booth. Scarlet got to know Mallory quite well, and they quickly became friends and started to do things together after work. They would go into Milwaukee for a concert or shopping at a local mall.

Life was turning around for Scarlet; she made some friends at the YMCA found a great job and felt she was ready to start dating again. Eight months after the trial, Scarlet sat up-front in a booth at Jimmy's with her laptop computer open. She wanted to go on a local dating site called WBHookmeup.com and try to meet someone. For obvious reasons, Scarlet was concerned. Michelle had warned her about going on social media. Mallory assured Scarlet that only local people went on the site looking for a date or partner. Mallory said, "in fact, nobody from outside our area even knows about this website. It was set up by people, for people around here to meet people from the West Bend area."

Scarlet logged onto the website and typed in what she thought was a reasonably good profile. Mallory took a picture of Scarlet with her phone and uploaded it to the WBHookmeup.com website.

Mallory said, "hey Scar, read me your profile."

"OK, I'm twenty-nine years old, five foot eight inches tall, athletic build, blue eyes, no tattoos, but not adverse to getting one, and an animal in bed."

"No! you didn't write that, did you?"

"No, I said I was five-seven, guys don't like women when they're too tall."

"I mean the animal in bed part, ya dork."

"No, I was kidding. I wrote I'm twenty-nine years old, five-seven, athletic build, blue eyes, single, no kids, no animals, but I like them, and no tattoos. I like to draw, but I'm not an artist and a non-smoker. Looking for someone active and interested in going on hikes, to the theater, concerts, or even a baseball game."

Mallory acting hurt said, "I'm getting the feeling you're trying to replace me?"

"No, I'm not replacing you. I'm just looking for more companionship than you can provide. You know what I mean."

"Yeah, of course, you need to get laid."

"Well, yeah, that's what I was thinking."

Mallory walked away and said, "I gotta get back to work, Jimmy's here."

Jimmy walked through the swinging door with his bagel and coffee and said, "Hey blondie, what are you working on?"

"I'm trying to find a date."

"You? Guys should be crawling all over themselves to go out with you. Sometimes you're gorgeous."

"Thanks, Jimmy, just sometimes?"

"Well, you know you keep coming in here in your running clothes, but when you clean up, you have potential."

"Thanks, Jimmy." *Potential for what, I wonder.*

"Why are you looking for a date, got something coming up?"

"No, it's just that Mallory can't meet all my needs."

"Oh, you need to get laid, huh?"

"None of your business, Jimmy."

"Alright, Blondie, good luck with that."

Each day Scarlet came into the restaurant for coffee; she and Jimmy would have these short sessions of banter. They start quickly and end just as fast. She completed the profile and posted it online and then packed up her laptop and sketchbook and headed to work. Scarlet spent the day designing and building beautiful centerpieces for a wedding this weekend. She stayed at work until nine that night because the arrangements had to be perfect. Mallory sent a text around seven to go out for a drink; Scarlet declined because it was crucial to finish this order tonight. She grabbed some sushi from the deli and drove home.

When Scarlet got home, she pulled out her laptop and logged onto WBHookmeup.com to see if there were any responses to her profile. "Shiiiit!" She said out loud to no one in particular. Fifteen guys were pinging her back for a date. She quickly picked up her cell phone and called Mallory.

"Hey Mal, I just got home, and I checked WBHookmeup, there's like fifteen guys that sent me messages and are asking me out."

"Any of um cute?"

"Yeah, some, do you want to see them and help me pick a few out to call?" Scarlet said.

"I work tomorrow until two, but after that I'm free. I can come over and look at who you've narrowed it down too, and help you pick a few out."

"Ok, see you tomorrow, Mal."

"Bye, Scar."

TWENTY-NINE

After eating her sushi, Scarlet walked upstairs and took a shower, brushed her teeth, and went to bed. In the morning, she made herself some coffee and logged onto WBHookmeup.com again. There were several more requests for dates. Scarlet looked at each profile and started deleting guys just on their looks. She thought *I'm acting awfully shallow here.* That left about ten pictures for Mallory and Scarlet to consider. Mallory showed up at two fifteen, and they looked at the final ten profiles together and decided to pick out five for Scarlet to contact. Her response was simple. *I like your picture and profile and would like to talk on the phone. Please send me a phone number, and I will call you this week.* Three of the five responded within a few minutes and gave her a phone number to call, and the other two a few hours later.

"Mal, will you and Adam double date with me if I decide to go out with one of these guys?" Adam and Mallory have been together for over a decade. Who knows if they will ever marry? If you ask either one about it, they say the other doesn't want to get married.

"Of course, honey. Adam can check them out and see if they're douche bags. But first, you should have them meet you at the diner for coffee some morning. Then I can check them out right away."

"Okay, I'm going to call one of them tonight."

"Which one?"

"I'm not sure. Maybe Austin. He's twenty-eight, single, never married, no kids, no pets, non-smoker, and he has a job. No job is a deal-breaker. Lawyers are deal breakers too. I hate lawyers."

"Me too. Lawyers are sucky tippers."

"Bloodsucking evil bastards, if you ask me," Scarlet said under her breath. Scarlet pointed at a picture on the screen and said, "What about this one? I like his smile."

"Who is he?"

"Garrett. He's twenty-nine, divorced, no kids, nice eyes, athletic, and gainfully employed. He wrote he was looking for a woman that enjoys the outdoors, water sports, the sun, sporting events, and good food. This profile sounds a lot like me. I like baseball and good food."

Mallory reaching for the laptop, said, "let me see that." Mallory looked at the entire profile and handed Scarlet the computer back. She said, "He's cute and has a nice smile, take a look at all his answers to the profile questions before you call."

Scarlet read over all his responses, and they seemed on the up and up. "I know people lie on these dating sites, so I want to be super careful. Ok Mal, I'll call Garrett tonight. And maybe Austin tomorrow."

"Damn, girl, you could be a Hookmeup slut."

"I am not. I just want options."

THIRTY

El Reno Federal Prison (Library)

As part of John Mancini's deal with the FBI, he accepted a sentence to El Reno Federal Prison for three years. He was eligible to get out in about two. Big Tony could easily have him killed in prison, so it was necessary to change John's name to Jack Mason before he was incarcerated.

Jack usually spent a few hours each day on the computers in the prison library looking for Charlotte. But today was different; he was in the library with a mass murderer named Louie Lee Laux comparing notes.

"Jack, you'll be amazed at how many chicks we hook up with here on dating sites," Louie said.

"In case you forgot Louie, we're in prison."

"Yeah, I know. It doesn't matter to some of these chicks. Over the past few years, I've had them put money in my account and send me shit like porn, cigarettes, and candy bars. It's like a drug for them. They love bad boys, man. We write back and forth, or they send me a phone number to call when I can. It eats up time, brother."

"Do they ever visit?" Jack asked.

"Sometimes, if they're from somewhere near OK Corral (Oklahoma). But you know this is Federal prison, there ain't no conjugal visits, right? Anyway, I post my profile all over the US, anyways. I look for chicks everywhere."

"That's crazy Louie, what do I do first?"

"Go to the website Match.com and sign up. It's free."

"Ok, I'm there. What do I say, I'm in prison in the middle of bum fuck Oklahoma, and lonely? Do you want a pen pal or some shit like that?"

"Yeah, pretty much, be honest. I'm telling you, man; these chicks eat this shit up."

"Okay, can I look at all the profiles and reach out to the babes, I think, are hot?"

"Yup, I do that all the time. I pick chicks with low self-esteem, though. I can tell by how they look in their picture, and how they describe themselves. They almost always write me back."

"That's fucked-up, Louie."

"I know, but it works dude."

"Do you happen to mention you're a mass murderer, or how many people you've killed? Or when you're gettin out?"

"Sometimes. But I ain't never gettin out, brother. These chicks love the fact they can talk directly to a killer.
Some of them, though, don't like murderers; they want like cybercriminals or white-collar guys. Fuck em, I ain't no cybercriminal, I'm the real thing baby, I kill for a living—and I like it."

"Louie, you are one weird dude."

"I know, so what? Look, Jack, fill in the questionnaire with the type of chick you want to get hooked up with. You know, first enter the height, tall or short, weight, build like fat, or skinny, or athletic, do you want them to like animals, kids, divorced, tats, or whatever. Then Match.com will hook you up and send you profiles to review and contact."

"I like tall women with an athletic build. Blondes with blue eyes for sure. I like nice tits too; can I say that?"

"You could, but you should trust that athletic build means nice tits too. Once you start emailing with em, they usually send you naked pictures. You can check out their body then. I gotta tell you, brother, cell phones have changed everything when it comes to sending pictures."

"Okay, I don't care where they live either, I want someone that's looking for someone like me, athletic and horny and willing to keep in touch and maybe visit if she lives close or passes through. Will they have phone sex with you, or send you CD's with sexy shit on it or dirty letters with naked pictures?"

"Yeah, man, they do all that shit. Sometimes these crazy bitches ask me about how I killed people, and what it felt like to watch em die. I tell em it was awesome, that's why I slit the asshole's throat and watched the blood drip down their chest. These women are fucked up, man."

"You're a sick bastard, Louie, that's for sure. I just shoot em between the eyes. It's nice and clean. I help clean up the scum of the earth. And best of all, I usually don't get any blood on me."

"To each his own Jack, we can agree to disagree on the best way to put someone down."

"Alright, Louie, I'm done with my profile, and the type of

chick I want. What do I do next? Should I press the post my profile button?" *Hopefully, Charlotte is on here, and I can locate her.*

"Hang on, call the guard to take a picture of you so you can post it with the profile. You'll get more responses if you have a picture. You're a good-looking prick. These sick bitches will eat you up."

The guard walked over and took a picture of Jack with his cell phone and uploaded it to the computer so he could post it with his profile.

"Louie, how long does it take to get some pictures of women to look at?"

"Usually, just a few minutes."

Jack sat there for a minute and watched as the screen filled with pictures of women who matched his profile request. Most of them were tall, athletic blondes with blue eyes. Many of them reminded him of Charlotte. He stared at the screen and suddenly became truly angry. Jack's mind took him back to the fact Charlotte went to the FBI. He still couldn't believe the bitch ratted him out with the Feds.

Jack was angry with himself for leaving the dry cleaning on the table and throwing the gloves in their garbage can. He knew better. He was always extraordinarily careful and paid close attention to every tiny detail. Jack knew he got careless around Charlotte and paid the ultimate price. Now it's his life's mission to find her and put a bullet in-between those blue eyes.

Jack used the rest of his computer time to surf the internet, looking for Charlotte. He looked at sites that had flower design contests every day. He regularly visited websites that talked about floral design and read the emails to and from the editors. Jack spent many hours searching for any trace of Charlotte on the internet.

THIRTY-ONE

"**U**m hi, Garrett, this is Scarlet from WBHookmeup.com, you sent me your phone number the other day to call you."

"Hey, hang on." Long pause. "Okay, how's it going?"

"Good, I liked your picture and your profile and thought we could talk and see where it goes from there."

"Sure. One second." Another long pause. "What do you want to talk about?" *I already don't like his tone.*

"I don't know; I wanted to get to know you." *He sounds like a dick. Like I interrupted something.*

"Sorry, I'm playing a video game with my friend here. Okay, well, I'm twenty-nine. I work out every day in the gym with free weights. I drive a Corvette, and I work as a salesman for a local car dealer. What about you?" *Playing video games? Works out with free weights and drives a Corvette. What is he a man child? A player?*

"I work in a flower shop. I design centerpieces for weddings and corporate events."

"Yeah, I just looked you up on WBHookmeup. We're looking at your picture on the big screen, wow, you're hot. Wanna hook up?"

"Um, thanks, but I don't think so." Charlotte ended the call abruptly.

That sucked! What an asshole. Arrogant asshole. She started pacing around the living room, wondering, is everyone out there like this? *This guy didn't even know who I was. He had to look me up while he was talking to me.*

Mocking his voice, "You're hot, wanna screw? Screw you!" *What a dick!*

Scarlet called Mallory next.

"Hey, Scar, how did it go?"

"What an asshole! This Garrett guy didn't even know who I was. He looked me up while we were on the phone and told me while he and his buddy were playing video games and looking at my picture. He told me I was hot, wanna screw?"

"Seriously? Did he really ask you if you wanted to screw?"

"No, but that's what he implied. He said he lifts weights, drives a Corvette, and wanted to know if I wanted to hook up. He was an arrogant asshole. I don't know Mal if this is for me. Do you have the last nice guy left in this world with Adam?"

"No honey, there are others, you'll find them, I know you will. Did you call any of the others?"

"No, I'm too scared now."

"You know you'll never know until you try Scarlet."

"I know. But what an asshole, the guy was such a dick."

"There are a lot of them out there, honey. You need to weed them out to find the good guys,"

"Ok, I'll try calling Austin next, he looked nice enough."

"Call me after, okay?" Mallory said.

"Yeah, I will. Bye."

Scarlet picked up the paper she had printed out with

Austin's picture and phone number and dialed it. He answered on the first ring.

"Hello, this is Austin."

"Um, hi, this is Scarlet from WBHookmeup.com. You gave me your phone number to call a few days ago."

"Oh yeah, I remember you. You're the blonde girl in Jackson, right?"

"Um, yeah, I guess I am. I thought we could talk and get to know each other before we meet. Is that okay?"

"Sure, do you work?" *Bad start, kind of condescending, wouldn't you say?*

"Um, yes, I work at Sendiks as a Flower Designer."

"That's cool, do you do it for like weddings?"

"I do, more than you would think, corporate events too. How about you, what do you do for a living?"

"I'm a day trader. Do you know what that is?" *Strike two, how is it this guy keeps insinuating I'm too stupid to have a job and too slow to know what a day trader does.*

"Yes, I do. Do you trade stocks or options?"

"Mostly stocks, I'm into tech stocks. It's extremely volatile; you know what I mean?" *Do I know what volatile means, or do I know how volatile tech stocks can be? You condescending asshole!*

"Yeah, I can imagine. Do you make money at it?"

"Duh, if I didn't, I wouldn't do it." *Strike three; you're out — you're an asshole!*

"Yeah, I suppose you're right. Hey Austin, I'm sorry I

have to go, I just wanted to reach out before I went to work. I have a big project I need to finish."

"Did I say something wrong?"

"No, I'll call you again later in the week. Bye." The line went dead. Scarlet pressed speed dial three and quickly called Mallory back.

"So, how did it go?" Mallory asked.

Pacing around the living room, Scarlet ranted, "condescending asshole, that's how it went."

"What do you mean, Scar?"

"He kept talking down to me." Mocking his voice, she said, "like do you know what a day trader does? And do you know what volatile means? Yes, asshole, I do, I went to college too. screw you."

"Calm down, Scarlet; it doesn't sound that bad."

"Look, Mallory, he did it three times, I had enough and practically hung up on him."

"Well, good thing you have five profiles picked out."

"Yeah, I'm done for tonight. Maybe I'll try again tomorrow."

"Don't give up, Scar; your prince charming is out there. It just takes time."

"Yeah, maybe I'll try girls because guys suck!" Scarlet said.

"Stay tough babe, I'll talk to you tomorrow."

"Ok, love you, Mal."

"Love you back, Scar."

Scarlet paced around the living room for a little while longer, thinking to herself how rude and arrogant these guys were. She just wanted to meet someone interesting, fun, and employed. After about ten minutes of pacing, she poured a glass of wine and walked upstairs to put on a pair of pajamas, sketched for a little while to take her mind off the calls, and fell asleep.

THIRTY-TWO

Scarlet woke up early and went for a three-mile run. On her way back home, she stopped at Jimmy's for a cup of coffee and a bagel. When she walked through the front door, many of the regulars waved. Most of them work the third shift at the Kerry factory across the street. To them, it was the end of their day, so a beer was a way to wind down. For everyone else in the restaurant, it was the beginning of their day, and they needed coffee to wind up. Scarlet took a seat at the end of the bar next to the cash register. Mallory was busy making a new pot of coffee.

"Hey Mal, how's it going this morning?"

"Oh, hi. What's going on? Feel better after a little sleep?" Mallory asked.

"I don't know. I'm just out for a run before I go to work. I have a big wedding I'm working on for this weekend."

"How far did you run?"

"Just three miles. Can I get some coffee and a toasted bagel with cream cheese, please?"

Mallory poured her a cup of coffee. "I'll be right back." And she disappeared through the swinging door that led to the kitchen.

While Scarlet waited for her bagel, she grabbed the newspaper off the bar and scanned the front page to see what was going on in the world. Nothing new, and more importantly, nothing on Tony Gambucci or John Mancini. Hopefully, they're tucked away in some supermax federal prison somewhere never to be seen or heard from again. She thought Siberia would be too good for both of them.

Scarlet flipped back to the entertainment page and found the crossword puzzle. She took a pen from a cup on the counter and began to complete some of the crossword answers.

"Hey, blondie, what are you doing with *my* crossword puzzle?" Jimmy asked.

"Ah, I didn't realize it was yours, Jimmy, sorry." Every day Jimmy comes into work in the morning and sits down at the same table in front with the crossword puzzle, a buttered bagel, and coffee.

"That's alright, how'd you do on it?"

"I got a few of the answers for you."

Mallory came back through the swinging door that leads to the kitchen with Scarlet's bagel and some cream cheese. "You two are funny, Scarlet, you look like Jimmy with your bagel, coffee, and the crossword."

Handing the paper to Jimmy, Scarlet said, "here you can have it. You know, Jimmy obviously needs the help. It takes him all morning to finish it."

"Hey, quit busting my balls blondie, I have a restaurant to run here."

Jimmy then walked around the bar and through the swinging door. A few minutes later, he returned with a bagel and his coffee, the crossword folded up under his arm, and a pen in his mouth. He sat at his usual table at the front of the dining room.

Scarlet walked over and set the rest of the paper down on the table. He said, "thanks, you didn't have to give it all back."

"Yeah, well, I don't want your whole day to be thrown off." Jimmy watched as Scarlet turned and walked to the barstool and sat down. She could feel Jimmy staring at her from behind.

While Mallory was at the other end of the bar, filling coffee cups and talking to some of the regulars, Scarlet sat quietly and ate her bagel. She used the pen from filling out the crossword to draw a picture of sunflowers in a field on a napkin. When she finished eating, Scarlet dropped a ten-dollar bill that she usually carries in her running clothes, on the bar, and walked out the front door.

It was a twenty-minute run to get home. When Scarlet got there, she jogged up the stairs, brushed her teeth, took a shower, and got dressed for work. She put on a pair of straight-legged jeans, a white tee-shirt, and some new flats. Because it was supposed to be a busy day, Scarlet pulled her hair back into a ponytail.

THIRTY-THREE

On her drive to work, she noticed there were a lot of people out walking their dogs. *Hmm, maybe I should get a dog. The house is so quiet*, she thought, and *I could use a partner to run with in the morning.* She thought, *what kind of dog would I want to get? It'll have to be big enough to run three to five miles each day, so a little dog wouldn't work. Maybe a Golden Retriever or a Lab, they like to run.*

Scarlet pulled into the parking lot and left her car in the usual spot, in the last row straight out from the front door facing the street. Sendiks is at the far end of a strip center. There's a Papa John's Pizza at the other end, and in-between there's a 24-Hour fitness place, a tanning salon, a place for men to get their hair cut, and a dry cleaner.

Scarlet walked in the side door by the flower shop. This entrance came in behind the flower coolers. It provided ample space behind the coolers to do design work and kept her from having to be in the front waiting on customers. Scarlet's day was spent building twenty-five guest table centerpieces. Tomorrow, she'll finish the order by creating the bride's bouquet.

It was five-thirty, and Scarlet was exhausted from standing all day. She walked to her car and drove home.

After parking in the driveway, she walked into the dark house. It was so quiet. And lonely. *The more I think about it, the more I think I want a dog. Someone happy to see me when I get*

home from work each day. Unconditional love and all that crap.
Scarlet made herself some dinner and poured herself a healthy glass of Pinot Noir.

THIRTY-FOUR

When she finished eating, Scarlet decided to take a chance and call the other WBHookmeup.com guys. She walked to the dining room table and reviewed the remaining three profiles that were printed out. *I think I'll try Bob next.* Bob was thirty years old, single, and never married. He wrote he's athletic and works at a furniture store. Scarlet picked up the phone and dialed his number.

"Hello, who the hell is this?"

"Um, it's Scarlet from WBHookmeup.com. You emailed me your phone number a couple of days ago to call you."

"Oh, I'm so sorry, I've been getting so many of those darn robocalls for health insurance that I'm fed up. Your number came up private, so I assumed it was a robocall. I mean it, I'm really sorry about that."

"That's okay; I get them too."

"So, how's it going?"

"Good, I thought we could talk a little and then decide if we want to meet."

"Great, tell me about yourself. What do you like to do?"

"Well, I've lived in Jackson for about a year, I'm from Ohio. I came to settle my family's estate after they passed, and I liked it here, so I stayed. I work at Sendiks in the flower department. I design centerpieces for weddings and corporate events."

"I'm sorry about your family passing." *Hmm, empathy, that was really nice to say.*

"Thanks, I appreciate that."

"I can't believe you would be that busy in the flower shop at Sendiks."

I like how this conversation is about me. He seems nice. "Yeah, I was surprised too. I'm swamped though; we do two or three weddings and a dozen corporate events a month. How about you, tell me about you."

"Well, I work at Ashley Furniture in the design department. I work with contractors to stage their model homes. Ashley supplies the furniture from our in-stock inventory. And I stage the model with what we provide."

Scarlet excitedly said, "You should get fresh flowers from me. They make a difference when someone visits a home. Plus, the right flowers can have an amazing fragrance."

"Hey, not a bad idea. I'll mention that to some of my clients and see what they say. I think that would be great, especially for open houses on weekends. What do you do for fun?"

"I like the theater, musicals mostly, and concerts. I enjoyed Summerfest this year; we saw Zach Brown at the Marcus; I've never been to anything like that before."

"Yeah, Summerfest is amazing. I think it's like one of the biggest music festivals in the US."

"I've heard that. I like baseball too. And I go to a Bucks game now and then, I love the Fiserv Forum, it's an awesome place to watch basketball. Also, I've never seen the Packer's play live, but I enjoy the Packer parties my friends have."

Bob jumped in and said, "I love the theater too." *Really?*
"I like to catch the train to Chicago and see a play before it goes to Broadway. It's a lot of fun to stay down there for a weekend and party on Rush Street."

"That sounds like fun. I'll have to try that sometime." *Maybe Mallory would like to go down to Chicago for a girl's weekend.*

He then said, "so do you want to meet for coffee sometime?"

"Why not? Do you know a place called Jimmy's in Jackson?" Scarlet asked.

"No, but I can find it."

"It's right off the 41/45 highway on 60, past the McDonalds and the Dairy Queen, across from Kerry the spice factory. You can't miss it. How about eight o'clock tomorrow morning?"

"I'll be there. I look forward to meeting you, Scarlet."

"You too, Bob, goodnight." Bob ended the call.

Scarlet jumped up from the dining room table and started doing her I got a date dance. She started singing, "I got a date, bop, bop, and I won't be late, I got a date, bop, bop, and I won't be late, I got a date..." She danced around the house until she fell onto the couch, exhausted, and then called Mallory.

"Mal, I got a date!"

"Yeah, who?"

"The WBHookmeup guy Bob. He seemed nice."

"When are you meeting him?"

"Coffee, tomorrow at Jimmy's, and you can tell me what you think."

"Cool, tell me about him."

"Well, he works at Ashley Furniture as a designer. He works with contractors to stage their model homes. He likes theater and didn't say anything about sports. But who cares? I got a date!"

"I love it, Scar; did you do the I got a data dance yet?"

"Yeah, of course!"

"You're such a dork, you know. What are you going to wear?"

"Hmm, I hadn't thought about that yet. I think I'll leave my hair down for sure; it looks sexier. Maybe just a pair of jeans and a tank top. My boobs look better in tank tops. I got a new bra from Victoria Secret that makes them look perkier. I don't want to look slutty, though."

"Are we talking a trashy white tank top or nice tasteful tank top from Black and White or Macy's?"

"The one I'm thinking of is from Nordstrom. It's very nice. I bought it a couple of weeks ago when we went shopping at the mall."

"I remember that one, you'll look awesome."

"Thanks, hon. I'm tired from doing the I got a date dance; I'll see you in the morning."

"Goodnight, Scarlet."

Time to finish my wine, go upstairs, and go to bed. I got a date, bop, bop!

THIRTY-FIVE

Scarlet woke up early the next morning and went for a run. She ran her usual route of about three miles. When Scarlet returned home, she took a shower and got dressed. She decided to wear a pair of jeans with lace down the side, her new favorite bra, and a simple white blouse. She slipped on a pair of ankle boots and headed to Jimmy's for coffee.

When Scarlet walked in, she first waved to the usual guys and asked Mallory where to sit.

"You look pretty this morning, honey. I like your hair down, and the new bra is working. Sit up in the booth by the window so you can see him coming."

Mallory brought over some coffee, and Scarlet sat there waiting for her first date in years. *I'm so nervous I can't sit still.* It was only seven-thirty, so she had a little while to wait. Jimmy walked into the dining room and went through his usual routine. He disappeared in the kitchen and returned with the paper, a bagel, and coffee.

"Good morning, Blondie. You look good this morning. You clean up well."

"Thanks, Jimmy, you too."

"Hot date, I hear."

"Mallory has a big mouth."

"She's loyal to me, girl; don't you ever forget that. I always need to know everything going on in my restaurant. Also, you should know we have a strict policy of no sex on the tables. You got that?"

"No worries, Jimmy; we're just going to have some coffee and talk."

And that was it; the daily banter was over. Jimmy took his usual seat as Scarlet looked out the window and saw Bob coming. Her first thought was, *at least, he looks like his picture. He drives a little red Hyundai. Don't judge, Scarlet.* He was wearing a pair of jeans with holes in the knees and a short sleeve casual shirt. *I guess I don't warrant dressing up a little.* His shoes were like deck shoes, but they looked filthy. He walked through the door. Mallory said, "Just sit where you want, I'll follow you with a menu."

He promptly said, "No need."

Scarlet stood up and waved. "Hi, Bob."

"Hi, nice to meet you, Scarlet." He went for a half hug, and Scarlet reached out to shake his hand. *Awkward.*

"Nice to meet you too, please sit down," Scarlet said.

Mallory came by the table and refilled Scarlet's cup with coffee and asked Bob if he wanted coffee too.

"No, I don't drink coffee; do you have tea?"

"Sure, what kind do you want?"

"What kind do you have?"

"All sorts of flavors, is there something you had in mind?"

"Do you have green tea with honey?"

"Sure, I'll be right back."

That was awkward too. He was sort of snarky toward Mal.

"So, you found the place, okay?"

"Yeah, I just used Google Maps. I don't work far from here; I work out of the Menomonee Falls store just up the highway."

Mallory returned with a green tea and set it in front of him. He quickly moved it to the side and gave her a dirty look. *OCD? She may slap him.*

"Are you guys ready to order?"

Without looking up at Mallory, he said, "We'll call you when we're ready."

"Ah, okay. Just let me know." Mallory looked at Scarlet and raised her eyebrows, then turned and walked back toward the bar. *Oh boy, she doesn't like him already.*

Scarlet started the conversation by asking, "Are you hungry? The food here is delicious. I eat here pretty often."

"Yeah, I just want to take some time and look at the menu."

"Oh, okay." She looked past Bob and could see Jimmy was staring at them. Scarlet could tell he was getting irritated with this guy's attitude toward Mallory.

Suddenly Bob turned around toward the register where Mallory was standing and whistled. He then said, "Hey, lady, I'm ready."

Oh my God, Mallory might not only slap him, but she may kick his ass too. This isn't going anywhere. How do I end this quickly?

He ordered two eggs over easy ("very easy"), bacon ("very crispy"), and home fries with whole wheat toast, dry. Scarlet ordered a bagel with cream cheese and a small side of fruit. They talked about their jobs before the food arrived, and then pretty much ate in silence. After they were done eating, Bob whistled again for Mallory to come and get the empty plates. *Oh, boy, she's pissed.* When Mallory put the bill down on the table, Scarlet reached for her purse and said, "let's split it."

Bob said he would take care of the bill. The total was eighteen dollars and twenty-five cents, and he dropped a twenty-dollar bill on the table. *That's it? What a cheap prick.*

As they got up to leave, Bob asked if he could see Scarlet another time, dinner maybe. She told him no, she wasn't interested in going out. He didn't seem to take it well.

Bob kept asking why Scarlet didn't want to go out with him. Scarlet kept saying, "I'm not interested, Bob." After a couple of exchanges, Jimmy got up from his table and stepped between them and said, "I think it's time for you to leave."

"Hey, this is none of your business," Bob said.

Jimmy grabbed him by the arm and started leading him out the front door. "Get the hell out of my restaurant. If I ever see you again, I'll break your arm."

"Hey man, we're just talking over here. There's no need for violence."

"Shut up and get out." Jimmy continued to push him out the door and then stood outside and watched as Bob got in his car and drove away.

Mallory walked over to the table, "are you kidding me?

What was up with that asshole?"

"Mal, I know he was a jerk. But on the phone, he was so nice."

"I saw Jimmy had to get rid of him. I bet it's not the last time you see him, Scarlet. He seems like a guy that won't give up."

"Funny I got that feeling too, I don't think this is the last time I see this guy either."

"Oh, and let's not forget the cheap-ass left a dollar seventy-five tip."

"I'm sorry, Mal," Scarlet said. She then reached into her purse for a five-dollar bill to add to the measly tip left by Bob.

Jimmy marched back into the restaurant and came over to the table to rub it in. "Blondie, what the hell are you Doing bringing this garbage into my restaurant?"

"Thanks for getting rid of him, Jimmy."

Jimmy could tell Scarlet was disappointed and said, "No problem, kid. Sorry, it didn't work out. You deserve better. The guy was an asshole."

Scarlet left Jimmy's about a half-hour later, all hyped up on coffee, and drove the twenty minutes to work.

THIRTY-SIX

At four-thirty, the phone in the back of the store rang.

Scarlet picked it up and said, "hello?"

"Hi, is Scarlet there?"

"This is she; can I help you?"

"Hi, this is Bob, from this morning. I wanted to say how much I liked meeting you and wanted to ask you out again for a drink tonight."

"Bob, that's so nice of you, but no thank you. I didn't think we really had a connection. I'm sorry. It didn't go so well this morning."

"Oh, I see. Do you mean that whole thing with the waitress? She was inept. I just wanted to talk to you; I didn't need her all over us."

"Yeah, Bob, that wasn't it. I don't see us together. I'm sorry. I have to go." Scarlet abruptly hung up the phone. *Well, that was a guy who has two giant balls on him. No way I would have called me after that disaster this morning.*

She picked up her cell phone and called Mallory. "You won't believe who called me."

"My guess is Bob?"

Nodding to herself, Scarlet said, "yeah!"

"I knew it, what an arrogant asshole."

"Yeah, the balls on this guy."

"Yup, you can tell. He's one of those men that won't give

up. He takes rejection as a challenge. He doesn't understand how creepy it is to be stalked by a psycho. Mark my words, Scar, you haven't heard the last from him."

"I know Mal; I'm a little put off by all of it. I'm deleting my profile when I get home."

"What are you doing tonight?"

"I was heading home to make some dinner. Why? Do you want to meet for a drink?" Scarlet asked.

"Sure, but I have to be home early, Adam's getting off work soon, and he wants to have dinner together."

"How about The Norbert in twenty minutes?"

"Okay, see you in a few."

There's a bar in downtown West Bend that looks and feels like it should be in New York City. It has large windows in the front-facing Main street so you can see inside. There's bench seating around the perimeter, a majestic bar that runs the entire length of the place front to back. Behind the bar are mirrors surrounded by antique- looking tin squares that also cover the ceiling. There are several hi-top tables, and the rest of the bar area is complete with low tables. Original hardwood floors and the artwork is all from local artists. The most impressive part of The Norbert is the antique chandeliers that hang from the ceiling. The owner, Anthony, is an excellent cook too. The martinis are great, the wine is good, and the bartenders are friendly and welcoming. Scarlet arrived before Mallory and took a seat at the bar. Her favorite bartender Ricardo was working. Ricardo is bi-lingual, and Scarlet pretends to be bi-lingual too each time she comes in. He teaches her phrases occasionally when they're not too busy.

"Hola Ricardo"

"Hola Scarlet, como estas?"

"Estoy bien, y tu?"

"Bien, Scarlet, gracias. Que te gustaria beber, un martini?

"Si Ricardo, un martini, con...um, four olives."

"Ok, your accent's a little weak at the end there, and obviously, the phrase four olives is not Spanish. What you want to say is con cuatro aceitunas? It means with four olives."

"Okay, si Ricardo, un martini, con cuatro aceitunas, por favor."

"Good, un momento, Scarlet."

"Gracias, Ricardo."

He returned a moment later and poured the martini into a glass with four plump pimento-stuffed green olives. Mallory showed up about ten minutes later and ordered a martini too.

Then she asked, "Did you two do your Spanish dance?"

"Of course, he taught me how to say four olives in Spanish. It's cuatro aceitunas."

"You're such a dork, Scarlet."

They sat at the bar and talked about Bob and how Jimmy had to get rid of the guy. Scarlet said, "I'm done with WBHookmeup.com. I'm erasing my profile as soon as I get home tonight."

"I don't blame you, Scar."

Scarlet also shared the fact she decided to get a dog and asked Mallory to join her tomorrow at the Humane Society.

Mallory declined because she had to work the whole day. About an hour and a half later, they walked out of The Norbert and headed home.

THIRTY-SEVEN

When Scarlet got home, the first thing she did was turn on her laptop and log onto WBHookmeup.com to erase her profile. Then, she made herself some pasta and a salad. She poured a glass of wine and sat at the table, eating, and drawing a new centerpiece. Afterward, she put her plates in the sink, and walked upstairs, brushed her teeth, and sat up in bed to read her book. At about nine o'clock, her cell phone rang. *God, I hope it isn't Bob.*

"Hello?"

"Hey, Scarlet. How are you?"

"Michelle, hi. I'm doing okay, how are you doing?"

"I'm well, thank you; I wanted to call and check on you and ask for a big favor."

"Um, what sort of favor?" Scarlet asked.

"Well, did you ever get a dog?"

"No, I was going to go to the Humane Society tomorrow to see what they had available. That's so weird that you would call and ask me that question tonight. Why?"

"Well, great minds and all. Look, I'm going to take an undercover assignment for a year or two, and I can't take my dog with me. Do you remember I was telling you about Duke on the plane? I'm wondering if you're interested in adopting him from me. Not just for a year or two that would be wrong, but permanently. It wouldn't be right to take him back after a couple of years."

"Are you sure, Michelle?"

"I am. Scarlet, this assignment will make my career. Do you remember I told you about Duke being an extraordinary dog? When I started at the FBI, I was his handler. I trained dogs for several years for the FBI canine unit. Duke was injured in a bust and had to retire. The FBI allowed me to adopt him. He healed up and is fine now. After I adopted him, I've continued to train Duke, and he's really amazing."

"Oh my gosh, Michelle. I'm so honored you would ask me. I would love to take care of Duke. Can I pay you for him?"

"No, of course not. Scarlet, believe me, I thought of you instantly when I decided to accept the assignment. I really think you could use someone to watch your back, and Duke can do that better than anyone I know."

"I would like that, especially after my last trip to New York. Everywhere I go, I keep looking around for another sniper or another bomb."

"As you should. So, here's the deal, Scarlet. To teach Duke to work with a new handler, I need to spend several days with you and Duke. Can you meet me on Friday?"

"Yes, of course."

"Great, I'll meet you at the same hanger in West Bend on Friday afternoon around three. I'll stay the weekend and leave on Monday night. We need about thirty-six hours to teach you how to handle Duke."

"Ok, I can't wait. I look forward to it. And thank you for thinking of me, Michelle. I really appreciate it."

"You're welcome; I'll see you on Friday. Bye, Scarlet."

"Bye, Michelle." The line went dead. *Wow, that is awesome. I now have a dog. Duke! That is so cool and a great name.* Scarlet read a little longer and then fell asleep.

The next morning there was a text on Scarlet's phone from Bob. She pressed delete without reading it. Scarlet got out of bed and took a quick shower, brushed her teeth, got dressed, and went downstairs to make coffee. As she was leaving the house, a quick scan up the block revealed what she thought was a red Hyundai. It may or may not have been Bob, though.

The day went by pretty quick. Scarlet finished the wedding order she was working on a day earlier than it was due. Tomorrow was Friday, and Scarlet was excited about meeting Michelle in the afternoon. So tonight, Scarlet wanted to go home, clean the house, and get ready for her new puppy.

As Scarlet drove toward home, she couldn't shake the uneasy feeling someone was following her. She kept peering in the rearview mirror to see if Bob's red car was anywhere to be seen. It wasn't, but the uneasy feeling never left.

After pulling into the driveway and going in the house, Scarlet put some Gloria Estefan music on her iPhone, closed all the shutters, and started cleaning the house to the song Conga. Two hours later, she called Mallory.

"Hey, Mal, how was work?"

"Good, I was busy all day. Are you okay, what's going on?"

"Yeah, I'm fine. Have you ever had the feeling someone

is watching you?"

"Yeah, why is someone watching you?"

"I don't know; I can't shake the feeling. I keep thinking Bob is following me."

"Did you see him or his car?"

"No, I thought I saw his red Hyundai this morning down the street. But I'm not sure, you know just because you don't see him, doesn't mean he isn't there. Plus, I wonder how he would know where I live?"

"I don't know what to tell you hon. The asshole may have followed you from here the other morning or from work. He obviously knows where you work. What are you doing? Do you want me to come over and stay the night?"

"No, I'm cleaning. I have a friend from Ohio coming to visit for the weekend with her dog. She's being transferred and asked me to adopt her dog. Funny how I was going to the Humane Society today, and she called last night."

"What kind of dog is it?"

"A German Shepard," Scarlet said.

"That's cool. Good timing, too, with Bob around. Maybe he'll bite the little pricks little prick off."

"Funny. Hold a little grudge, do you, Mal?"

"Yeah, just a little one. That guy was an asshole and a shitty tipper. You know I can forgive a lot if they're a good tipper?"

"I can't argue with that logic. Well, I'm gonna finish cleaning my house and get something to eat. Love ya."

"Love you." The line went dead.

Scarlet spent the next hour cleaning the upstairs and then went back to the kitchen to make some scrambled eggs with cheese and salsa. She ate at the dining room table, drank her wine, and sketched a beautiful floral arrangement.

When she finished eating, she walked upstairs, brushed her teeth, and went to bed.

THIRTY-EIGHT

The next morning, Scarlet woke early and went for a five-mile run. She stopped by Jimmy's on the way home and talked to Mallory for a few minutes. Jimmy stopped in and went through his usual routine. He did say hello, but that was pretty much it. There was no witty remarks or banter.

Scarlet left jimmy's and went home to shower and go to work. She spent the day working on a centerpiece for an awards banquet at the West Bend Mutual convention center. The centerpiece design started as a drawing Scarlet had made several years ago. It was magnificent. Scarlet created an arrangement of apple-blossom sprays, hydrangea, and nandina. She added polyester florals for additional color and carefully placed them in an antiqued mirror mottled-gold and silver-leaf accented planter that brought the entire arrangement to life.

It was so beautiful her boss insisted on taking a picture of Scarlet holding the drawing and standing next to the final arrangement. For obvious reasons, Scarlet didn't like her picture taken. Still, it was her boss, and she was so excited for Scarlet to be able to make something she had spent so much time drawing.

THIRTY-NINE

At two-forty-five, Scarlet left work and drove to the West Bend Airport to meet Michelle. A little after three, the FBI plane landed and taxied to the hanger where she was waiting. The plane stopped, the door dropped open, and at the top of the stairs, Michelle and Duke appeared. *Oh My God! Duke is beautiful.* Duke was all black with a little brown on his ears. His paws were enormous. His posture was majestic like Mufasa in the Lion King movie. A big barrel chest, a bushy tail, and dark, scary eyes.

Michelle stepped forward and said, "Scarlet, hi, it's so nice to see you."

"Hi Michelle, Duke is so beautiful."

"Yes, he is, thank you. I'll miss him dearly."

"I bet you will." Michelle walked down the stairs with Duke and hugged Scarlet; then, she opened the back door of the Jeep. She swept her hand from right to left without saying a word, indicating Duke should get into the back seat. Duke jumped up into the Jeep and sat there, staring at every movement Michelle made. She then turned and walked back up the stairs of the plane and returned with boxes and duffel bags that filled the back of the Jeep.

"Boy Duke doesn't travel light."

"Most of this is for training. I need you to focus and pay attention to what I tell you over the next three days. Scarlet, remember, Duke, is very special. He's smart, strong, and extremely dangerous if he wants to be. He weighs more than a hundred and twenty-five pounds, and it's all muscle. He could bite a hand and the wrist clean off in less than a minute, and he can kill a person in five seconds or less by crushing their carotid artery. I've spent years training this dog to be a killing machine."

"Um, Michelle, that's a little scary."

"Yes, it is scary. That's why I need you to understand what you have here; this is a serious responsibility. It's more responsibility than owning a gun, Scarlet. Duke is as gentle as a baby, loving, and playful too. He loves to play catch, run, jump, and retrieve. You'll love having him around as a companion. He's as close to a human being as you will ever find in an animal. And most importantly, he's extremely loyal in that he'll give up his life to save yours."

"That's reassuring," Scarlet said.

They drove straight to the house and unloaded the Jeep while Duke took care of some business in the front yard. The first thing Michelle did was walk Duke around the perimeter of the house outside first and then inside. As she did this, she spoke to him in German. After about an hour, they sat down in the kitchen, and Michelle said, watch this. Michelle looked at Duke and said, "Duke, pass auf."

Suddenly, the dog stood up and started walking the route she had taught him inside the house. He sniffed every inch along the way, and then he walked upstairs and did the same thing. He returned to the kitchen and barked once, and then he opened the screen door by using his nose to push the handle down and walked the perimeter of the yard. When he was done, he returned to the kitchen door, barked once again, and sat there waiting for Michelle to let him back in the house.

Michelle said, "If there was an intruder inside and he was outside, Duke would've jumped through this screen door or broke a window to get in to protect you. The one bark indicates everything is okay, no intruders. Scarlet, if he doesn't bark, something is wrong, and someone is inside your home. It's crucial to remember if Duke doesn't bark, there's someone in your house. He'll need instruction as to what to do about the intruder. He doesn't assume all intruders are bad. You might have a house guest, for instance. Duke doesn't know the difference. He won't do anything but stop and guard the intruder unless you give him a command. Scarlet, it's important to remember that you must always be in control."

"I'm, I'm so impressed and astonished at the same time."

"The command I gave him is called guard alert. He needs to do this regularly, so he'll remember the route. I would recommend you have Duke perform guard alert every time you come home. I'll leave you a card with all the commands you need to memorize."

"Are they all in German?"

"No. Duke knows two commands in English."

"What are they?"

"Attack and kill."

Again astonished, she said, "Really, the only two words he

knows in English are attack and kill?"

"Scarlet, Duke will attack. That means to disable or disarm a person. If a person pulls a gun out, or knife, he'll chew off their wrist if he senses you're in danger. Even if they drop the weapon, he will continue to bite them until you stop it. Once they are disarmed, he'll hold his mouth on a person's neck and wait for the kill command. Or if you're really in danger and it's a matter of life and death, he can be told to kill. And he'll kill that person in seconds. He is fast, strong, smart, and very stealthy."

"Holy crap, Michelle. Are you kidding me?"

Michelle stood and let Duke back in the house. "Good boy Duke." She gave him a treat. "No, I'm not kidding you. You also need to know Duke will only eat his own food and snacks. We'll teach him to only take food or water from you. It's too easy to poison a dog, so he must learn to only take his food and water from you. His food and snacks are special order from the number on this card." Michelle handed Scarlet a card with only a phone number on it.

"Okay. Can Duke run with me in the mornings?"

"Oh, yes, of course, he'll love it. When you return home, though, have him on guard and alert to make sure no one is in the house tell him Pass Auf while you wait either outside or just inside the door."

"Okay."

"Scarlet, you can take Duke anywhere. He will behave like no other animal you have seen. If you're in a crowded room or even if you're in a different room, we'll teach him to only listen for your voice and your commands. If you're in trouble, he'll find a way to help you. This weekend I'm going to teach you to be Duke's handler. You will become the center of his world. He will depend on you to take care of him, just like he will take care of you. He will only be loyal to you. However, if you start dating someone regularly, he'll eventually learn their routine and their actions too. But remember, Duke will only take direction from you. He'll only listen for your voice, and for now, only go on alert at this house. Duke will learn to trust only you."

Scarlet said she understood, but she wasn't too sure that she really did.

"Scarlet, this is a great responsibility. Remember, Duke can kill quickly, so you must always be in control. He is more lethal than a gun or a knife. He's extremely fast and enormously powerful. You're the only person who can control him. So, if he attacks someone, they're as good as dead unless you stop him."

"Michelle, I'm not sure I can handle this, are you sure I'm the right person for Duke?" *What have I gotten myself into now?*

"I'm positive Scarlet, I know you can do it, and you'll appreciate the power and security he brings to you. You'll be fine; it just takes a little time and patience. By Monday night, you'll be a pro at it. I promise."

"If you say so." *I'm not too sure about this.*

FORTY

Over the next three days, Michelle spent twelve hours a day teaching Scarlet how to "handle" Duke. Scarlet picked up the commands quickly but had a little trouble with her tone. She tended to yell commands at the dog. Michelle explained how Duke has incredible hearing. You can whisper, and he'll respond. They worked inside the house, in the yard, and at the park. Michelle explained over and over the importance of always being in control. Reminding Scarlet that Duke can severely injure and kill quite quickly. After the first twelve to fifteen hours of working with Duke, he and Scarlet began to bond. It became apparent Michelle was right, Scarlet and Duke belonged together.

Duke slept in Scarlet's bedroom each night with the door slightly open. He would leave and search the house occasionally throughout the night. Michelle said, "this is because the house is old; he must hear it settling, and he's not used to the sound of air conditioning or the furnace. He'll become familiar with it, and the nighttime searches will eventually stop."

On Monday morning, Michelle, Scarlet, and Duke went for a three-mile run. On the way back, they saw Mallory outside Jimmy's on a smoke break. They walked over, and Scarlet introduced Michelle and Duke to Mallory.

Mallory immediately said, "Oh my God! How beautiful. Duke is magnificent, Scarlet, and he's not exactly a puppy, hey."

"He's gorgeous and, he's so smart," Scarlet said.

"Do you guys want a coffee to go?"

Scarlet nodded and said, "That would be awesome."

"Come on in through here." They walked in the door that led directly to the kitchen. "Duke can stay in the office over there (pointing at Jimmy's office) if you want to go in the dining room and sit down, I'll be right there; I need to wash my hands."

They left Duke in Jimmy's office with the door open. Scarlet tested her training by pointing to the office and saying, "bleib" (stay). He walked into the office, looked at her, and sat down. Michelle and Scarlet slowly walked through the swinging door into the dining room. Duke never moved, he just watched them walk away. Mallory brought them some coffee and a bagel for Scarlet. Michelle didn't want anything to eat. And Duke, of course, refused food and water too. About twenty minutes later, Jimmy came through the door and asked, "Whose horse is in my office?"

"He's my new dog, Jimmy, what do you think?"

"He looks pissed you left him in there by himself."

"Naw, he's just making sure nobody spits on my bagel."

"Funny girl, who's your friend?"

"Jimmy, this is my friend Michelle. She's being transferred and can't take Duke with her. She asked if I would adopt him."

They shook hands, and Jimmy said, "Good friend, that's a beautiful animal."

"Yes, he is, thank you," Michelle said.

"Jimmy, Duke is amazing too. Besides, do you remember that date the other day?"

"Who the bum I needed to toss?"

"Yeah, that one, I think he's stalking me now."

Michelle turned to Scarlet and looked shocked; she said, "Stalking? Are you sure?"

"Well, no, I'm not. But with Duke around, I doubt he'll be much trouble."

With a seriously concerned look on her face, she said, "Scarlet, we need to talk about this before I return to New York."

"Okay, sure, what is there to talk about?"

"Finish your bagel, and let's get out of here. I want you to call Duke from here at a normal voice level. He'll find you, and we can leave out the front door."

Scarlet said, "Duke hier" (Come) About 5 seconds later he came flying through the swinging door that led to the kitchen and sat right at her feet. *Amazing.*

Mallory and Jimmy were astonished.

As they walked out the front door, Michelle said, "Nice to meet you both, and thank you for the coffee. Come on, Scarlet, let's go."

FORTY-ONE

They walked out of the restaurant, and Michelle explained that "when you're in witness protection, you need to report any incident of a stalker to ensure you're not compromised." Michelle asked for all the details about Bob. She took detailed notes and said Vincent will get a full report when she returns to New York. Listen, Scarlet, "We'll run a background check on this Bob, and if it's nothing, we'll file it in your record. However, if something's hinky, we'll contact the local FBI office in Milwaukee, and they'll reach out to the local police, to have him detained until an Agent can interview him."

Michelle explained that the FBI version of witness protection is different than the US Marshal's WITSEC program. The FBI tries to keep a close watch over their witnesses; they're protected for life. "Scarlet, I can't tell you enough times how important it is to stay off social media sites. You need to understand there are people out there searching social media who want to kill you. The FBI must know anytime you have trouble with someone like a stalker. You must notify Vincent. Okay?"

"Yes, of course, thank you, Michelle. I'll be cautious. The WBHookmeup.com site is supposed to be only for the Jackson area, not national. So, I honestly didn't think of it as social media. I think of social media like Twitter or Facebook. Also, it turns out Bob was an asshole. So, I learned my lesson quickly and deleted my profile the next day."

"Good. Now have Duke do a quick scan of the perimeter."

Scarlet unlocked and opened the side door to the House, then looked down and said, "Duke pass auf."

Duke did his perimeter check and barked once. All safe, so they entered the house and discussed the training regimen they would go through today.

At five-thirty, they packed up the Jeep with all of Michelle's training props and headed to the West Bend Airport. On the drive, Michelle kept reminding Scarlet how important it was to keep training and practicing with Duke. She said, "The more you practice the commands, the easier it will become on both of you. Scarlet, the most important thing for you to remember, is Duke will lay his life down to protect you. You must respect this and treat him with dignity. Work with him every day, talk to him like he's human, he needs to learn to focus on your voice only, and that comes with practice. Be sure to take him everywhere you go, he loves the car, and he loves to go places. He will soon learn to respond to your feelings, your moods, and, most importantly, your fears. One other thing you need to know is because he is so beautiful everywhere you take him people respond to him. They want to pet him. It's okay; he's friendly until he senses it's time not to be friendly. Do you understand this is a tremendous responsibility?"

Scarlet nodded and said, "yes, of course." It became evident Michelle is going to miss Duke when her eyes were starting to tear up. Her voice began to crack when she talked to him in the back seat. There is no doubt, Michelle will really miss this dog.

When they arrived at the airport hangar, the plane was already there, and the door was open. Bob (a different Bob) met them and helped unload the Jeep and put the training props on the plane. Michelle opened the back door so Duke could get out, and Michelle knelt and began to hug her dog as tears rolled down her cheeks. "I'll miss you, boy. You take really good care of Scarlet, you hear me?"

You could tell the dog knew what was going on too. And then Michelle got up, gave Scarlet a firm hug, and told her to take care of Duke. Scarlet thanked her repeatedly. A few minutes later she walked up the stairs of the airplane, the door closed, and the plane began its taxi.

Scarlet and Duke stood for a few minutes and watched the plane taxi to the end of the runway. It accelerated rapidly and then lifted off the ground and disappeared. Scarlet's eyes became watery as they watched the plane disappear in the eastern sky. Duke nuzzled up against Scarlet's leg like a friend would do to show comfort and understanding.

FORTY-TWO

It was about six o'clock in the evening, and Scarlet decided to cheer Duke up by taking him to the park to play catch. Scarlet drove to Riverside Park in Downtown West Bend and played with a tennis ball for about thirty minutes. When it was time to go, Duke jumped in the back of the Jeep, and they drove home. As soon as Scarlet climbed out of the vehicle, she let Duke in the house and told him to check the perimeter "Duke, pass auf." He walked through the entire house and returned, barked once — all good.

Scarlet told him what a good boy he was and then put down some food and refreshed his water bowl. She poured some wine and sat on the couch with her sketch pad and drew a portrait of Duke. When he finished eating, he climbed up on the couch and laid next to Scarlet and put his head in her lap. They fell asleep a little while later. At midnight Duke jumped off the sofa, barked once, and ran to the front door.

"I heard it too, boy. It sounded like someone had checked to see if the door was open."

Scarlet walked to the door, unlocked it, and slowly pulled it open. Duke put his head through the opening to see what was there. They didn't see anything or anyone out front. She let him out into the front yard to check things out and maybe do a little business before they went up to bed. Scarlet said, "Pass auf." Duke walked around the yard and then came back in and walked around the house and returned. One bark. *Everything must be okay. Who or whatever it was is now gone.* So, Scarlet locked the door and climbed the stairs to go to bed.

The next morning while Duke and Scarlet went for a run, she looked up the street from her front yard and said out loud to no one in particular, "I knew it!" She saw Bob's red Hyundai parked down the street. Scarlet turned around and marched right for it. He immediately started the car and drove off. They continued their run and stopped by Jimmy's on the way back. Mallory told her to park Duke in the office and come into the dining room. Duke waited in Jimmy's office, and Scarlet walked into the dining room and took a booth near the front.

"How's it going with Duke?" Mallory asked.

"Good, I think he's a little sad that Michelle left."

"Yeah, probably, dogs have feelings too, I guess."

"Hey, I caught Bob this morning, stalking me. He was in his car up the street from my house. We jogged up toward it, and the chicken shit took off like a bat out of hell. How does he know where I live anyway?"

"He probably followed you home from work one night. I pity the little bastard if Duke ever gets ahold of him," Mallory said.

"Amen, sister. What are you doing tonight? Wanna go out?"

"Well, Adam's working late on some project, so yeah. Meet you at the Sunset Bar?"

"Yeah, seven's good. Adam said it would be at least

eleven before he gets home."

Jimmy walked in and said, "are you out, running the horse this morning?"

"I am, and you better watch it, Jimmy, he doesn't take a lot of shit from people."

"I believe you, Scarlet. Good thing we're friends."

"Awe Jimmy, we're friends? That's the nicest thing you've ever said to me."

"Don't get used to it, Blondie. I'm just playing nice until you get that giant horse out of my office."

"Jimmy, you know he won't bother you. He'll sit and wait for me to tell him it's time to go."

"Yeah, I noticed that. Jose (the chef) tried to give him some bacon this morning; he wouldn't even look at it."

"He's taught to only take food from me, Jimmy. That way, he can't be poisoned. Besides, I'm not sure bacon's actually good for a dog."

"Oh, blondie, bacon makes everything taste better. Even for a dog. In fact, I think I read, dogs love bacon."

"Funny, Jimmy. Duke hier." (come) All of a sudden, Duke came running through the door and sat by her side.

"Damn Scarlet, that's amazing. How the hell does that dog hear only your voice when all this is going on in here?" Jimmy asked.

"Excellent training. My voice is the only one Duke's listening for. Even in a crowd, I can almost whisper, and he can hear me. Good boy Duke let's go home. Mama's gotta clean up and get to work. Thank you, Jimmy. Love you, Mal, see you tonight."

"Love you back, Scar, be careful."

"Oh, I will. Duke fuss." (heel) They left out the front door waving to the regulars and walked home. All the while, Scarlet's head was twisting and turning, looking for Bob. When she arrived home, they went through the usual routine of Scarlet walking in the side door and waiting in the kitchen. Duke walked the perimeter of the house and gave her the all-clear one bark, and then she came in all the way. Scarlet climbed the stairs to take a shower and got ready for work, while Duke finished his breakfast.

FORTY-THREE

No one minded Duke coming to work with Scarlet. In fact, hardly anyone noticed. She stayed in the back all day and worked on flower arrangements, while Duke laid in the corner and slept all day. *A dog's life!*

At six-thirty, Scarlet packed up and left work. They walked to the Jeep, and Duke jumped in the back seat. Scarlet drove to downtown West Bend and parked in a lot near the bar she and Mallory were meeting at. Since they were only having drinks, they wouldn't be too long; it seemed okay to leave Duke in the Jeep. He would just lay across the back seat and sleep. Scarlet cracked all the windows so there would be plenty of airflow, locked the doors, and started walking toward the bar. Duke followed her with his eyes the entire way. Scarlet began to get that uneasy feeling inside again like she was being watched. She looked around and didn't see anything out of place or unusual, but she couldn't shake the uneasy feeling in her gut.

Scarlet walked in the front door and saw Mallory was already at the bar with a beer in her hand. The Sunset Bar is a hole in the wall bar. It's what some might call a biker bar. A lot of Harley Davidson riders stop there on the way to Harley headquarters and the Harley museum in downtown Milwaukee. It can get rowdy occasionally. The bar is on the right when you first enter the front door, and there are a few tables behind the bar stools. Toward the rear, there's another room off to the left that has a pool table, dartboards, and the restrooms. Mallory waved her over and introduced her to the bartender.

"Elizabeth, this is my friend Scarlet."

Reaching over to shake hands, "Hi Scarlet, what can I get you?"

"Hi, I think I'll have a Summer Shandy."

"One Shandy coming up."

"Mal, I got that feeling again when I was walking over here that Bob is out there watching me."

"Is Duke in the Jeep?"

"Yeah, of course."

"Then, don't worry about it."

As soon as the words came out of her mouth, Bob walked up to them and said, "Hello ladies."

"Are you following me?" Scarlet asked.

"No, are you following me? I was here first," Bob retorted.

Scarlet stood up, turned to face him, and said, "are you kidding me? You were parked on my street this morning, stalking me. Stay the fuck away from me, you freak."

"Hey, it's a peace offering. I just wanna buy you, ladies, your drinks, and apologize for what happened at breakfast the other morning."

Scarlet raised her voice a little higher and said, "No, thank you. Look, Bob, my dog, can sense danger, and he'll act on it. I'm warning you to stay away from me."

"Yeah, I saw him, he's huge."

"He is, and he's trained to kill. If you want to keep your

balls, I suggest you move on and find someone else to stalk."

"Whatever." Bob turned around and walked back toward the other room, never looking back.

Scarlet sat back down on the barstool and said, "do you think he got the message this time?"

"Honestly, no, he's a little prick." Turning to Elizabeth, Mallory said, "Crappy tipper too."

"Mal, you know if Duke hurts him, I'm responsible?"

"Look, Scar, he's a little asshole. Don't worry, Elizabeth and I both heard you warn him."

Elizabeth leaned over the bar and quietly said, "that guy is such a dick; he hits on everyone and is constantly turned down. I strongly suggest you stay as far away from him as you can."

"I know I'm trying too, but he's stalking me. I know the little bastard was down the street in his car this morning watching my house."

Shaking her head, Elizabeth said, "better you than me, honey. I'm fairly sure he's got a small dick, and he's trying to make up for it by hitting on all these women."

They laughed and then moved on to a new topic. After about an hour at The Sunset Bar, they decided to go somewhere else for food. But first, Scarlet wanted to drop off Duke at home and feed him. They drove to her house first, and Scarlet parked in the driveway. Mallory parked at the curb. Scarlet opened the side door by the kitchen and said, "Duke pass auf." Off he went checking the house.

"What's that all about?" Mallory asked.

"He'll walk the perimeter of the entire house and make sure it's safe. Once it is, he'll return to the kitchen and bark once. If he doesn't bark, someone's in the house."

"No, shit?"

"Yeah, amazing. Mallory, I'm telling you, Michelle thought of everything. The things Duke can do is nothing short of incredible. Let me feed him, and then we can go. Do you need a beer roadie?"

"Naw, we're only going up the street."

Scarlet proceeded to feed Duke and give him fresh water. She let him wander around the backyard for a few minutes while Mallory smoked a cigarette.

FORTY-FOUR

The girls climbed into Scarlet's Jeep, and they drove twenty minutes to a city called Hartford, to a restaurant called the Mine. The place was busy, so they decided to eat at the bar. They each ordered a beer and a steak sandwich with fries. Scarlet felt she had been so busy with work and Duke that she lost touch with Mallory. It was great to catch up.

Mallory said Adam was doing fine as usual, and work was okay. Jimmy was a good guy to work for. She kept insisting Scarlet ask Jimmy out on a date. Scarlet kept saying, "he just tolerates me; he doesn't really like me."

Mallory went on, "Scar, you should see how he looks at you when you're not looking. In all the years I've worked for Jimmy, I've never seen him pay that close attention to a woman. Sometimes he asks about you in passing. Like he doesn't care. I know he does, though, just by the way he asks."

"Come on, Jimmy wouldn't have anything to do with me. I'm not his type," Scarlet said.

"Scar, he always watches you walk away from him, and he sometimes checks you out when you're sitting at the bar. He must like your ass." Scarlet thought, *I work on it, and it is a nice ass.*

They spent a couple of hours at the Mine watching several drunk people sing karaoke. Scarlet said, "It's incredible how you think you can sing when you're drunk." They both laughed and ordered a couple more beers and just kept talking about Jimmy, work, and Bob. It was great to just laugh and laugh over nothing at all. When they finished the last of the beer, they walked to the Jeep and drove back to Scarlet's house and parked in the driveway.

When Scarlet climbed out of the Jeep, she could see something going on a couple of houses away. There was an SUV parked in the middle of the street. Standing around it were some people trading money for small envelopes. Mallory came around the back of the Jeep and stood next to Scarlet. They watched what was going on down the street for a couple of minutes. As they turned to go into the house, Scarlet noticed Duke was pacing in the window staring at them. He was anxious and panting like something was wrong. Then they heard someone yell toward them in the driveway. Both girls turned around and looked.

One of the men from the house, a couple of doors down, came walking up the sidewalk. You could smell him before he reached Scarlet's driveway. He smelled like a skunk. He was about five-nine, Latino, tattoos up and down his arms and a black widow spider tattoo on his neck, short black hair, dark eyes, and dressed in a plain black t-shirt and jeans around his ass. *Not his waist.* He had a pistol stuck down the front of his pants. When he walked, it looked as if he took a step and dragged his other leg.

"Hey, Bitches!" Both girls turned and stared at him. Pointing, he said, "yeah, you two bitches."

Scarlet spoke first, "Who're you talking to, us?"

"Yeah, you two. Wait a minute I want to talk to you."

"Hey, if the cops come round asking questions about us,

you dint see nutin. Got it?"

"We didn't see anything, so I don't think it's going to be a problem," Scarlet said.

"Good, then we won't be having any issues wit choo bitches," pointing his finger at Scarlet's chest, he said, "Now will we?"

"We didn't see anything, so don't worry about it," Scarlet said again. Then, she turned to walk away.

The gangbanger reached out and grabbed Scarlet's arm to try and turn her back around toward him. As she pulled away, he said, "Hey, bitch, you don't turn your back on me, and nobody talks to me that way, I get respect, or maybe I'll pop yo cracker white ass."

Right then, Duke came around the corner running at full speed and growling with his teeth showing. Suddenly, it seemed like everything slowed down for Scarlet — this massive animal is running full speed right at the gangbanger. Duke leaped in the air from about four feet away and knocked the gangbanger down flat on his back. Duke continued to stand on his chest, and stare into his eyes while growling. The banger tried to squirm away, but Duke wouldn't move; he put his jaws around the banger's neck and continued to growl. He patiently waited for Scarlet to tell him what to do next.

The banger started screaming, "get him off me! Get this motherfucker off me!" When he reached for the pistol in his pants, Scarlet quickly yelled, "Don't do that, he'll chew off your hand. I'm not kidding; he's trained to disarm if he sees a weapon or senses danger."

The banger froze, he put his hands above his head and move another inch; he didn't say anything else; he just laid there as still as he could be. Everyone at the house up the street turned and began to stare at what was going on. A couple more bangers started to walk toward Scarlet's house. Finally, after a long minute, Scarlet said, "Duke fuss." (heel) The dog stepped off his chest and came to stand by her side.

Duke was still on guard when she said, "Look, he's very protective. He sensed danger, and he acted. That's what guard dogs do. He won't bother you anymore unless you try to touch me again. We don't want any trouble; we didn't see anything anyway." Mallory, Duke, and Scarlet then walked up the driveway back toward the house, leaving the banger on the ground, acting angry.

"Damn bitch keep that Cujo mofo away from me. Or I be poppin one in his mofo ass." The gangbanger got up off the ground and started walking back to the house up the block. He was still complaining, as his friends were heckling him and laughing. Duke never bit him, he just stood on his chest and was ready to bite his neck. Scarlet said, "he would have chewed through his wrist if he drew the gun, and in less than five seconds, this guy could have been dead."

"Damn Scar, Duke is a real badass. Did you see how fast he was on top of that guy? No hesitation, just boom, and the bangers on the ground. What did you say to get him off the guy?"

"Heel in German. I tell you, Mallory, I seem to attract

them, first Bob, and now this guy. They could be a problem living just up the street. I doubt these guys are going to let this go either."

"They'll be pretty careful around the house now, though; I can tell you that. Come on, let's go inside and have some wine."

"Duke hier (Come), let's get you a treat, good dog." She patted him on the head, and he followed her inside the house. They walked around the house and looked for where Duke got out. Mallory noticed in the downstairs bathroom, he jumped on the vanity, and through the screen in the window. He busted right through it. That must be a five-foot drop. Scarlet shut the window, and locked it, and made a mental note to get the screen fixed this week. After several glasses of wine *(maybe bottles, she lost track)*, Mallory finally called an Uber around one in the morning and went home.

Scarlet called Michelle's cell phone and wanted to leave a message. She surprisingly answered, and Scarlet shared the story of how Duke jumped through the screen with no hesitation and knocked the banger, "right on his ass." Scarlet made it clear she told Duke to heel, and he got off the guy but continued to stand guard.

Michelle told Scarlet she handled the situation perfectly. Also, she reminded Scarlet once again that Duke won't do anything unless he senses danger to her, or he is told to attack. Finally, Michelle said she would report it to Vincent, and he would update the file and call the local office to have the bangers, and the house checked out.

It was nearly two in the morning when they finally

climbed the stairs and went to bed. Scarlet didn't sleep well; she tossed and turned all night. She couldn't get the image out of her head of Duke standing on the banger's chest with his jaws around his neck. Even though she felt safe because of Duke, she was frightened by what he was capable of doing. The dog is a killer. *The responsibility of handling a killing machine is scary.*

FORTY-FIVE

The next morning, Scarlet woke early, hungover, and unsteady. She threw on an old pair of Levi's, a t-shirt, sandals, and put her hair up. They climbed into the Jeep and drove over to Jimmy's for breakfast. She couldn't shake that uneasy feeling like she was being watched or followed.

Mallory was outside on a break smoking when Scarlet pulled into the parking lot. They walked over to see her first. Mallory patted Duke on the head and told him what a badass he was last night.

"Oh my God, you're not even hungover, how is that possible?" Scarlet asked.

"Lots of practice, honey, lots of practice! I think they start teaching us here in Wisconsin to handle our liquor as soon as we come out of the womb."

Mallory put out her cigarette, and they walked in the side door. By now, Duke knew the routine, Scarlet pointed at Jimmy's office, and he walked over and laid down next to an empty chair. Mallory washed her hands, and they walked into the dining room together, everyone started clapping.

"You told them?" Scarlet asked.

"Of course, it was so exciting. Duke, the badass, jumps through a window to take out the banger. He's a superhero, you know a wonder dog."

"Oh Lord, can I have scrambled eggs, crispy bacon, fruit

instead of hash browns, and a toasted bagel with cream cheese for breakfast, please? And don't forget the water and coffee, please."

"Are you sure you don't want a Bloody Mary?"

"I have to go to work at some point, so no, I don't think so."

"Alright, coming right up." And off she went to the kitchen to put in the order. Mallory returned with the coffee and the bagel with a side of cream cheese. Scarlet sat at a booth up by the window and held her pounding head in her hands. Jimmy walked over and slid into the booth across from Scarlet.

"How's it going, Scarlet? You look like shit."

"Thanks, Jimmy, I'm not feeling so well either."

"I heard you had a little trouble last night."

"Yeah, I guess so. You know Jimmy, Duke is amazing. Loving, loyal, sweet, smart, but scary as hell. You should have seen him, no hesitation, he just leaped in the air and landed on the guy. It was as if everything slowed down for that moment in time. I don't know if I can handle him."

"Oh, sure you can, kid. He saved your ass last night. He's an awesome animal; you need to get used to having a bodyguard around you all the time." *If he only knew.*

"Yeah, maybe." Mallory showed up with the rest of the food, and Scarlet dug in like she was on death row, and it was her last meal.

"Are ya a little hungry this morning, Scarlet?" Jimmy asked. "You could feed a small army on all that food."

"I'm hungover because your waitress doesn't know when

to quit drinking."

"I hear she can hold her liquor."

"Yeah, I suppose. Tell me, Jimmy, what do you do all day?"

"Well, I start my day with the paper and the crossword puzzle and a buttered bagel, as you know. When I've finished the puzzle around ten, I go into the kitchen and make all the sauces from scratch for the dinner crowd. I bet you didn't know I can cook. I started this place as the chef. I use all my family sauce recipes from Italy, and we make homemade noodles too."

"You know I've never eaten dinner here. I'll come in and try it out sometime."

He put his thumb and forefinger together up to his mouth and said, "Oh, Scarlet, my Osso Bucco is the best in the world."

"Veal?"

"No, Osso Bucco."

"That's veal, Jimmy. You can dress up the name all you want; it's still a baby cow."

"How about a nice plate of my baked ziti and bracholas?"

"What's that?"

"It's a homemade pasta baked in my homemade sauce, covered in imported Romano cheese from the old country and a side of homemade meatballs made from scratch. A brachola is a meatball."

"Really? It sounds delicious."

"Well, how about you come on Saturday night with Mallory and Adam, and we eat baked ziti and bracholas?"

"I'll ask Mallory," Scarlet said.

"Good, just let me know or have Mallory let me know."

"Okay, thanks, Jimmy."

"Anytime, kid."

Jimmy got up and walked back into the kitchen. By all measures, Jimmy was a handsome man. He's six-one, green eyes, dark hair styled like Al Pacino, and chiseled facial features. He has an athletic build in that he has a flat stomach, a big chest, and muscular arms. Not like a bodybuilder but defined and toned. He shaves every day, and he looked very Italian. He usually dressed in slacks and a short-sleeve silk shirt and shined laced up shoes. He didn't step out of GQ, but he's a stylish guy with good taste in clothes and shoes.

When Scarlet finished eating, she called for Duke. As soon as he came through the door, he got another round of applause. Scarlet said, "take a bow, boy." Duke was much too humble. They climbed in the Jeep and headed to work, still hungover, and stuffed from breakfast.

Scarlet's drive up the freeway was only three exits. She kept her eyes peeled in her rearview mirror. When she exited on Washington Street, three other cars exited behind her. She turned right on Sendiks way, and two of the three vehicles followed. When she turned into the parking lot, only the black Chrysler 300 followed. Scarlet parked the Jeep in her usual spot and watched the Chrysler drive slowly past her to the end of the parking lot, where they stopped near the Papa Johns.

She looked at Duke and said, "What do you think, boy,

were they following us?" Duke didn't respond.

FORTY-SIX

Around three o'clock that afternoon, Heather, Scarlet's manager, excitedly pulled her aside. She told Scarlet that she had submitted her drawing and design for the West Bend Mutual event to the National Association of Florists contest. Heather said she thought Scarlet had a great chance of winning. *Oh crap, this is national publicity. I can't have my picture out there.* Scarlet smiled, thanked Heather.

Scarlet grabbed some Sushi off the Sushi bar and a bottle of Pinot Noir from the wine area before walking to the Jeep with Duke. After she opened the door and let Duke in the back seat, Scarlet climbed into the driver's seat. Suddenly, Duke jumped over the center console and started barking and jumping on her. He wouldn't allow Scarlet to start the engine. Scarlet kept saying, "What's the matter, boy, why are you barking?" It quickly became apparent he wanted both of them out of the vehicle, now! He kept pushing Scarlet into the door with his head. She finally opened the door, and he continued to nudge her out of the Jeep. Once they were standing in the parking lot, Duke sat down behind the front tire and barked twice. Scarlet knelt and looked under the Jeep and saw what was going on. There was what looked like a stick of dynamite duct-taped to the pipes coming out of the engine. She ran back toward the store, Duke followed. Scarlet pulled out her cell phone and dialed 911 and told the operator, "there's a bomb under my car."

The West Bend SWAT team showed up. Along with the fire department and what appeared to be a bomb squad. One of the bomb squad officers dressed like he was going to outer space crawled under the jeep and removed the explosive. About an hour later, the ATF showed up and asked about any recent trouble Scarlet was having in her life. Scarlet explained about Duke and the bangers and told them she also had a stalker named Bob, but she couldn't believe either could have done this. Scarlet kept the fact she was in witness protection from everyone involved. The problem was it could have been John or the New York mob that planted the explosive. When Michelle brought Duke to West Bend, she reminded Scarlet that Tony Gambucci still had a contract out on her life.

A uniformed officer from the bomb squad walked over to Scarlet to explain what was under the vehicle. He said, "Whoever put it there wasn't all that smart, in that they duct-taped a stick of dynamite to the pipes leading to the muffler."

"How was it supposed to blow up?" Scarlet asked.

"I'm certain the plan was, when the pipe got hot enough, it was supposed to blow up the car. I'm not sure that would have worked."

"Where in the world does one get dynamite?" Scarlet said.

"The dynamite looks like it came from a construction site. It was probably stolen from the demolition box they keep near the on-site office. Dynamite is regulated and a controlled explosive, so we can track where it's used and where it's stored. The contractor may even have a camera so we can see who stole it. Dynamite is commonly used around here, with all the commercial building going on."

While Scarlet waited, she called Vincent and explained what happened. He told her to stay calm, and he would check into it too. Finally, after a couple of hours of questioning and reports, they cleared Scarlet and Duke so they could leave.

FORTY-SEVEN

As soon as the police cleared Scarlet, she called Mallory.

After explaining the whole incident, she said, "Mal, I'm so shaken up, will you meet me for a drink?"

"Of course, where and when?"

"The Landing, now, I have Duke so we can sit outside with him." She tossed the sushi in the garbage, threw her wine on the front seat, and drove into downtown West Bend and parked the Jeep. Scarlet walked over to the bar with Duke, and they sat at a table out by the river. The Landing is on the Milwaukee River. It's a two-story building where at the street level, there's a bar with tables and bar food. There's also a balcony that looks over the patio below and has unobstructed views of the Milwaukee River. Downstairs there's another small bar; pool tables and dart machines. The door in the lower level walks out onto the patio bar that sits on the Milwaukee River. They don't mind dogs, so Mallory and Scarlet like to go there with Duke.

The waitress came by and brought Duke a bowl of water (which he never touched) and Scarlet a shot of Gentleman Jack Daniels and a Summer Shandy beer. Mallory and Adam showed up about twenty minutes later.

Scarlet waved and said, "Hi, guys. Adam, it's so good to see you." They hugged.

"You too, Scarlet, what in the world happened today?"

"Well, Duke jumped in the Jeep and started barking. He

wouldn't let me start it. He kept nudging and pushing me to get out. I finally got out, and he sat down next to the tire and barked twice. I finally got down on the ground and looked under the Jeep and saw the dynamite taped to the muffler pipe. I about shit myself."

"Oh my God, how scary. Who do you think did this, the bangers from the other night?"

"I don't know Mal, could be. Hell could be Bob for all I know. But I can tell you this; I have never been so scared in my life. Thank God, Duke was there." She reached down and patted him on the head. He just laid there, panting as if nothing had happened.

Mallory reached down below the table into her purse and pulled out her cigarettes and a lighter. "Mal, give me one of those, please."

Astonished, "why? You don't smoke?"

"I used too, and I think I could use one now. Maybe it'll help calm my nerves. Hell, I may take it up again if this shit keeps happening to me."

Mallory handed over a Camel cigarette and lit it for her. Scarlet drew the smoke deep into her lungs and coughed a little. She then turned her head away from Adam and blew out the smoke in the opposite direction. Looking down at the cigarette between her shaking fingers, she said, "It's been years since I smoked a cigarette, especially a non-filtered one."

Mallory gave her a look of surprise and said, "you look funny, smoking. I just never pictured you with a cigarette in your hand."

Looking down again, Scarlet said, "How do you smoke these unfiltered things?"

"I don't know, I just do. Unfiltered cigarettes taste better to me than the filtered ones. Scarlet, I've been smoking since I was thirteen. I think the first cigarette I stole from my Dad was an unfiltered Lucky Strike. I thought I was going to puke. Now, that's all I smoke are unfiltered cigarettes."

"When I used to smoke, I smoked Marlboro Lights. I quit after a couple of years cold turkey. I never smoked again, until now. Hell, I never wanted another one, until now." The Camel Mallory gave her tasted awful. Scarlet took a few more drags off it and then put it out. It made her lightheaded.

The waitress saw Adam and Mallory sit down and came over to take their order. Adam ordered a Bud Light, and Mallory ordered a brandy old fashion sweet.

Scarlet looked at Mallory awkwardly and said, "brandy old fashion, sweet?"

"Yeah, it's the unofficial official State of Wisconsin drink. Jimmy told me B&G sells more brandy in Wisconsin than any other state. In fact, I heard they have a distillery that serves just the state of Wisconsin."

Scarlet responded, "That's just weird,"

Scarlet was still nursing her second beer when the waitress brought their drinks and some pretzels. Scarlet used the pretzels to try and get the awful cigarette taste out of her mouth.

"How did Duke know there was a bomb under the car

anyway?" Mallory asked.

"Michelle told me he's trained to identify bombs from their smell. She said every bomb type has an odor signature that you can teach dogs to recognize and respond too. Duke knows dynamite and C-4 supposedly. His response is to identify, locate, and bark. I guess dogs can only sense bombs or drugs, not both. But thank God Duke could smell bombs."

"What does she do that she had a dog trained to smell bombs?" Adam asked.

"She was a canine trainer for the FBI. I know her from my hometown back in Ohio. We went to high school together."

"Did she know your ex-husband?" Mallory asked.

"Yup, she did. But she moved to Quantico to train dogs and then New York to become a Special Agent for the FBI. We used to hang out and do stuff together. Oh, speaking of doing stuff together, Jimmy invited the three of us for a baked ziti dinner on Saturday night at the diner. Are you guys up for a night with Jimmy?"

"Um, like a date? Did Jimmy finally ask you out on a date?" Mallory asked mockingly.

"Well, I didn't take it as a date, but now that you mention it, he might be thinking it's a date."

"Ooooh Scarlet has a date, get the diaphragm out."

"That's just sick, Mal. I told you Jimmy is nice to me because he likes Duke. Why else would he let us park the dog in his office all the time?"

"He likes you, that's why he lets Duke hang out in the

diner."

"So, will you do the I got a date dance for Adam?" Mallory asked.

"Oh, Funny Mal. Bite me." Scarlet mockingly said.

"Come on, I got a date, I got a date, bop, bop, and I won't be late bop, bop." Mallory proceeded to show Adam the gyrating hip motion of the bop Scarlet uses for the I got a date dance. Mallory kept dancing around the table, singing and thrusting her hips back and forth against Adam. They all laughed until they cried, except Duke, he just ignored her.

They stayed at the Landing while Adam and Mallory had a couple more drinks each. Scarlet nursed her third beer, and then they all walked across the street to a Mexican restaurant for dinner. Duke had to go back to the Jeep; the Mexican restaurant didn't allow dogs inside.

Adam ordered plenty of chips and salsa, margaritas, and burritos for everyone at the table. After the day Scarlet had, she forgot she was hungover from last night while working on getting hungover tomorrow. When they finished eating, Adam walked Scarlet back to her vehicle like the gentleman that he was. She kissed him on the cheek and gave him a firm hug. Scarlet climbed into the Jeep and drove home with Duke in the back seat, watching her back.

FORTY-EIGHT

Scarlet pulled into her driveway, parked, and then went through the usual routine of having Duke walk the perimeter of the house. However, this time, Duke returned to the kitchen and sat next to Scarlet, no bark. *That means someone's in the house. Did John get out of prison? Did Big Tony find me? Shit, who the hell would break into my house?* She froze, trying to process the moment; she felt a little buzzed and not entirely thinking straight. First, Scarlet called Mallory and Adam, and they said they would turn around and drive back to her house right away and told her to stay outside and call 911. Scarlet didn't want to cry wolf when it was unnecessary; she, of course, had a killing machine right in front of her. So, she did what Michelle told her to do.

"Duke voran!" (search) Suddenly the dog tore off upstairs, and then she heard a loud thud on the ceiling above her head. The next thing she heard was Duke barking several times, and then he was quiet. The house was entirely silent except for the faint sound of a person whimpering upstairs in the hallway. Scarlet dialed 911 and said, "there's an intruder in my house, and my dog has him cornered."

The Jackson police arrived in five minutes with three squad cars. *Who knew they had three squad cars in this small town?* Mallory and Adam got there about ten minutes after that. The officers had Scarlet walk upstairs behind them to control Duke. They had their guns drawn and aimed in front of them.

Scarlet peeked around the officer, and there in the hallway lying flat on his back on the floor was Bob the stalker. Duke was standing on top of his chest with his jaws around Bob's neck, waiting for Scarlet to give him the next command."

Bob was whimpering, "please get him off me. He's hurting me."

"Duke, fuss." (heel) Duke released his light grip on Bob's neck and stepped off his chest. He walked over next to Scarlet and sat down. Duke never took his eyes off Bob.

One of the officers commented, "that's a beautiful dog, he must have been professionally trained."

"Yeah, my girlfriend was a canine trainer at Quantico."

"Good thing this dumb ass wasn't armed, eh? The dog might have killed him."

"Yeah, a good thing, Duke can kill a person in less than five seconds."

"Miss, you realize it's a tremendous responsibility having a dog that's trained to kill. It's like owning a gun; you need to be in control at all times."

"Yes, I'm aware of that, officer," Scarlet said, "But Duke won't do anything unless I give him a command. He was holding that idiot on the floor, so he didn't move, waiting for me to tell him what to do next. He'll act on his own only if he senses I'm in danger."

The officers picked Bob up off the floor and cuffed his hands behind his back. Scarlet noted the red marks and slobber on Bob's neck. He didn't draw blood, but he was awfully close. If

Duke closed his jaws, Bob would be dead. They walked Bob down the stairs and put him in the back of one of the police cars.

Scarlet said to Bob as he passed by her, "Bob, I warned you Duke could kill you, stay the hell away from me. Next time I'll have the dog bite your little wiener." When she got downstairs to the dining room, Mallory and Adam were sitting at the table.

Mallory said, "Scar, it was Bob, right?"

"Yeah, I knew he wouldn't listen. He may have shit himself; I smelled something when I walked upstairs. Duke nearly killed him. He had his jaws around Bob's neck, ready to crush his throat. The little prick was crying and whimpering." Scarlet mocked his voice, "oh he's hurting me, please get him off me, boohoo."

"I told Adam, I bet it was Bob. Did they ask him if he planted the dynamite too?"

"No, I forgot to mention it to the cops."

"Go do it, hurry before they leave," Mallory said.

Scarlet walked down the block to one of the police cars still parked on the side of the street and knocked on the window. The officer rolled down the window and asked if she needed something. Scarlet told him the story about the dynamite in her Jeep earlier in the day and asked if they would question Bob about that too?

"I heard about that. It was at Sendiks in West Bend, right?"

"Yup, that was me."

"Well, this guy will be out on bail in a few hours, we'll

book him for breaking-and-entering, but if he set a bomb, it may be several years until he gets out. I'll question him when I get to the jail. We're taking him to the Sheriff's jail in West Bend."

"Is there any way for you to call and tell me if he's the one who put the bomb under my Jeep?"

"Of course, if he admits to it, which I doubt he'll do. I'll call you. Otherwise, you can assume he didn't say a word."

"Thank you, officer?"

"Delgado, James Delgado."

"Thank you, officer Delgado."

"You're welcome, Ms. Maxwell. And keep that dog close to you, he clearly has your back."

FORTY-NINE

About midnight, Duke and Scarlet climbed up the stairs to go to bed. She brushed her teeth extra hard to get the cigarette taste out of her mouth, and then crawled into bed, and quickly fell asleep. The next morning, they rose later than usual and went for a short run. On the way back, they strolled past the house where Scarlet saw the drug deal going down. This morning, there were no cars parked in the driveway. It didn't seem like anyone lived there, so they just walked by and went back home.

"Duke pass auf." Duke walked through the house and returned a few minutes later and barked once. All clear. Before Scarlet climbed the stairs to take a shower, she filled Duke's water bowl and fed him. Next, she went up to take a shower, brush her teeth, and put on jeans and a floral blouse for work. She put her hair up because it would take too long to dry. They climbed into the Jeep and headed to work.

All the crime scene tape was gone from the parking lot, from all the excitement the day prior, so Scarlet parked in her usual spot. She spent the entire day working on an upcoming corporate event, where she had to design floral arrangements for several tables and a large piece for the head table. Throughout the day, several people came by to ask about the bomb under her car. Scarlet just responded with, "I don't know who did it or why." She was secretly hoping it wasn't Big Tony and the Mob from New York.

After work, Scarlet went home for a quiet evening. She drew a couple of flower arrangements, read her book, and went to bed. Saturday morning, they jogged past Jimmy's and didn't see anyone outside, so they just continued trotting home. Tonight, Scarlet was having dinner with Mallory, Adam, and Jimmy. It was important for her to get home and finish some of her housework. "Duke pass auf." Duke ran off, checking the house while Scarlet waited by the kitchen door. When he returned to her side, he barked once, all clear.

Just after the noon siren (*for some reason, a siren sounds every day at noon in Jackson*), Scarlet and Duke climbed into the Jeep and drove to the park to get a little exercise. They played catch for a while, watched the Milwaukee river flow by, and just hung out relaxing. Scarlet brought along a sketchbook and drew several pictures of Duke sitting and watching the river flow by, and one of a cute bridge that crossed over the river.

They got back home at about three o'clock. Scarlet parked in the driveway but had a sinking feeling in her gut—again. Thankfully, the bangers weren't out in front of their house, and Bob was probably still in jail or perhaps too afraid to come around. *So, what was the problem?* She wondered to herself. Scarlet walked out onto the sidewalk in front of her house and looked around. It all seemed clear, her neighbors were out working in their yards and waved. Kids were playing on the sidewalk and in the street, and nothing seemed out of whack. But she still couldn't shake the uneasy feeling.

Scarlet immediately turned to Duke and said, "Duke pass

auf." He took off around the house and came back with one bark, all clear. She repeated this when she opened the side door to the kitchen. It was the same result, all clear.

Scarlet spent the rest of the day painting her fingernails and toenails, doing her hair, and pretty much girl stuff so she would look and feel pretty for her...date? She called Mallory to make sure they were coming and would be on-time.

"Mal, want to meet for a drink before we go to Jimmy's?"

"Yeah, Adam's ready to go, I'll be ready in twenty. We'll pick you up, okay?"

"Yup! See ya then, hon. Bye!" Scarlet slipped on a black skirt, her favorite bra, a sexy black silk blouse *that probably showed a little too much cleavage*, earrings, and a matching necklace. She decided to wear stilettos that would add about two inches to her already five-seven frame.She left her hair down and just pulled it behind her ear on the one side. About thirty minutes later, Adam and Mallory pulled up in their Ford Explorer. Mallory came to the door. When Scarlet answered, she said, "Holy shit, girl, you look beautiful."

"Thanks, honey, I tried. I haven't dressed up in a long time. I'm really excited and so looking forward to tonight. You look beautiful in that sundress." Mallory never wears dresses. She had on a sundress with white sandals. Her hair was down for a change, and she wore earrings and a neckless.

Adam drove about ten minutes to a local bar up the street in Jackson called The Owl's Nest. They all ordered beers and talked about the week's events with Bob, the bomb under Scarlet's

Jeep, and the bangers down the street.

"I can't believe all this shit is happening to you, Scarlet. Usually, Jackson's pretty quiet," Adam said.

"I know, I thought my life here would be simple and quiet. What does a girl have to do to get some peace?"

Adam laughed and said, "well, you may start with not screwing with gangbangers."

Noticeably perturbed, Scarlet said, "Oh, fuck them, they shouldn't even be out on our street. Little kids are playing on the sidewalk and in their yards, for Christ's sake. Who do they think they are selling drugs around little kids? That's fucked up."

"The mouth on you, girl. I don't disagree, but still, your dog almost ate one of them," Mallory said.

Adam just kept nodding, and finally said, "Scarlet, Duke *is* a little intimidating. Especially if he's standing on your chest growling at you. Frankly, his stare is scary as hell."

"Well, he is a little overprotective, I get that. Maybe that's something we need to work on," Scarlet said.

They drank their beers and ordered a second round. The night was warm, so they were able to sit outside and enjoy the weather. It became awkwardly quiet for a moment, then Scarlet asked, "What do you guys really know about Jimmy?"

"What do you want to know?" Mallory asked.

"Come on, just give me some insight," Scarlet said.

"Well, he's about 35 years old. I would say pretty cute." Turning toward Adam, Mallory said, "Not as cute as you, Adam, honey."

"Yeah, I was going to ask," Adam responded.

"Never honey, nobody is as cute as you. Jimmy's a good boss, you know. He treats us well, pays us well, and never lets anyone mess with his staff. Everyone says he's a great cook. He stopped cooking for the restaurant before I started and hired a chef. He still makes sauces every day and cooks for his Grandmother and her friends, usually on Wednesdays. He doesn't cook for the customers anymore, though. I've been working at Jimmy's for more than five years, and I haven't seen him cooking in the kitchen for customers in all that time."

"Is he a mobster, Mal?"

Mallory and Adam turned to look at each other and started laughing. "I don't think so." She said, "We never see gangsters around the restaurant. Jimmy's clientele is Judges, lawyers, the chief of police, the mayor, I think he knows the Governor. You know, influential people. Not thugs or gangsters. But remember, I usually work for the breakfast crowd, mobsters aren't usually up at five AM? Why are you asking?" *If they only knew!*

"I don't know. I'm trying to uncomplicate my life. I have Bob stalking me, the Bangers trying to blow me up. You know, trouble just seems to find me, even when I'm not looking for it. And, for the record, I don't think mobsters are up at five AM. Only crazy people."

Mallory said, "I don't think Jimmy's a mobster. He's at work all the time. I know he started the restaurant as the chef and built the business up from there. He expanded a few years ago to add-on to the kitchen. Hell, he plays golf. How many mobsters do you know who play golf?"

"None," Scarlet said. "I do think Jimmy's cute, and I like his wit. I enjoy our daily banter too." She looked down at the time on her phone and said, "Hey, guys, we should get going."

They finished up their beers, paid the check, and walked to Adam's SUV.

FIFTY

The drive to Jimmy's was less than fifteen minutes. The group walked into the restaurant, and the entire ambiance was different than at breakfast time. It even smelled different. Garlic, tomato sauce, and fresh bread, it was amazing. Jimmy had the lights dimmed, and lit candles on every table. He also put white tablecloths on all the tables too. Scarlet barely recognized the place. Jimmy greeted them at the door and led them to a table toward the rear of the dining room.

"Scarlet, you look gorgeous tonight," Jimmy said.

"Thank you, Jimmy. You look good too." Jimmy was dressed in black slacks, a light blue dress shirt, and a sport coat.

"Where's the horse tonight?"

"At home, guarding my *domicile*."

"Your domicile, is that a fact?"

"Yeah, Duke is very busy guarding my domicile."

"From what, may I ask?" Jimmy asked.

"Unsavory characters and stalkers."

"I see."

"Jimmy, it looks nice in here tonight. Very romantic."

"Thanks, I try. Would all of you like wine?"

Adam and Mallory both nodded and said yes.

Scarlet joked and said, "If I have too."

"Red good?" They collectively nodded. And off he went, returning with a bottle of red wine. The wine had a gold label and was called Ruffino Classico Chianti Reserva Ducale Gold.

"Jimmy, you're not waiting on us, are you? Aren't you going to sit down and eat with us?" Scarlet asked.

"Yes, of course. I just wanted to grab this wine. It's one of my favorites."

"What's for dinner?" Adam asked.

"I made stuffed mushrooms to start. They're large button mushroom heads stuffed with Italian sausage and imported cheese and baked to perfection. They'll be out shortly. Then, a Caesar salad, no anchovies, and homemade dressing, followed by my homemade baked ziti and a brachola on the side. I made everything from scratch today."

"I'm so excited to taste your cooking, Jimmy," Scarlet said.

"Blondie, tell me how the hell you keep getting into all this trouble? Did I hear someone stuck a stick of dynamite under your Jeep yesterday?"

"Sort of, the dumb ass duct-taped dynamite to my muffler pipe. He supposedly thought once it heated up, it would blow up the car. The cops told me it likely wouldn't have, but the potholes in town might have set it off."

"That's simply crazy, Scarlet. Who'd you piss off enough that they want you dead?" *If he only knew. Let me see, Big Tony, my ex-husband hitman, gangbangers, a dumb ass stalker named Bob, my senior class English teacher, my last boyfriend. The list goes on.*

"Maybe the gangbanger's next door. I think one of them

followed me to work the other morning from here. I watched someone get off the highway and follow me into the parking lot at work. But they drove to the other end by Papa Johns and parked. So, who knows? Good thing Duke was with me."

"That dog is something else. How did your friend Michelle end up with him in the first place?"

Scarlet told the fake story about how she and Michelle were friends in high school back in Ohio, and how she went on to become a canine trainer for the FBI at Quantico. "He was injured in a bust and had to retire. I think he broke his leg or something. Anyway, they let Michelle adopt him after the injury. She continued to train him once he healed up."

"Well, the horse has my vote for the man of the year."

"Yeah, mine too. Duke is the most reliable man I know. Did Mallory tell you how he jumped right through the bathroom window that's five feet off the ground to get to the banger?"

"Yeah, she did, that's crazy. Was Duke in the front window watching what was going on?"

"Yeah, I saw him pacing and panting. He knew something was off. Mallory and I were standing in the driveway when the banger walked up to us. We turned to go into the house, and he grabbed my arm and pulled me back toward him. Duke saw this and went crazy."

Mallory then said, "You guys should see when Scarlet brings Duke home, she says something in German, and he goes on guard by walking through the entire house. He then comes back and barks once. If he doesn't bark, then someone's in the house, and he waits for her to tell him what to do. That's how she knew Bob was in the house, stalking her."

He doesn't automatically rip the person apart when he finds someone in your house?" Jimmy asked.

"Well, no, unless he senses I'm afraid of the person, but it might be a guest, and Duke wouldn't know the difference. He sort of keeps tabs on them until I tell him what to do next. I think if they tried to run away or jump out a window, Duke would sense something is wrong and stop them. That dumb ass Bob sure found out what happens next. His pants were soaked around his little dick, and I smelled shit, when I walked up the stairs, he had to have crapped his pants and pissed on himself."

"I'll remember that if I ever spend the night. What did Duke do to him?" Jimmy asked. *Spend the night? Hmm, was that a Freudian slip?*

"He jumped on top of him and knocked him down, and then he stood on his chest, growling at him. When I got upstairs, Duke had his jaws around Bob's neck waiting for the kill command."

"What's the kill command?"

"Funny story, its kill. Michelle wanted it to be in English, so you don't have to think how to say it in German, you just say Duke kill. In less than five seconds, the dog can crush your neck, and you die; he knows exactly where the carotid artery is located. Duke has more than 200 pounds of biting power; only a rottweiler has more. Michelle told me if he senses fear or danger and sees a weapon, Duke will attack to disarm and could chew through someone's wrist in a few minutes. Honestly, it scares the shit out of me."

Together they ate great food and drank fantastic wine, talked, and laughed. Jimmy was a perfect host. He was charming, funny, and sweet. He even served homemade cheesecake for dessert. Then, after dinner, Jimmy brought over a bottle of Anisette, an anise-flavored liqueur. He explained how it helps settle your stomach after a big meal, the same way red wine helps your digestive system. *That's obviously good for me, I like red wine...a lot.*

"Why do you think they have red wine at every meal in Italy?" Jimmy said.

Mallory and Adam went home at ten-thirty. Jimmy offered to drop Scarlet off at home later, so she stayed. They sat at the table, talked, and held hands for another hour. Jimmy then asked if she wanted to have a drink someplace else.

"Why not? Everything was so perfect. You're a wonderful cook and a great host, Jimmy. Thank you again."

"It's my pleasure, Scarlet, I really enjoyed your company. Do you want a doggie bag for the horse?"

"Yeah, I don't think so, you know he wouldn't eat it anyway, he only eats his food, that's how he's trained."

"Sounds boring. Alright, come on, let's get out of here."

They climbed into Jimmy's Range Rover and drove about twenty minutes to a bar called The Peak. Harold's is a small nightclub off the beaten path in a city called Mequon. The first thing you'll notice is how small and intimate it is. The lights were low, and a trio of musicians were playing jazz on a small stage in the back. It wasn't exactly a dive bar, but a classy, jazzy sort of joint, like one of those places in New York City or Chicago where you might see a famous musician show-up and sit in with the band.

When they walked in, the bartender immediately said hello to Jimmy by name. *Of course, they knew each other.* He asked Dan the bartender for Champagne. And then turned to Scarlet and asked, "Is Champagne ok, or is it too sweet this late at night?"

"No, it's fine, but please get me a glass of water too."

They sat close to the bar because all the tables near the stage were taken. The waitress brought over the Champagne and a glass of water. Jimmy was a perfect gentleman again, polite, kind, generous to the wait staff at both his place and The Peak. They didn't talk while the musicians played, they held hands and listened to the music. The band stopped playing a little after one AM, and the bass player walked over to the table. Jimmy stood and gave him a man hug and said, "Kurt, great to see you. Kurt, this is Scarlet, Scarlet this is the best damn bass player this side of the Mississippi."

"Hi Scarlet, nice to meet you. I hope you enjoyed the set."

"Yes, I did. It was great. I liked that last song by Stan Getz."

"Ah, you know your music. Yeah, that was Stella by Starlight. Did you hear us play One Note Samba?"

"No, sorry, we just got here a little while ago, maybe next time. I love that song too."

"You need to come back. We do a mean version of it. Well, hey Jimmy, great to see you, and Scarlet nice to meet you, I need to go help tear down." Kurt turned and walked away.

"Bye."

They finished their drinks and climbed back into the Range Rover and headed back to Jackson toward Scarlet's house. Jimmy pulled into the driveway behind Scarlet's Jeep at 1:45 AM; Duke was in the window watching them closely. Jimmy got out of the SUV and opened her door. Just like a perfect gentleman, Jimmy walked her to the front door, where Duke was waiting.

"I'll leave you in the most capable paws of your killer dog." Then Jimmy leaned in and lightly kissed Scarlet on the lips. He said, "goodnight, kid." Then he turned and walked back to his SUV, climbed in, waved, and drove away.

Scarlet walked into the house on cloud nine. No one has ever treated her like this. Jimmy was so polite, kind, and gentlemanly. In all the time she visited the restaurant, she never saw the romantic side of Jimmy. *Sometimes it's hard to see what's right in front of you.* Scarlet texted Mallory to see if she was awake, but never got a response. Scarlet gave Duke a treat for guarding the house, and they walked upstairs to go to bed. *A perfect date, I hope he's not a hitman.*

FIFTY-ONE

Sunday morning, Scarlet woke up late and hungover—again. *How do these people drink so much?* Her head was pounding, her mouth was dry, and her eyes were held shut with sleep. She climbed out of bed and washed her face, then walked downstairs to let Duke outside. She quickly fed him and then literally crawled back into bed. Around noon Scarlet finally dragged her sick, tired, hungover body out of bed. She walked downstairs to make some coffee and toast and then called Mallory.

"Hey Mal, what a night. I didn't get home until almost two."

"Did you sleep with Jimmy?"

Sounding disappointed, Scarlet said, "No, he kissed me goodnight and left. I think Duke scared him off."

"I doubt it. Did you guys hang out at the restaurant all that time?"

"No, we went to Mequon to a place called The Peak. We listened to jazz and drank champagne. Big mistake!"

"Yeah, champagne is not a good finish after beer and wine, and that liqueur Jimmy brought to the table."

"Ugh, I am so hungover, again, and I feel like shit."

"Yeah, Adam, too, and he didn't have nearly as much to drink as you. Great wine, though, huh?"

"Yeah, really good. By the way, thanks again for coming along, it helped to have you there. It helped fill the awkward moments."

"No worries sweetie, I'm so glad you had a good time. Jimmy's a great guy; I hope he treats you right. Did he ask you out again?"

"No, he didn't say anything. He didn't even say he would call."

"Well, give it a few days, he will. You looked so beautiful last night; he would be crazy not to want to go out with you again. Hell, if I weren't with Adam, I'd ask you out."

"Awe, thanks, that's so sweet. Look, Mal, I'm seriously hungover, I'm going back to bed."

"Talk to you later," Mallory said.

"Love you, Mal." With a pounding headache, and hungover, Scarlet and Duke stuck around the house, mostly in bed all day.

FIFTY-TWO

Monday morning, when Scarlet woke up, she jumped out of bed and put on her running clothes. The sun was out, and they ran for miles. There was a slight breeze and all the fresh air you could breathe in. It was a spectacular Wisconsin morning. On her way home, they stopped at Jimmy's for some coffee and a bagel. They walked in the front door, and Duke immediately planted himself in Jimmy's office. Scarlet took a stool at the bar and waved to the regulars. Mallory was polishing wine glasses at the opposite end of the bar.

"Hey Mal, can I have some coffee, please?"

Putting down the glasses and walking over to hand her a cup, "Here you go, are you feeling better?"

"Much better, it took me all day to recover. I don't know how you do it."

"I told you, lots of practice, honey, lots of practice." Then, Mallory being philosophical, said, "Champagne is bad, it goes in like sweat cream, and comes out like the devil's breast milk."

"No, kidding. Will you make me a bagel please?"

"Be right back."

Scarlet reached over the register and grabbed the newspaper. She immediately turned it to the crossword page and started trying to figure out the answers. It was Monday, so they were all easy. She avoided writing in the answer's because she didn't want to ruin Jimmy's morning. Right then, he strolled into the dining room from the kitchen.

"Good morning, blondie. How are you today?"

"I'm good, Jimmy, thank you again for such a great night Saturday."

"You're welcome, do you want to go out again sometime?"

"Yeah, of course, what did you have in mind?"

"Brewer's game? I can get us some great seats. I know the ticket manager."

"Of course, you do. You know I love baseball, don't you? Can Duke come?"

"Yeah, No, I don't think so," Jimmy said.

"Okay, I'll let him down easy. He can watch it on TV. I'll tell him to look for us in the stands."

Jimmy darted off into the kitchen to get his morning coffee and bagel. Scarlet had his paper, so he'll have to wait to get that back.

Mallory came back into the bar with Scarlet's bagel and refilled her coffee. "It's so funny; the chef is in there talking to Duke in Spanish, I think he's asking him why he doesn't like bacon. Duke is trying to ignore him. He keeps moving his head back and forth, refusing to eat the bacon."

"I tried to explain to him before; Duke won't eat or drink from anyone but me."

"He doesn't care; he keeps trying."

"Hey, Mal, Jimmy just asked me out again."

"I told you he would, where are you going this time?"

"Brewer's game."

"I think Jimmy knows the ticket manager; he comes in here with his wife to eat pretty often."

"Yup, that's what he said." Scarlet finished her bagel and coffee and called for Duke. He came through the swinging doors and sat by her side until she got up to leave. They walked home slowly, thinking about her next date.

FIFTY-THREE

When they arrived at the house, Scarlet opened the side door and said, "Duke pass auf," and he walked through the house and returned. Duke sat down and barked twice. Scarlet was confused; Duke had never done that before. Scarlet didn't enter the house; instead, she called Michelle and asked what it meant when Duke did his routine and returned with two barks.

"Michelle, I had Duke pass auf, and he came back sat next to me, and barked twice, not once. Does that mean something? My file's in the house, and I don't want to go in unless I knew it was safe."

"Good thought Scarlet, it's better to be safe than sorry. It does mean something; it means someone *was* in your house. They're gone now, but they were there. Duke picked up an odd, out of the ordinary scent. He'll show you where they spent most of their time when they were inside your house. A scent will linger if they stand in one spot too long. Fabrics like carpets, curtains, and bedspreads, for example, capture the smell and retain it. Use the command *spur*; it literally means to track. Duke will identify where the scent is the strongest and then guide you to that spot, just like he did the bomb. He'll sit and bark twice while staring at the spot."

"Um, okay, then what?"

"Well, call your local police and tell them someone was in your house. They'll send over a patrol car to take a report, and then they should keep an eye on your house for a few days. I'll let Vincent know too. He'll need to put it in a report in your file here at the FBI. What's going on, Scarlet?"

Scarlet told her about the car bomb and the bangers. She said she would take care of it from the New York side by letting Vincent know all the details. She also insisted a local FBI agent come out to the house and visit with her to discuss the level of threat the bangers may cause. They'll cover some additional protocols Scarlet should be aware of around reporting an incident like this.

"Scarlet, this is very serious. Please don't downplay the seriousness of this incident."

"I know Michelle. It's frustrating. What am I supposed to do, become a hermit?"

"No, but make sure you keep Duke near you at all times, he will always have your back, okay?"

"Yes, of course. So, Michelle, when are you leaving?"

"In a few more weeks. I'm in training to learn what it's like being in a deep undercover role. Let me tell you; it's intense work."

"I'm sure you'll be great. Take care, honey, and thank you again, Duke misses you."

"Yeah, I miss him too. Bye, Scarlet." Michelle ended the call.

"Duke spur." Duke walked around the house, sniffing, and then climbed up the stairs. Scarlet followed him to the bedroom, where he stopped in front of the dresser, sat down, and barked twice.

Next, Scarlet called the Jackson Police, and officer Delgado showed up. She explained to him that Duke sensed a strange scent in the house. He then insisted they walk through the entire house together and see if anything is missing and if they can figure out how a stranger got in. They walked around the entire house, and Scarlet didn't notice anything missing or moved. She told him Duke thinks he was just in my underwear drawer. She explained how a scent will linger in the carpet or bedspread if they spend time in one spot. It's much like cadaver dogs who catch a whiff of a scent and can identify a body's location. The officer wrote all this down in his report and left.

It felt weird knowing someone had been in the house, much less her underwear drawer. Scarlet knew she was safe with Duke there but still couldn't shake the uneasy feeling. She thought, *maybe it would be a good idea to leave Duke home today to guard the house.* In the end, Scarlet decided it was smarter to have Duke by her side. He'll recheck the house when they got home later tonight.

On the way to work, she called Mallory and told her about someone being in the house that morning and how they were in her underwear drawer. All she could say was "freak." Scarlet couldn't agree more.

FIFTY-FOUR

Scarlet spent the day working on a head table centerpiece for the Gehl Company. At five-thirty, her cell phone rang, Jimmy wanted to know if she was up for a cocktail.

"Sure, why not?" Scarlet said.

"Do you want to meet me at the Polar Inn downtown?"

"Yeah, can we sit outside? I have Duke with me."

"Of course, meet you there in twenty minutes."

Heather, Scarlet's boss, came rushing in the back and said, "Scarlet, you won! I can't believe it; you actually won!"

"Excuse me? Won what?" Scarlet asked.

"You won the national contest for your floral arrangements and centerpiece at West Bend Mutual."

"Really? How is that possible? That's crazy."

"Yes, it'll be published in their national magazine with the picture I took, and the drawing you made. I'm certain the magazine is sent all over the world, Scarlet, you'll be famous. You also get a prize of five thousand dollars."

Her heart sank as she faked a smile and pretended to be excited. *I can't have my picture in anything national much less worldwide. I need to call Vincent or Michelle. They need to know about this. Maybe the FBI can stop the picture from going into the article.*

After the news from Heather, Scarlet and Duke packed up and headed toward downtown West Bend to a restaurant/bar called the Polar Inn. The Polar Inn is an old house from the eighteen hundred's that was converted into a swanky restaurant and bar in the 1970s. It's a two-story home with the downstairs, mainly dining, and the kitchen and the upstairs is both a bar with a limited amount of dining in an adjoining room. All the floors were original hardwood, and the windows looked incredibly old too. The place felt like something out of a Norman Rockwell Painting. The stairwell up to the second floor was old, narrow, and creaking, yet charming.

It only took about ten minutes for Scarlet and Duke to arrive. She parked on the street in front of the restaurant and walked behind the building to the courtyard. Scarlet and Duke sat outside in the courtyard at one of the tables. It was beautifully landscaped. There were rose bushes planted in the ground along the inside of the fence, and large pots with a variety of flowers sprouting out at the corners. There were even hanging plants, and some gorgeous trees to block out the sun. Scarlet wasn't sure she could have done a better job of landscaping or planting the flowers and the trees. The entire courtyard was surrounded by a solid wood fence that was eight feet tall. There were flower gardens planted around the outside of the fencing that was just as pretty as the inside. They had ten tables and a fire going in an outdoor fire pit. It was a beautiful night, warm, but not too humid.

The polar Inn provides music several nights a week on the patio. Tonight, a guitar player named Charlie Lango was playing Latin music. The waitress took Scarlet's order as she got lost in the music waiting for Jimmy and worrying about winning a national flower contest. Duke laid next to her chair without a care in the world.

The waitress brought over a glass of red wine and set it down on the table, disrupting Scarlet from her thoughts. Jimmy arrived about ten minutes after that. He walked in through the restaurant shaking hands and waving to everyone. It was apparent the staff all knew him here too. He finally arrived at the table, and the first thing he did was pet Duke on the head, and kiss Scarlet lightly on the lips. *Nice!*

"Been waiting long?"

"Nope, we just got here. Why aren't you working tonight?"

"We close on Monday nights. You're aware that even God had one day off?"

"Yeah, I suppose so, you deserve it."

"Are you okay? Mallory told me someone was in your house this morning."

"I think so; I'm not sure what's going on. I keep thinking it was the bangers, but oddly enough, it could be Bob again. You would think he knows better, though. Duke figured out they were in my underwear drawer. Duke also searched for another bomb; you never know what these asshole bangers are going to do next."

The waitress brought Jimmy a glass of red wine too and asked if they wanted to look at menus? They both declined.

"How did Duke know there was someone in the house?"

"He smelled the scent they left. He can tell where they spent most of their time in the house by the smell they leave on the carpet or curtains. Dogs have an amazing sense of smell; it's like ten-thousand times that of a human."

"What are you going to do about it?"

"What can I do, Jimmy? Duke will check the house each day when we come home for intruders, bombs, and whatever. I don't know what else I can do, should I move?"

"That seems a little extreme."

"Yeah, I thought so too. It's getting old, though. I'm tired of all the cloak and dagger crap between Bob and the bangers." *The contract out on my head, and my ex is a hitman. I don't know what to do.*

"My Grandmother always told me; this too shall pass. So, I'm telling you, Scarlet, this too shall pass. It will all work out, you'll see."

"Yeah, when? It's not like I'm out looking for trouble. I'm just going through life with a few friends, some wine, and a few good times. What the hell, Jimmy?"

"I couldn't have said it any better, Scarlet. What the hell?" They touched glasses and toasted to, what the hell! Jimmy then said, "So how about Friday night going to the Brewer's game?"

"Yeah, sure. I'd like that. Just you and me?" Scarlet asked.

Sounding hurt and pulling his hands up to his chest, Jimmy said, "What are you afraid to be alone with me? Do we need a chaperone or something?"

Backing off, Scarlet said, "no, Jimmy, I was just asking."

"Well, to be honest, my cousin Frankie and her boyfriend are coming with us."

"You crack me up, you're giving me shit about being alone together, and when I push back, you go down like a fat kid on a seesaw."

"Blondie, you're so damn funny, it kills me."

They stayed at the Polar Inn for a few hours and knocked off a bottle of red wine and some appetizers. About eight-thirty, Jimmy walked Scarlet and Duke to her Jeep and asked if he should follow her home to make sure she's safe. Scarlet agreed with Jimmy and thought that was a great idea. She put Duke in the back seat and turned back toward Jimmy. He put his arms around her waist and kissed her lightly on the lips. Duke stared him down from inside the Jeep.

"Wait here for me; I'll pull my car around and follow you home." Jimmy turned and ran toward his Range Rover. *Hmm, nice ass!*

Scarlet and Duke drove back to Jackson, and parked in the driveway, while Jimmy parked his SUV on the street out in front of the house. When she got out of the Jeep, she looked down the street and didn't see any bangers outside, or Bob's little red Hyundai. Scarlet thought, *maybe I'll have a quiet night.*

FIFTY-FIVE

El Reno Prison

John Mancini spent every day on the computer searching websites for Charlotte. He subscribed to blogs, newsletters, and searched for her name constantly. Over the past year, he kept coming up with nothing, until today. John received a newsletter from the National Association of Florists announcing their winners of the most unique and beautiful centerpiece contest. There on the first page was a picture of Charlotte, her drawing, and a picture of the centerpiece she designed. "I got ya!" He said to himself. "You bitch, I got you!" Her new name was Scarlet Maxwell.

The article says she's from Jackson, Wisconsin, and works at a local florist. The story never mentioned the name of the florist or any other details about Charlotte. The article focused on the sketch and how she transformed a picture into the reality of a beautiful centerpiece.

John now had something to look forward too. It had been well over a year, and every day, he thought about what went wrong. The mistakes he made with the gloves and leaving the dry cleaning on the dining room table. But worst of all was how he took the job with Charlotte in the car. That was the biggest mistake. He should have driven home, dropped her off, and then gone back to Queens that night and take out the Fletcher's.

Sure, it was hypocritical to be angry at Charlotte for going to the FBI when John himself testified against Big Tony to get such a light sentence. Still, the bitch put this whole mess in motion. John's anger built every day he spent in prison.

John spent hours thinking, scheming, and planning how he was going to kill Scarlet. John wanted to make sure she knew it was him. He planned to look Scarlet in the face, maybe screw her once more, and then shoot her between the eyes. A one-shot kill, excited John. He started to get a rise in his pants.

FIFTY-SIX

Scarlet, Duke, and Jimmy walked in the side door by the kitchen, "Duke pass auf." And off he went checking the house, he returned, sat down, and barked twice again.

"Damn it! Someone's been in my house again."

"Want me to go check it out?" Jimmy asked.

"No, they're gone. Duke would warn me if they were still here. Come on in, let's see if they stole anything. Also, I can't seem to figure out how they keep getting into the damn house? Duke spur" (track)

Duke walked directly upstairs to her bedroom and sat down in front of the dresser and barked twice. "Son of a bitch, they were in my underwear drawer again. What's wrong with these people?"

Jimmy and Scarlet walked around the house and didn't notice anything missing or any windows ajar. This time she didn't bother to call the police. She fed Duke and poured Jimmy some wine. Scarlet put on a CD of Chris Botti's called Night Sessions. They lounged on the sofa and listened to music, talked, and kissed. *Maybe a little second base too.* About midnight, Jimmy lifted Scarlet from the couch, took her hand, and walked upstairs to her bedroom.

At two-thirty in the morning, Duke was standing and staring out the window and began to bark. From a sound sleep, both Jimmy and Scarlet jumped out of bed. They ran to the window to see the backyard by the garage on fire. Scarlet quickly grabbed her phone and dialed nine-one-one. They both slipped on pants, and Scarlet threw on a sweatshirt and ran down the stairs to let Duke out.

He tore off after someone behind the garage. Jimmy quickly followed. Scarlet trotted toward them, and at the end of the ally, Duke had someone on the ground. Jimmy kept yelling at Duke to get off him. When Scarlet arrived, she stopped and stared. It was the same gangbanger as before, the one who grabbed her arm. *You would think he would have learned his lesson previously when Duke had him on the ground. The little prick set my garage on fire I should have Duke bite him.*

"Get this dog off me, bitch. I'll kill you, get him off."

"You know what you little asshole, maybe I'll have the dog eat your balls. Duke bleib, kehle" (stay, throat) Duke put his jaws around the banger's throat and stayed put. Duke growled each time the banger swallowed. When Duke didn't move or get off his chest or remove his jaws from the bangers' throat, the banger stopped squirming and just laid there as still as he could.

Scarlet continued to stand over them, staring at the desperate banger. He seemed scared but more pissed off about a hundred and twenty-five-pound German Shepard standing on top of him. She warned him not to move, or the dog would bite him. "And don't even think of pulling a gun," she said, "or the dog will chew off your wrist."

Jimmy walked back to the house and summoned the police to come down the ally and get the banger. When they arrived, officer Delgado recognized Scarlet and said. "Miss Maxwell, Hello! Busy night for you, hey? Why don't you save me some time and the State of Wisconsin some money and just instruct the dog to eat him?" the officer said.

"Believe me; I wanted to. But you know the dumb ass would probably sue me, and then I'd really be screwed."

"Yeah, messed up world we live in, isn't it? Can you get Duke off him so we can arrest this piece of shit?"

"Duke hier, sitz" (Come, sit) Duke released his grip and walked over to Scarlet and sat down.

"That dog is incredible. Get up, asshole, you're under arrest for stupidity, and let's throw in arson for good measure." The officer pulled the banger up and turned him around to put cuffs on his hands. As the officer led him back to his police car, the banger turned his head and yelled, "The dynamite should have taken care of yo ass, bitch." *Now we know who bombed my Jeep.*

"Thanks, asshole, I hope you rot in jail," Scarlet said.

"This ain't over, bitch!" the banger replied.

Jimmy, Duke, and Scarlet walked back to the house, and the fire was basically out, but still smoldering a little. The neighbors were in their yards, looking at what was going on. The banger didn't start the whole garage on fire; just the one side burned a little. He was trying to start it all on fire, but it looked like he burned the newspaper in his hand using gasoline. Scarlet said, "thankfully, our bangers are stupid." As they were walking back into the house, Scarlet noticed the window to the basement was ajar. *That was how the little bastard was getting into my house.*

Pointing to the basement window, Scarlet said, "Look, Jimmy, the window's open."

"Never a dull moment with you and super dog blondie."

"Thanks, Jimmy, let's go back to bed. I'm exhausted."

They climbed the stairs to the bedroom and went right to sleep. About nine-thirty the next morning, Scarlet rolled over and realized how late it was. She jumped out of bed and ran to the shower. After showering, Scarlet walked downstairs, and there was a cup of freshly brewed coffee and a toasted bagel on the table with a note. *Blondie, I had a great time, next time let's stay at my place...it's safer. J*

FIFTY-SEVEN

After Jimmy left, Scarlet called Michelle to tell her about the magazine article. She explained how Heather, her boss submitted the information because she wanted to do something nice for Scarlet and surprise her if she won any of the prizes. *Who would have thought I would win?* The picture they used was from Heather's cell phone. She took the picture the day they delivered the centerpiece to West Bend Mutual. She submitted it without Scarlet's knowledge or permission.

"Scarlet, there's nothing we can do about this now. You need to be hyper-aware of your surroundings now. Let's hope anyone looking for you doesn't see the article." Michelle said.

"Michelle, I also wanted to let you know the gangbanger who Duke attacked struck again. He lit my garage on fire last night. Duke ran him down and attacked him again. The guy admitted to the police he put the dynamite under my Jeep."

"Well, that's one mystery solved. Are you and Duke okay?" Michelle asked.

"Yes, of course," Michelle said she would update the file and brief Vincent on the dynamite mystery being solved.

FIFTY-EIGHT

After talking with Michelle, Scarlet fed Duke and let him out before they climbed in the Jeep and drove off to work. Fully awake, and not really tired, just angry over the gangbanger, Scarlet called Mallory.

"Mal, did you hear what happened last night?"

"Now what?"

"The banger tried to set my garage on fire."

"What? Are you kidding me?"

"Nope, the dumb ass messed it up by using gasoline as the accelerant and newspaper. It looks like he started the paper on fire in his hands and then threw it at the garage. Duke woke up and barked, I let him out, and he tore out after the guy. He caught up to him at the end of the ally. Duke damn near ate him. It was the same asshole from the night we were out together. What a dumb ass, oh yeah, and he admitted to putting the dynamite under my car too."

"They're too stupid to believe they'll ever be caught," Mallory said.

"It was so funny Mal; Jimmy was yelling at Duke to get off the guy, Duke just stood on the assholes chest and growled at him."

"Wait, what? First, I want to know how much fire damage there was. Then I want to know about Jimmy sleeping over."

"Well, he didn't do much damage, mostly to the yard,

flower beds, and the corner of my garage. Also, I found out how he was getting in the house. The basement window was ajar. I think he was sniffing my underwear drawer too. The freak."

"Well, at least you know now, and you know who put the Dynamite under your car, it was a good night, hey? And Jimmy spent the night? Tell me more!"

"Yeah, well, I got a new dance. It's called the I got laid last night dance!"

"Seriously, and?"

"We met for drinks after work at the Polar Inn, and then went back to my house. And get this, when I got up and went downstairs this morning, he left me a fresh cup of coffee and a toasted bagel on the table with a note."

"That is too cute. How was it?"

"Mal, I was so horny, are you kidding, I almost killed him. I think what we did was illegal in half a dozen states. At least the ones south of the Mason Dixon line."

"You're such a dork Scarlet; I need to see the new dance."
"I'll show you later. I gotta get to work, love you, girl."

FIFTY-NINE

Even though Scarlet didn't show up for work until close to eleven, it was a slow day. She spent a good portion of the day drawing a new design for a big party at John Deere in Horicon. At six, Scarlet packed Duke up, and they climbed back in the Jeep and headed home. It was only Tuesday, and she was already looking forward to the Brewer's game on Friday night with Jimmy. *I wonder when Jimmy will call me back.* Maybe I'll stop over and get some dinner to go on the way home. *I bet he's at work.* Suddenly, her cell phone started to vibrate.

"Hello."

"Blondie, what are you doing?"

"Driving home, thinking about you."

"Yeah, what are you thinking about me?"

"How I miss you already, and I just saw you a few hours ago when I woke up. Scares the shit out of me."

"Don't be afraid; I'm harmless."

"I'm fairly sure you're not harmless. But what the hell, I'm adventurous. I can take on a stalker, banger, fire, car bomb; I don't care, keep throwing shit at me, I'm good."

"Are you hungry?"

"Famished, why?"

"I just made some fresh gnocchi; thought you might like it."

"Gnocchi? What's that?"

"Italian potato, homemade, you'll like it."

"Sounds fattening."

"I doubt you have to worry about that, the way you and the horse run."

"Well, I have a new boyfriend now, and I can't get fat."

"Funny girl, stop by; I'll make you a plate you can take home."

In her best pouty voice, she said, "you're not going to join me?"

"I gotta work kid, how about I stop by after work? Will that be too late for you?"

"No, that would be great. I'll see you in a few; I'm just leaving work now."

Scarlet drove directly to Jimmy's. She let Duke out of the back, and they walked in through the kitchen door, where the chef and staff were busy making dinners for the guests.

Jimmy was out in the dining room, so she left Duke in Jimmy's office and walked through the swinging door that opens into the dining room. He was schmoozing at a table. Jimmy looked up and waved her over.

"Scarlet, these are good friends of mine, Mike and Rachel Stanley. Rachel is a Federal Judge for this part of the United States, and Mike and I play golf every week. Actually, the truth is I play golf; Mike just rides around in the cart bitching for four hours."

Mike responded, "funny guy Jimmy, it's nice to meet you, Scarlet. Don't believe a word this guy tells you, especially when it comes to golf. He's the one riding around bitching about his putting, and his slice. Besides, I'm paying for a vacation home on my golf winnings."

Scarlet genuinely laughed and said, "nice to meet you both," as she reached out to shake their hands.

Jimmy had to tell them about Duke. "Mike, Rachel, Scarlet has a dog that was trained by the FBI, you should see this horse, he's amazing. No matter where Scarlet is, Duke is listening. Is he in the office, honey?"

"Yes, of course."

"Call him, will you?" Turning to the Stanley's, Jimmy said, "you've gotta see this."

In a very calm, almost whispered voice, she said, "Duke hier" (Come) Suddenly Duke came tearing out the side door and stopped next to her. His full attention was on Scarlet. "Sitz." (sit) Duke sat right down and looked over at Rachel. She patted him on the head.

"He's so beautiful, Scarlet, and that's amazing. How did he learn to do that?" Rachel asked.

Jimmy said, "Rachel, you wouldn't believe what this dog is capable of doing." He proceeded to tell them the story of the banger, setting the garage on fire, and Duke chasing him down the ally. Jimmy made it sound extra heroic. They were awed."

Mike asked how much he weighed and how much he ate.

"He weighs about a hundred and twenty-five pounds, and he eats a lot. He'll only take food from me and only eats his own dog food and treats. It's too easy to poison a dog if they take food or water from anyone but their handler. So, he was taught to only take food from me."

"Honey I have a plate made up for you in the kitchen, come on I'll get it for you."

Scarlet smiled again and said, "It was nice to meet you both. I look forward to seeing you again. Duke fuss." (heel)

The three of them walked back into the kitchen, and Jimmy grabbed Scarlet around the waist and kissed her hard and deep. Scarlet realized that she felt something like never before. Her body melted into Jimmy's. Duke flinched at first and then relaxed. *Quite sure, Jimmy almost shit himself.* "Damn blondie, I may never get used to him doing that."

"Maybe the more you kiss me, the sooner he'll get used to it."

"Sounds like a great plan." And he proceeded to kiss her again. *This time Duke didn't respond.*

"You know Jimmy, he already responds to you. He usually ignores most people."

"I know, he's still a killer dog, and he's still unpredictable. Don't you know the story of the turtle and the scorpion?"

"Yeah, I know, the scorpion stings the turtle after he takes him across the river because that's what scorpions do. Just remember, he's really not unpredictable, Duke won't do anything unless I tell him."

Semi laughingly, he said, "I'll try to keep that in mind."

Scarlet grabbed the bag of food and said her goodbyes. Jimmy kissed her once more, and she drove home.

SIXTY

When Scarlet arrived at home, she opened a new bottle of wine, poured herself a glass, and tried the gnocchi. The gnocchi was good, a little heavy for her, but thankfully Jimmy put a salad in the bag too. And a note. *"Can't wait to make love to you again. J" I like the way he thinks.*

It was just after ten when Jimmy knocked on the front door. Duke barked once and realized it was Jimmy, so he laid back down. Scarlet had dozed off on the sofa sketching a new idea for a centerpiece, so at first, she was a little out of sorts. She walked to the front door and opened it to let him in. He kissed her and gave her a giant hug. Duke didn't respond, he just looked up and then laid his head back down. Jimmy walked over to pet Duke on his head and ask if he was protecting Scarlet for him. Duke didn't bother to respond; he just ignored Jimmy.

Scarlet first offered Jimmy some wine. Jimmy skipped it; he took her hand and immediately led her up the stairs to the bedroom. It wasn't until about one AM that Scarlet fell asleep. After they made love, she laid next Jimmy listening to the rain beat down against the roof. Scarlet stared at the ceiling and watched the clock for more than an hour, trying to figure out why her gut still felt unsettled. Since Scarlet went into witness protection and moved to Jackson, she formed a great friendship with Mallory, a boyfriend she's head over heels crazy about, and landed a great job. That's when it hit her. *Jimmy! He was Italian, from New York and she didn't know anything else about him. Is he connected to Big Tony somehow? Is he related? Maybe Vincent can run some kind of background check for me on Jimmy.* She slowly dozed off to sleep in Jimmy's arms.

The next morning, Jimmy rose early and left. The rain had stopped sometime after two, so Scarlet climbed out of bed, put on her running clothes, and went for a 3-mile run with Duke. On the way back, they stopped and talked with Mallory at the diner. Duke sat in Jimmy's office while Scarlet sat at the bar drinking coffee and eating a bagel. Mallory had to serve some food, so Scarlet grabbed a napkin and started to sketch a picture of a calla lily. Jimmy came through the door, and the first thing he did was kiss Scarlet on the lips. The usual customers at the bar all made noises, and Jimmy said, "shut up, I'm in a good mood; the beers are on the house!" There were cheers all around.

He sat down next to her and said, "that's a great picture, it's beautiful. How in the world do you do that so quickly?"

"I don't know, I just do, I see it in my head, and then put it on paper. I've always been able to draw, it's a way of expression when I can't say the words, I think. So, where did you run off too so early this morning?" Scarlet asked.

Jimmy apologized and explained how he had to run his Grandmother to church. She has this volunteer thing for the morning mass on Wednesdays and must be at the rectory early to help the priest.

"Well, if it's a Grandmother thing, then it's okay. I forgive you for leaving me in bed alone and naked. Especially with my stalker Bob running around, and the bangers breaking into my house. By the way, when am I going to meet your Grandmother?"

"Soon, Babe, she'll love you. She'll try to fatten you up, though. And the beast in my office, she'll go crazy over him, she loves dogs. She'll try to feed him Lasagna."

"Yeah, you know he won't take it?"

"I know, but she'll badger him until he does."

"That's funny. So, when? Huh? When am I going to meet her?" She playfully poked him in the midsection. *Nice Abs!*

"Are you free for lunch today?"

"Sure, I have a little project I can put aside and meet for lunch."

"Well, then come here at lunchtime. Noni's going to be here. She usually comes here after church on Wednesdays. I'll make something special for all of us to eat."

"That's a date. Then I better get going. Duke hier!" (come)

They left out the front door and walked back home. Duke did his pass of the house, all good, one bark. Scarlet walked upstairs, brushed her teeth, and showered. She put on a yellow sundress, sandals, earrings, and a simple cross necklace. She left her hair down the way Jimmy likes it, and then put a bandana on Duke so he would look handsome too. They climbed in the Jeep and drove the three exits up the freeway to work.

SIXTY-ONE

At noon, Scarlet roused Duke, and they drove back to Jackson to Jimmy's Diner. She walked through the front door, and Jimmy immediately greeted her with another hard kiss and long hug. *It felt good to get this much attention.*

"Scarlet, you look so beautiful, come meet my grandmother." Then, with his arm around her waist, he walked her to a table where a little Italian woman was sitting. She couldn't have been five feet tall, beautiful olive complexion; She had a stocky build and short grey hair. She was wearing black slacks with black closed-toe flat shoes, and a pink striped blouse. For jewelry, she had on a beautiful cross necklace hanging around her neck, diamond stud earrings, and a gold diamond ring on her ring finger. The ring looked like it was very old. The diamond in the ring was small but beautiful.

"Duke sitz." (sit) Scarlet bent at the waist to give her a half hug and said, "How nice it is to meet you."

She stood up right away and put her arms around Scarlet's neck and hugged her. The woman had a faint smell of garlic. In her broken English Italian accent, she said, "It's so nice to meet you too, Scarlet. Jimmy has told me so much about you." She then bent down and said, "And this must be Duke." She began to pet him and said, "What a handsome scarf you're wearing Duke."

Duke had never responded to someone like this. Duke stood and wagged his tail. He nuzzled up to her leg like he was enjoying her petting his back. Her old-world accent was so charming.

"Duke gib laut." (speak) Duke barked one time.

Jimmy looked down, "That's new."

"He likes to talk. He said, nice to meet you too...um?"

"Please call me Noni, everyone does."

"Ok, Noni. We're so excited to meet you."

"Can the horse go in the office now, please?" Jimmy was trying not to bother his other customers.

Scarlet pointed at the kitchen door and said, "Duke voraus" (go out) Duke walked to the swinging door while Mallory was coming through it. She held it open for him and said, "Sucks to be you, Duke, banished to the office, huh? Too bad, you don't eat bacon, buddy."

Mallory brought out iced tea for Noni and a bottle of red wine for Jimmy and Scarlet to split. They ate a Caprese salad to start, and shrimp scampi with vegetables and plenty of bread and olive oil as their main meal.

After eating, Scarlet excused herself from the table to check on Duke. She really wanted to talk to Mallory. As she entered the kitchen, Mallory said, "Scarlet, what do you think of Noni?"

"Oh my God, she's soo cute and sweet too."

"Yeah, Jimmy's awfully close to his Grandmother. She often comes in with her girlfriends to eat lunch. Jimmy always cooks special meals for them, never anything on the menu."

"What happened to his parents, Mal?"

"Mob hit!"

"What? Are you shitting me?"

"Yeah, just kidding, I wanted to see your reaction after you asked me if he was a mobster the other night. They died maybe ten years ago in a boating accident on Lake Michigan. Weird, because his Father was supposedly deathly afraid of the water. His business partner convinced him to go out on a yacht, and the damn thing sunk. Everyone died."

"That's so tragic. Thanks for telling me that Mal, I need to get back in there. I'll talk to you later tonight."

Scarlet quickly checked on Duke; he was lying in Jimmy's office. He looked up with sad eyes when she peeked in on him. Scarlet patted him on the head and said, "It's alright, boy; I'll be right back."

She walked back into the dining room and sat down. Jimmy and Noni were deep into a conversation in Italian. They stopped when she sat down and welcomed her back. Jimmy asked, "Is Duke okay?"

"Yes, of course. Duke likes it in your office. Keeps the kitchen staff company and on their toes."

"Yeah, Noni, he's in there all the time. It's so funny, Jose keeps trying to get him to eat bacon, but he won't take it. He's trained to only take food and water from Scarlet."

For the next forty minutes, they talked about Jimmy's cooking, Duke, and the fact that Scarlet wanted to visit Italy. Noni said she still had plenty of relatives in the southern part of Italy in a province called Calabria. "My sister lives in Cosenza in a town on the sea called Paola."

Noni kept telling Jimmy how he needed to take Scarlet to meet the family in the old country. He just kept saying, si Noni, si, Noni. Jimmy said, "They live on the side of a mountain facing the Tyrrhenian Sea; it's so incredibly beautiful Scarlet, you would love it. They grow olives to make olive oil to sell, make bread from scratch, and have a garden filled with vegetables that would make you cry."

At one-thirty, Scarlet said, "I have to get back to work." She stood, and Noni stood to hug her goodbye. Jimmy kissed her on the lips and walked her back to the kitchen to pick up Duke. He told Scarlet he would see her tonight. Duke and Scarlet climbed back into the Jeep and drove back to West Bend.

SIXTY-TWO

When Scarlet arrived back at work, she was walking through the parking lot and heard someone call out her name. She turned around to see that it was Rachel Stanley, the judge she had met the other night at Jimmy's. Her long thick red hair was up in a ponytail. She was wearing a pretty summer dress, cute pumps, and an impressive diamond ring that Scarlet hadn't noticed before.

"Hi Scarlet, nice to see you again. You look so pretty." Looking down at Duke, she said, "Nice to see you again too Duke. Nice bandana you're wearing." She patted him on the head.

"Hi, Rachel, thank you. It's good to see you too. What are you up to?"

"I'm just picking up some food trays and wine for a party we're having this weekend. You?"

"Oh, I work here. I design flower arrangements for corporations and weddings."

"That's so cool, how fun is that? You get to be around beautiful flowers all day every day."

"Yes, I like it very much. It's calming, and it keeps me pretty busy."

"You and Jimmy should come to our house on Saturday night for the party. It'll be a lot of fun. Jimmy will know most of the people that are going to be there."

"I would love that, but of course, I need to check with Jimmy."

"Scarlet, he's a great guy. We've known Jimmy for a long time, and he has never looked at a woman like he does you. My mother would say it's so obvious he's smitten with you."

"Awe, that's so sweet to say. I really like him. He's kind and a real gentleman."

"That's great; I hope we see you on Saturday night."

"Bye, Rachel." And off they went in the side door by the flower department.

About fifteen minutes later, the phone in the back rang. "Flowers, hello, this is Scarlet."

"Scarlet, there's someone upfront to see you."

"Okay, thank you. I'll be there in a few minutes."

She looked through the two-way mirror, and Rachel was standing at the flower counter. Scarlet walked out front and said, "Hi again, can I help you."

"Scarlet, can you make me a centerpiece for the party?"

"Um, yes, of course. How much do you want to spend?"

"Something around a hundred and fifty dollars."

"Give me fifteen minutes, I have something I was working on, I can make some changes, and you can have it. It's gorgeous."

"Great, I'll swing back by in a little bit."

About twenty minutes later, Rachel returned to the flower shop counter. Scarlet took the centerpiece she had been working on out front to show her.

"Oh my God, Scarlet, it's absolutely beautiful. I can't believe you designed this so quickly."

"I was already working on it, so it was no problem. The

flowers are so pretty, and they smell so good. This arrangement has all freshly picked flowers." Pointing at each flower, Scarlet said. "There are orange roses and carnations, yellow Asiatic lilies and daisy poms; Peruvian lilies, Athos poms, white monte casino, and I added accents of salal tips. Also, don't worry about the Peruvian lilies, the buds will bloom in a couple of days, maybe sooner."

"Scarlet, thank you so much. Please make sure you and Jimmy come to the party."

"We'll try. Goodbye, Rachel."

She took the flowers, two cases of wine, a meat and cheese tray, vegetable tray, several pounds of shrimp, and assorted loaves of bread and oils and went to the checkout counter to pay. *Hmm, it must be a hell of a party.*

SIXTY-THREE

Thinking about meeting Noni and then the interaction with the Judge, Scarlet picked up her cell phone off the desk in the back and called Vincent.

"Special Agent Patterson, how can I help you?"

"Hi Vincent, this is Scarlet Maxwell. Do you have a moment?"

"Of course, Scarlet, what's going on?"

"Vincent, I'm starting to date a guy, and it's moving pretty quickly. I was wondering if you could check him out for me. I wouldn't ask, but I clearly have a bad track record with men, and I really like this guy."

"Of course, Scarlet, what's his name?"

"Jimmy or James Fanto. He owns a restaurant in Jackson called Jimmy's Italian Family Diner."

"You wouldn't happen to know his date of birth, would you?"

"Yes, February 24, 1987, born in New York, I think."

"Is there something, in particular, you're looking for?"

"Well, let's start with, is he a hitman? I'm just kidding—sort of. I want to know if he's a gangster, I guess. I don't know what I want to know Vincent, other than should I invest in this relationship, or run like hell? He's a great guy, but I thought John was a great guy. I don't want to make the same mistakes I made before. Do ya know what I mean?"

"I understand Scarlet, give me half an hour, and I'll call you back."

"Okay, thank you, Vincent." The line went dead.

When Vincent hung up, Scarlet felt a little deceitful, or maybe duplicitous. Running a background check on Jimmy didn't seem right. Thinking about John, however, Scarlet felt like she may never trust her own instincts again with men. Digging deeper, she thought, *I must have a type because Jimmy is a lot like John. Italian, from New York, knows food and wine. Same basic build. What's wrong with me?* Twenty minutes later, her cell phone rang. It was Vincent calling back already.

"Hi Vincent, that was quick."

"Yeah, we are the FBI, I have access to a lot of information you know."

"What did you find out?"

"Alright, Scarlet, he was born James Michael Fanto, in Queens New York to Vendetta and Nicolina Fanto on February 24, 1987. He has no prior convictions, no warrants outstanding; I don't even see a parking ticket in the past ten years. His fingerprints and DNA are not on file with us, and that's a good thing. It means he's not in any national database for anything at all. He and his Grandmother own the restaurant you referred to as Jimmy's. They bought it over ten years ago. He drives a year-old green Range Rover. No aliases on record, and we don't have any record of him associating with any known criminals. Once again, that's a good thing. His credit score is 774. No debt on the restaurant, they own the building outright; in fact, it looks like they own the entire corner. He has a small mortgage on a house in Jackson, and he leases the Range Rover he drives. Scarlet, I don't see any red flags, as far as I'm concerned, he's clean as a whistle."

"Thank you so much, Vincent. I feel better already. He seems to be a decent guy, and I want to trust him. But I'm scared after John."

"I understand. I would be hesitant too. It's good that you called me. Is everything else okay?"

"Yes, I think so. The gangbangers are still a little scary. It would be nice if the police got them off my block. But Duke is watching out for me. I'm good. How's Michelle doing?"

"I can't say, but I think she's well."

"I understand, she's undercover."

"Yes. Well, Scarlet, let me know if you need anything else. I'm here for you."

"Thanks again, Vincent, bye." Scarlet ended the call.

SIXTY-FOUR

The rest of the week flew by, nothing special happened.

Jimmy spent the next two nights with Scarlet at her house. They talked about going to the party on Saturday night and decided they would. Scarlet wanted to go, but Jimmy was hesitant.

Friday night, Jimmy picked her up at home at five o'clock to head into Milwaukee to go to the Brewer's game. She, of course, had to dress the part. Scarlet had her hair up in a ponytail and a Brewer's hat on, and she put on her oversized men's Yelich jersey over a tank top. She wore shorts and a pair of Chuck Taylor tennis shoes. Of course, she left the TV on and set to the game so Duke could try to find them in the crowd.

They drove south toward Miller Park and stopped along the way in a city called Wauwatosa to pick up Jimmy's cousin Frankie and her boyfriend.

Scarlet stayed in the front passenger seat, while Frankie and JD (her boyfriend) climbed into the back. Frankie was five foot three, dark eyes, black hair, and very dark Mediterranean features. You could tell she was Italian. Her arms were covered in tattoos of roses, lilies, lotus, and a large sunflower along with some Chinese symbols on her wrist, and just behind her left ear was a snakehead. The rest of the snake ran down her neck and back, but you couldn't see it because her hair covered her neck, and her blouse covered her back. Frankie also wore jeans with holes in them, closed-toe flat shoes, a super tight Brewer's t-shirt, and a

Brewer baseball cap on backward. When she spoke, she had a distinctly east coast New York accent Scarlet immediately recognized from growing up in New York.

JD, on the other hand, was very tall. Six four, blonde hair, several earrings in the right ear and one ring in his left eyebrow, a thin mustache, and one of those beards that are just a wad of hair on his chin that if it weren't blonde, it would look like dirt. He had deep brown bloodshot eyes, and a little scar by his left ear. His nose looked like it had been broken one time or another. He, too, had several tattoos. His right arm was entirely covered with all sorts of pictures, sayings, figures, characters, and a skeleton head. On his left arm, he had a picture of a devil riding a Harley.

He was odd-looking, sort of gangly, and he smelled like marijuana. He was wearing skinny jeans and what Scarlet thought was a dirty t-shirt. It was hard to read JD because he seemed cagey and elusive. JD had a very deep voice that didn't fit his look, he moved gracefully like a giraffe, for a guy so tall. Scarlet immediately recognized his east coast accent too. It was probably New Jersey.

They chatted on the way to Miller Park, and he said he was a consultant for a manufacturing company in South Milwaukee. He never elaborated beyond that. Scarlet got suspicious when he asked so many questions to be "just interested." His presence made her feel extremely uncomfortable. *I can't wait to get him away from me.*

Jimmy parked up close to the stadium. Once again, he knew someone. They decided it was too late to tailgate, so they took the elevator up to the TGI Fridays in left field and had drinks and dinner. All night Scarlet had this uneasy feeling in her stomach that JD was watching her.

Jimmy, of course, had great seats right behind home plate. The Brewer's ticket manager obviously set Jimmy up with seats and parking. The roof was open, the air was warm, and the best part of the night was when Scarlet won twenty dollars from Jimmy on the sausage race. At Miller Park, in the seventh inning, five people dressed in costumes like a giant hot dog, brat, Italian sausage, chorizo, and polish sausage. They run a race from the left-field corner, around third base, home plate, and finish at first base. They bet each other twenty dollars on the winner. Jimmy chose the Brat, and Scarlet chose the Italian sausage. The sausage won. The Brewers won the game 9-3 over the Mets. Scarlet rubbed it in teasing Jimmy and Frankie because they were both from New York. *Scarlet thought of herself as a cheese head now.*

After the game, Jimmy wanted to check out a couple of bars in the area. Scarlet said she wasn't feeling well and wanted to go home. *I need to get away from JD; he's creeping me out.* Jimmy dropped Frankie and JD off at her house in Wauwatosa, and they drove the rest of the way home with Scarlet napping in the passenger seat.

SIXTY-FIVE

When they pulled up to the house, Duke was in the window watching. Jimmy woke her up, and they walked to the front door.

"Do you feel any better?"

"Yeah, Jimmy, sorry about that, I don't know what came over me. Maybe all the drinking the last few weeks finally caught up with me."

He snickered and said, "No problem, blondie; let's just get you into bed." *I like the way he thinks.*

Scarlet let Duke out the back, refreshed his water, gave him a treat, and then walked up to the bedroom. She brushed her teeth, got naked, and crawled into bed next to Jimmy.

The next morning, they sat at the kitchen table in their underwear and t-shirts, having coffee and a bagel, and Scarlet said, "What's the deal with JD?"

"I don't know him well, but I think he's from New Jersey or Philly. Frankie met him when she lived out east."

"He creeps me out. He asked too many questions and kept staring at me."

"Look, baby, he's harmless, and he was staring at you because you're so beautiful." *That's my guy; he thinks I'm beautiful.*

Jimmy left at nine to go home and clean up, and then returned to the restaurant to make the sauces for the dinner crowd.

Scarlet and Duke went for a three-mile run and then to the park to play some catch.

On the way home from the park, Scarlet called Mallory. "Hey Mal, do you know Jimmy's cousin Frankie?"

"Yeah, of course, why?"

"Well, her boyfriend creeped me out last night at the Brewer game. He asked a lot of personal questions, and then I felt like all night he kept looking over at me and staring. It was unsettling. He was creepy, slimy, and smelled like a skunk."

"Frankie brought him around a few times to the restaurant," Mallory said. She didn't like him much either. Her advice was to ignore the feeling. After talking with Mallory, Scarlet went out back and started to clean up the yard and then came inside and cleaned the house.

SIXTY-SIX

Scarlet was standing in her closet, trying to decide what to wear to Rachel's party. She finally settled on a colorful floral summer dress she bought at Nordstrom's at a nearby mall. After deciding on an outfit, Scarlet slipped on a pair of white sandals and a necklace with a small cross on it. She wore her hair down because Jimmy liked it that way.

Jimmy arrived at seven sharp. He came to the door holding a bag. When Scarlet answered, she said, "What's that?" pointing at the bag.

"It's a present for you."

"Really? Why?"

"Why not, I want you to have it."

"Well, what is it?"

"Open it."

She immediately recognized the box. It was baby blue, Tiffany blue. She opened the box, and inside was a beautiful white gold necklace with diamonds and sapphires. "Holy crap, Jimmy, it's beautiful. But it's too much; I can't accept this. It must have cost a fortune."

"Scarlet, I want you to have it. It's almost as beautiful as you. It will look great around your neck."

"Why, what's it for, it's not my Birthday or anything?"

"It's just a gift, sweetheart, because I want you to know how much I care about you."

"Awe Jimmy, do you love me?"

"Maybe blondie, turn around, let me put it on you."

Scarlet turned around, and Jimmy gently removed her cross necklace and put the Tiffany necklace around her neck and fastened it from behind. He gently kissed the back of her neck right on the clasp. It sent shivers down her spine. Scarlet looked in the mirror and said, "It sparkles like nothing I've ever seen before." *No one had ever treated me like this. I think I'm falling in love.*

They climbed into the Range Rover and drove directly to the party. When Jimmy pulled up to the judge's house, Rachel appeared at the front door. She stepped out and greeted them immediately. "Hi guys, come in. Scarlet, what a beautiful necklace." As she first hugged Scarlet and then hugged Jimmy.

"Thank you; Jimmy got it for me."

Rachel turned and winked at Scarlet and said, "Good taste, Jimmy boy. Good taste." She stepped back and said, "Come on in." They entered the foyer and walked to the living room. Rachel followed behind them and said, "there's a bartender in the far corner, get yourselves a drink. And there's plenty of food in the kitchen, help yourselves. Oh, Scarlet, your flowers are a big hit; everyone thinks they are so beautiful. The sun is starting to set behind the trees across the lake. It looks incredible on the water, so don't waste too much time in the house."

The house looked like it came out of Architectural Digest. When you enter the living room, the windows run from floor to ceiling. The view of the lake was stunning. It looked like a postcard. The main area of the house had a giant stone fireplace and beautiful leather furniture. The hardwood floors made the living area even more attractive; they were probably cherry. When they walked through the living room to the kitchen, there was a Wolf stove with eight burners and a large built-in double-sided Sub-Zero refrigerator. The Island was ten feet long and filled with a spread of appetizers, crockpots filled with meats, and desserts. Scarlet's flower arrangement was in the middle of all the food on the island. Underneath the island, there were two wine refrigerators filled with dozens of bottles of wine. The artwork on all the walls was nothing Scarlet had ever seen before. *Scarlet recognized many of the paintings on the walls. She was particularly interested in Sunrise by Claude Monet. It looked like the original. A beautiful painting of a sailboat on the water with two people in the back.*

When she looked back toward the living room, there was a winding staircase that led up to the bedrooms. Rachel said there was a pool tournament going on in the basement, but it was too rich for her blood.

They walked to the bar first and asked for a couple of glasses of Merlot. Jimmy commented on how beautiful the flower arrangement was that Scarlet designed and built. She realized Jimmy had never seen any of her work before. Then they strolled out onto the veranda that faced the lake. There were several people on pontoon boats enjoying the sunset with their cocktails in hand. A few fishermen were out trying to catch dinner, and a young couple was sitting at the end of Rachel's pier, watching the sun peek behind the trees from across the lake. They continued to walk around the property for a little while, taking in all the beauty of nature.

After about an hour, they walked back into the house and chatted with a few couples. Jimmy knew a lot of the people and introduced Scarlet to many of them. Some were local politicians, and others were business owners, a few Judges, and Lawyers too. She even got to meet the Governor of Wisconsin; you could see Jimmy was bored with it all. It was just not his scene. Finally, at ten, Scarlet said, "Do you want to go?"

"Yeah, let's go somewhere and get another drink," Jimmy said.

They said their goodbyes with hugs and kisses and drove to the West Bend Country Club. The place was busy for ten-thirty at night, the bar was full of people watching the end of the Brewer game, and several tables in the bar had patrons still eating. They took a table near the window facing the eighteenth hole. The waitress came over, and they ordered Martinis *(con cuatro aceitunas)*. A few moments later, an incredibly attractive couple walked over to the table.

The man said, "Hi, Jimmy, we haven't seen you in a while."

"Hello Mark," Jimmy nodded and said, "Lindsey, I've been kind of busy. Scarlet, this is Mark and Lindsey Bogart. Mark is the chief of police here in West Bend, and Lindsey is the District Attorney."

Mark was forty years old and six one with a full head of dark brown hair, dark brown eyes, goatee, and an athletic build.

You can tell he was either ex-military or law enforcement

by the way he carried himself. He was wearing a dark blue suit with a simple light blue dress shirt, opened at the top. Lindsey was gorgeous. She was petite, maybe five two, pretty blue eyes, athletic build, blonde, and dressed to the nines in a beautiful dress, expensive jewelry, and kick-ass shoes, with the red bottoms. Hmm, *I think they're called Louboutin.*

Lindsey spoke first, "Hi Scarlet; it's nice to meet you; that necklace is so beautiful."

"Thank you; Jimmy just got it for me. I love it."

"Yes, I can see why. You look familiar, have we met before?"

Scarlet, now feeling a little uncomfortable, said, "I don't think so; You're so pretty, I'd remember you." *I wonder if she knows I'm in witness protection. Do they notify local law enforcement?* To change the subject, Scarlet turned to Mark and said, "You may recognize me, though. I was the one that had the bomb in her vehicle at Sendiks."

"Oh yeah, that was a new one for us. I hear the Jackson Police caught the gangbanger who did it. I guess he admitted to it. Dumb ass bangers."

"Yeah, we were there, he was trying to burn down my house."

Lindsey said, "What happened? You had a bomb in your car, and someone tried to burn your house down?"

"Yes, a gangbanger was stalking me, and he taped some stolen dynamite to the pipes under my Jeep. Then a few days later, he tried to burn down my garage, and I guess my house in the middle of the night."

"No way, in West Bend?"

"Jackson. My dog discovered the bomb, and then when the idiot tried to burn the house down, Duke chased him down an ally and damn near ate him. Jimmy caught up to them in the ally while my dog sat on the guy's chest, growling at him."

"Really? That's crazy. How did all this start? Why is a gangbanger trying to burn down your house or blow up your car?"

"A few weeks ago, my friend Mallory and I were coming home from dinner and standing in my driveway. We looked over and saw the banger was probably doing a drug deal on my street. I think they have a drug house like a few doors down from mine. One of them walked over to us and tried to intimidate me. He grabbed my arm, and my dog went crazy and attacked him. You would think the idiot would have learned the first time Duke nearly killed him."

Jimmy interrupted and had to tell the rest of the story. "Lindsey, the dog jumped through a window to get to the guy. He knocked him down and then stood on him with his jaws around the banger's neck. It was amazing. Something out of the movies."

"Oh my gosh, that's an incredible story. Could your dog have killed this guy?"

"Oh, for sure. Duke's trained to kill if he's told."

"Where did you get this dog? Did you train him yourself?"

"The FBI trained him; my girlfriend was a canine trainer for the FBI at Quantico."

She turned to Mark and said, "That's what we need on the

West Bend police force, dogs."

"Yeah, I've looked into it. It's not all that easy, you need specially trained officers to handle the dogs, and the liability is off the charts. It has been good to see you, Jimmy, we should get back to our friends, nice to meet you, Scarlet. Jimmy, let's play a round of golf again soon."

"You got it, chief." Lindsey looked at Scarlet one more time as if checking her memory; Finally, they turned to walk back to the table where their party was very lively.

Scarlet turned to Jimmy, "She is stunning, and seems nice."

"Yeah, they're alright. He cheats at golf; I hate playing with him."

Scarlet laughed and hugged Jimmy. "Let's finish this drink and get out of here; I've got a special treat for you."

SIXTY-SEVEN

New York, NY

"**D**om, I got news for Big Tony."

"What is it, JD?"

"I think I found the hitman's ex-wife."

"What? Are you kidding me?"

"No man, we were out at a Brewer's game the other night with Frankie's cousin, and I think he's dating her."

"You mean Mancini's, old lady? Are you sure?"

"Yeah, she changed her name to Scarlet Maxwell."

"What do you want me to do?" Dominick asked.

"Can you find out if the contract is still good on her. I can tell you exactly where she is and where she works. I asked her like a million questions. Also, can I get paid for finding her?"

"I'll let Big Tony know; he hates that bitch. Tony blames her for why he's in prison. If the drunk bitch had kept her mouth shut, he would be out. Do you wanna do her?"

"No man, my old lady would freak, and her cousin would kill me. He's really into this chick. She's a fox man, with a great body. I just wanna get paid for finding her."

"Ok, I'll check with Big T and let you know. He'll have to send someone out there from New York. Where are you again, in Ohio somewhere?"

"Naw man, Wauwatosa, Wisconsin. it ain't horrible."

"Wa, what Wisconsin? You're crazy for living there. How's the pizza?"

"Yeah, it's bad, and I'd kill for a good cheesesteak sandwich about now." The line went dead.

SIXTY-EIGHT

El Reno Prison, Oklahoma

The El Reno prison guard pushed a clear plastic bag across the counter, "Here are your things when you checked in, please sign here, and you're a free man Mr. Mason."

John Mancini (AKA Jack Mason) signed his release papers and was ready to walk out the front door exactly seven hundred and eighty days after walking into El Reno federal prison in Oklahoma. It took a little longer than he had hoped because of a little fight he got into over the use of the computers in the library.

As soon as Jack went through the exit process, Special Agent Vincent Patterson met him in the office. Vincent led Jack to a private room to go over the rules of the FBI witness protection program. When Jack entered El Reno, he was processed under his new name; Jack Mason, so no one knew his real identity. This is now the name he'll use when the FBI relocates him permanently.

"The rules are simple, mind your own business, stay out of trouble, and you're free to roam the state of Arizona. If you get an itch to visit one of our other fine states, you need to let the FBI know about it before you travel. Do you understand?" Vincent asked.

"Yeah, I understand," Jack said.

"Good, just a few other rules. You are not to try and find or contact Charlotte. If you do, and we find out, you're going straight back to prison for all the murders you committed. That's basically for the rest of your miserable life. Are we clear on this point?"

"Sure, whatever," Jack said dismissively.

"Mr. Mason, we take witness protection very seriously at the FBI. As you know, Charlotte is also being protected by us. If we feel she's in any danger, by you or anyone else, you're going back to prison, and maybe we'll be lucky, and you'll get the needle."

"Can we get outta here now? I'm tired of all this bullshit," Jack replied.

"Look, you piece of crap; she wants nothing to do with you. She's safe and happy now. Stay the hell away from her."

Jack gave Vincent a mock salute and said, "Yes, sir."

"Jack, you need to know one more thing."

"Yeah, what?"

"Jack, Tony Gambucci still has a contract out on you. You need to be aware of this. You know the lengths he'll go to if he finds out where you're hiding."

"Bring it on; I know all those incompetent pricks. That's why the families used me all the time. Most of those idiots couldn't kill a goldfish in a bowl."

"Big talk for a guy that got caught by a ninety-eight-pound girl."

"Yeah, it pisses me off I got sloppy. Are we done? can we get the fuck out of here?"

When John Mancini (Jack Mason) entered prison, he

weighed a hundred and eighty pounds. A lot of his weight was muscle, but he had some belly fat. Now, Jack Mason is two hundred and fifteen pounds of all muscle. He's ripped in the abs, chest, legs, and especially his arms. He's now, ironically, a killing machine. While in prison, Jack had a tattoo etched on his shoulder blade of a skull and cross bone with the name Charlotte spelled out in a circle, and then a bright red arrow right through the center. In El Reno, that was a symbol of death. Jack wanted Charlotte dead. He thought about it every day for seven hundred and eight days.

Vincent drove Jack to the Sundance Airport outside of Oklahoma City. They boarded the FBI Jet that would take them to Pulliam Airport outside of Flagstaff, Arizona. The flight was mostly quiet. Jack and Vincent didn't like each other to begin with, so there was no small talk. Once they landed, they were met by a man standing next to a black two- year-old Jeep Grand Cherokee. As part of Jack's deal, the FBI gave him a small one-bedroom house outside of Flagstaff, the Jeep, $25,000 in a bank account, $30,000 of his own money from his and Charlotte's savings account, and a lead on a job.

Vincent slid in behind the wheel, and Jack climbed into the passenger seat. They drove about forty minutes to a small house on a quiet street outside of Flagstaff. Vincent went over the rules once again and gave Jack a packet of information regarding his new social security number, a verifiable resume, a Visa card with a credit limit of $20,000, a bank book, credit history, and the keys to both the house and the Jeep.

Vincent then called an Uber and went back to the airport to

fly back to New York.

Jack's now on his own with a new identity, new location, and $55,000 in the bank. It wasn't New York, and it wasn't the $1,000,000 he had hidden away in the Caymans, but in a few months, it'll be great. He'll take care of Charlotte, get his money from the account in the Caymans, and set up shop again. This time near Scottsdale. *Screw agent Patterson and screw the FBI.*

SIXTY-NINE

Jack spent months thinking about how he was going to kill Charlotte when he got out of prison. He was staring out into space, going through his checklist. He needed to get a new driver's license and a credit card to rent a car and hotel room in Wisconsin. A gun, some luggage, and clothes to start.

Jack was angry with Scarlet, himself, and the world. He felt he didn't belong in prison. Everyone he killed deserved it. They were terrible people, murderers, thugs, and thieves, stealing from the family that supported them. Jack believed Scarlet should have confronted him when she saw him eliminate Fletcher. He could have explained why he chose to be a hitman. Jack felt he was making the world a better place, making a difference. Charlotte would have understood this. Besides, he really wanted to surprise her with the million dollars he had hidden away in the Caymans.

The first thing Jack did was drive to Best Buy and use his new Visa card to purchase a powerful laptop computer, printer, router, and a big screen monitor for the house. Next, he stopped at the local Verizon store and bought the latest iPhone, and at the same time, tossed the phone the FBI provided him in the garbage.

His new identity and $55,000 in the bank gave him a certain amount of freedom and opportunity. On Saturday morning, Jack withdrew $9,900 in cash from his bank account. That way, it was under the $10,000 transaction limit when the bank must report it to the Feds. He returned home and set up his new computer system. Jack logged onto the web to locate a place where he could purchase a fake driver's license and credit card. The fact that the FBI issued his new license in his new name told him they could track his movements. The Visa card they gave him probably sent notices to the FBI if he bought a gun or a plane ticket. To be able to move around the country without the FBI knowing where he was and what he's doing, he needed the best credentials he could find. Luckily, he located someone in Phoenix on the Dark Web that could produce identification that was TSA proof in a few hours.

Sunday morning, Jack drove three hours to Phoenix to meet with the counterfeiter he found on the Dark Web. He was working out of the back of a dry cleaner shop on the north side of Phoenix. When Jack arrived, he told the man that he needed a driver's license that could get him through airport security, and a Visa card that he could use to rent a car and hotel room.

The counterfeiter was not what Jack expected. He was a small Asian man, about five feet five inches tall, dark black hair, and wearing an apron with the name of the dry cleaner on the front. Jack was concerned this guy wasn't professional enough. The man assured Jack he did excellent work. He introduced himself as Alan and told Jack he's been doing this for many years. The new ID will cost twenty-five hundred cash, and the Visa is five hundred. The ID will have the required hologram, but the visa is stolen. The owner doesn't know it, though. Alan explained to Jack how he could reserve a car or hotel, but he must not charge anything to the card. He'll have to pay cash when the vehicle is returned, or when he checks out of a hotel. Otherwise, the card owner will realize their card number was stolen, and that will compromise its use.

Alan further explained that all he had was Arizona driver's licenses, so that was going to have to do. It'll take about two hours to produce the credentials. Jack posed for a picture and pulled out a wad of hundred-dollar bills to pay Alan, the full amount. He then drove to a local mall in Scottsdale to kill time. Jack used his new Visa card the FBI gave him to purchase some luggage for his trip, new clothes, shoes, and toiletries.

Two hours later, Jack returned to the dry cleaner and picked up his new ID and credit card. The quality was excellent, just as Alan had promised. The license was issued for a man named Keith Banes of Phoenix, Arizona. Alan warned Jack once again not to use the credit card to charge anything. He explained that rental car company's scan your license into their system. Hotels also require picture ID when you check-in. So, it wouldn't be hard to match your face to the stolen card. Jack nodded and said he understood.

On the drive back to Flagstaff, Jack thought hard about killing Charlotte. He wanted to look her in the eye, screw her once more, and then put a bullet in her pretty little head. *I wonder if she's still pretty...the bitch!*

When he arrived home, he turned on his new laptop and logged onto the Hertz website to reserve a car with his fake ID and credit card for pick up the next day. He didn't bother booking a hotel yet. Jack's plan was to drive to Jackson, from the airport and then figure out where to stay.

SEVENTY

On Monday morning, Jack drove down to Phoenix Sky Harbor Airport to a long-term parking lot. He parked his Jeep and took the shuttle to the terminal. Using his new ID, Jack purchased a one-way ticket to Milwaukee. He didn't have any trouble with the TSA when he showed his new driver's license. Jack boarded the plane, sat in his semi-comfortable seat, and enjoyed his flight to Milwaukee.

When Jack arrived at General Mitchell Airport in Milwaukee, he grabbed his carry-on from the overhead bin and walked to the Hertz counter. They had a light blue Ford Taurus ready for him. Once again, he didn't have any trouble with the Visa or his driver's license. Before exiting the parking garage, he programmed the GPS on his new iPhone to Jackson, Wisconsin.

The mapping software estimated the drive to be forty-nine minutes with light to medium traffic. Jack exited the airport on Highway 94 and connected to 41/45 northbound and exited at Highway 60 toward Jackson. He drove past a McDonald's and a Dairy Queen and a factory called Kerry.

Jack thought to himself, *what a dumpy little town, how the hell does she live here after living in New York.* Jack drove around a few neighborhoods for about an hour to get a feel for the area. He noticed an Italian diner called Jimmy's Family Italian Diner and thought to himself; *I need to check that place out; I haven't had a good Italian meal in a couple of years.*

Jack got back on the highway and drove up a couple of exits north to a larger town called West Bend. He noticed a Hampton Inn right off the highway. They had rooms available, so Jack used his fake ID and credit card to reserve the room and planned to use cash to pay for it after he disposed of Charlotte. Just around the corner about a mile up the road, he drove to a Buffalo Wild Wings restaurant and ordered a beer and some wings for dinner.

The next morning Jack drove south down the freeway to the diner he saw the day before for breakfast. When he walked in, the waitress had her back to the door. "Sit wherever you want; I'll bring over a menu in a second."

"Thanks, I will," Jack responded.

Jack sat in the front window in a booth. He ordered coffee and toast and sat there, watching people come and go in and out of the diner. He thought to himself these people must come from that Kerry factory across the street because they're all at the bar drinking beer, and Bloody Mary's this early in the morning.

After about an hour, Jack dropped a ten-dollar bill on the table and got up to leave. The waitress, Mallory, seemed friendly enough. On his way out, he must have passed the owner because everyone said: "Hello, Jimmy." They passed each other and nodded.

All the years, Jack knew Charlotte; she loved drawing and working with flowers. Her winning some contest was just dumb luck on Jack's part. Jack got back in his car and spent the rest of the day driving around Jackson, West Bend, Hartford, and a couple of other small towns in the area. He was looking for florists, grocery stores, and taking note of anywhere else they sell flowers.

Before ending up in El Reno, Jack would arrive on a job early and drive around getting the lay of the land. He would follow the mark for days and learn their routine. Jack meticulously planned every little detail before he eliminated a person. He felt it was like a screenplay, in that he first developed the script, and then he would act it out in perfect detail and harmony. He needed to know everything. His approach, weapon, escape, etc. every little detail mattered.

Taking the hit from Big Tony was a giant mistake that he was never going to make again. Jack, by nature, was a planner, no more spur of the moment work.

SEVENTY-ONE

Springfield, MO, Supermax Federal Prison

"Tony, we found Mancini's ex."

"Yeah, where?"

"Some little town in Wisconsin called Jackson."

"How'd you find her?"

"Do you remember Frankie Sabatini from the old neighborhood in Queens?"

"Yeah, well, her boyfriend JD, recognized her from pictures we had floating around the neighborhood. He called his cousin Dominick Panzica, and Dom called me."

"What about Mancini, seen or heard from that asshole?"

"No, not hide nor hair from him. I'm sure he's hiding in some shithole somewhere in the world."

"Do you think he's looking for her too?"

"Hard to say, he's an egotistical prick, you know. I wouldn't doubt it. It's just by accident we found the ex-wife. I don't know how Mancini would find her, though."

"Tony, what do you want me to do about the ex?"

"Send Carmine and Gino to see her."

"How about JD? Should we slip him a finder's fee?"

"Yeah, have Carmine give him a g-note."

"Alright Tony, consider it done."

"Yeah, okay." Tony hung up the phone.

SEVENTY-TWO

Jimmy left Scarlet's house at seven and headed to the restaurant. While Scarlet showered and then put on a pair of jeans, a short-sleeved cotton top, and sandals. She never took the necklace off Jimmy had given her the night before. *It was so beautiful.* She fed Duke and packed up her purse to go to work. Tonight, she planned to meet Jimmy, Adam, and Mallory, for drinks.

Scarlet got to work a little after eight in the morning when her cell phone buzzed. She didn't recognize the number, so she let it go directly to voicemail. The phone buzzed once more, indicating the person calling left a message.

Scarlet immediately dialed her voicemail to listen to the message. "Hi Ms. Maxwell, this is Special Agent Kate Baxter with the FBI Milwaukee office. Can you please call me back at 4-1-4-5-5-5-1-2-2-2 regarding your case and witness protection status? Thank you. Again, this is Special Agent Kate Baxter with the FBI 4-1-4-5-5-5-1-2-2-2."

Scarlet's hands were shaking when she dialed the number and asked for Special Agent Kate Baxter.

"This is Baxter."

"Um, hi, this is Scarlet Maxwell. You called and left a message to call you back."

"Ms. Maxwell, Thank you for returning my call so quickly. Is this a good time to talk?"

"Um, yes, of course." *I thought this was about the gangbangers. Michelle told me the Milwaukee office of the FBI was going to call me.*

"Ms. Maxwell, our office, has been contacted regarding your relocation status. It appears your identity may have been compromised."

"What? How is that possible?" Her voice went up an octave and began to quiver.

"We tape all conversations between visitors and inmates at our federal prisons. And we heard a conversation between someone and Tony Gambucci. The entire discussion was around the fact that they, and I quote, we found the hitman's ex-wife in Wisconsin. Mr. Gambucci told the other party to send two people to Wisconsin. We believe that is an order for a hit, specifically on you."

"What? They found me. Why do they care about me anymore? Tony's in jail; John's locked away, and my life is finally turning around. Why do they want to bother to kill me now, after all this time?"

"I'm sorry ma'am I'm not familiar with all the details of your case. But Ms. Maxwell, it's our responsibility for your safety, and we believe it's enough of a threat that we
need to relocate you once again. I can come by this afternoon and help you pack your things. An FBI airplane can be in route to pick you up in a few hours."

"No way. I won't go."

"Well, ma'am, it's your choice, but we can't protect you

when you're exposed like this. And it looks like Mr. Gambucci is serious about finishing the job. He won't give up. These guys don't forget who testified against them. As you probably know, revenge is part of their DNA."

"I don't care about their DNA, I won't leave. I love it here."

"Ms. Maxwell, I'll report this conversation to Agent Patterson, and he'll most likely reach out to you shortly. Good day, ma'am." The line went dead.

Scarlet began to pace back and forth. *Holy shit, what am I going to do? Do I tell Jimmy? Do I tell Mallory?* She looked down at Duke, and tears filled her eyes. Scarlet got down on the floor and hugged Duke and sobbed. *Why now?*

After lying on the floor with Duke for a few minutes, Scarlet rose and called upfront to tell Heather to tell her she didn't feel well and was going to go home.

SEVENTY-THREE

Tears poured from Scarlet's eyes, making it hard to see as she drove back to Jackson. Scarlet pulled into the driveway and walked to the side door by the kitchen and unlocked it. Through her tears, she said, "Duke pass auf." Duke searched the house and returned one bark. All good. Scarlet walked into the house, locked the doors, and went upstairs and laid down on her bed and started sobbing uncontrollably. Duke jumped up on the bed and laid down beside her and put his paw on her shoulder, clearly understanding just how distraught Scarlet was feeling.

Scarlet's cell phone started to buzz under her, and it woke her up from a sound sleep. She first looked at the clock on the nightstand, and it was already six pm. She slept away most of the day.

"Scarlet, are you okay? Where are you?"

"I'm fine, Jimmy, I just came home to rest and fell asleep."

"Thank God, we've been worried sick about you. I called the store, and they said you left early this morning because you didn't feel well. Are you okay?"

"I'm fine, Jimmy."

"We're all at the bar, are you still up for a drink?"

"No, I don't think so, I'm going to stay in tonight. I'll see you tomorrow."

"Scar, are you sure you're okay, do you want me to come

over, can I bring you anything? I can stop at the restaurant and bring some food—"

Cutting him off, Scarlet said, "no honey, I'm fine, I just need a night alone. I love you, Jimmy."

Silence

"I Love you too Scarlet, just call if you need me to come over."

"Ok, bye." Scarlet pressed the end button on her phone. Scarlet kept hoping Michelle would call when she heard what had happened. Scarlet felt hopeless and didn't know what to do. She laid her head back down on the pillow, and her phone buzzed again. It was from a two oh two area code.

"Hello, Michelle?"

"Scarlet, it's Vincent."

"Oh, thank God, Vincent. I'm so confused. Is there any chance Michelle is still available to talk?"

"Sorry, Scarlet, she's undercover now. I understand you're likely to be compromised, and you don't want to relocate again. Michelle filled me in on this gangbanger on your street who is after you too. It sounds like a good time to relocate."

"Vincent, it's not like I go looking for trouble, it just seems to find me. Look, I love my life now. I have a boyfriend I'm crazy about, friends I adore, and a job that I love. I don't want to leave and start all over again. And besides, Yelich might win the MVP in Baseball."

"Whose Yelich? What are you talking about? Scarlet, the threat is real. Tony is sending two very scary hitmen from New

York to kill you. We can monitor the airports and ask the locals to keep an eye on you, but we can't protect you there twenty-four seven forever. They won't stop coming after you. You're too exposed, you're in the open."

"Vincent, what if I left the country for a few weeks or a month? I could go to Europe or somewhere on vacation and then come back when it all blows over."

"I doubt it would fool anyone, Scarlet. Also, you should know John was released from prison last week. I personally relocated him out west. I don't think he got the message. There's no doubt in my mind he's trying to find you too."

"Vincent, do ya think he knows where I am?"

"I don't know Scarlet, I spoke with him about it, and warned him to stay away from you, but he's a sly bastard, you never know what he knows or what he's thinking. He plays his cards very close to the chest. Plus, I remember you saying he's rather good with computers. You're not on any social media, are you? Twitter, Facebook, or Instagram?"

"No, no way. I hope he didn't see that damn contest picture a few months ago."

"Yes, that's right. Well, in any case, be sure to stay off all social media. Scarlet, I believe you should seriously consider relocating again. We can have you out of there in a matter of hours. Maybe this time you can go to California or Florida, you know someplace warm."

Scarlet quietly started sobbing. "Maybe Duke will keep me safe." Through her sniffles, she said, "Vincent, I'll think about it, but I don't want to move again, I don't want to start over. I'm not even sure I could start over again. My life has finally panned out the way I want it. I love it here."

"Look, Scarlet; you still have my personal cell phone number, you can call me anytime you like. I'm here for you if you need me."

"Thank you, Vincent, goodbye." Vincent ended the call.

SEVENTY-FOUR

As they hung up the phone, Scarlet began to cry and sob. Duke was there by her side trying to console her, but it didn't help. She was so sad she just wanted to curl up in bed and wait until it was all over. About midnight, she got a text from Jimmy, *"Scar, miss you so much, I love you."* She put the phone down on her wet pillow, with Jimmy's picture on the screen next to her head and cried until she cried herself to sleep again.

The next morning, Scarlet called in sick. Together Scarlet and Duke took a long walk. She didn't have the energy to run. They skipped stopping by Jimmy's because Mallory was off this morning, and she felt she looked like hell. Jimmy texted her for breakfast, but she turned him down. Scarlet wasn't ready to talk to Jimmy or anyone for that matter. Mallory called several times, but Scarlet let the calls go to voicemail.

Finally, about noon, Scarlet called Mallory back. *I think I'm ready to share my secret.*

"Mal, can you come over I need to talk to you."

"Sure, honey, I'll be right there. Are you okay?"

"No, I'm not, I need someone to talk too." They hung up, and Mallory was on her doorstep in about fifteen minutes.

The moment Scarlet opened the door, Mallory grabbed her and hugged her hard and said, "Oh Scarlet, you look awful, like you've been up-all-night crying. What happened?"

"I've been crying for two days. Mallory, what I'm going to

tell you, you can't tell anyone. Not even Adam. Do you swear you won't say anything to anyone? Not Adam, or Jimmy, no one, your life could depend on it."

"You're scaring me, Scar. Of course, I swear not to tell anyone, what's wrong?"

"Mallory, I'm in witness protection. My ex-husband was—is a hitman."

Mallory gasped. "Wait, what, how can that be?"

"Please wait before you say anything else. I'm actually from New York, and I accidentally saw John, my ex-husband, kill two people in Queens. They were friends of ours. He shot Greg in the head and my friend Carol in the chest. I was mortified Mal. Greg's head just blew off. It was so scary and gross, and Carol's eyes were so wide when he shot her, I couldn't get the image out of my head for months. I had to testify against the New York mob. It was a mob hit that was ordered by a gangster named Tony Gambucci. He also put a contract out on me. Somehow, they found me here in Jackson, and there are two assassins on their way here from New York to kill me." Scarlet started crying again.

Mallory put her arms around her friend and held her tight and started crying too. "I'm, I'm stunned. But it explains a lot of things. What are you going to do, Scar? Does Jimmy know?" asked Mallory.

"No, he doesn't, I'll tell him later tonight. I'm not sure what to say; it could change everything. I don't know what to do. The FBI wants to relocate me again. I can't do it. I love you guys too much. My life here is great. I don't want to run and hide any longer. I can't start a new life again." They sat on the sofa and held each other and cried. "Mallory, what would you do?"

"Run, I would run honey. I would take Duke and Adam and run as far away as I could go. Then in a year or two, I would come back. You know we'll still be here. Jimmy will still love you."

"Mallory, I can't run anymore. Oh yeah, wait, it gets worse. I forgot to tell you this. To add insult to injury, the FBI told me last night that my ex-husband is now out of jail, and he's probably coming for me too."

"How did he get out of jail so soon if he killed your friends?"

"He cut a deal with the FBI and the prosecutors to testify against Gambucci, the mob boss. He only spent a couple of years in prison. He's still obviously pissed at me and wants me dead for going to the FBI in the first place. Oh, Mallory, I'm so screwed." Scarlet's cell phone buzzed on the table. It was Jimmy calling. "Hello?"

"Are you crying again? Scarlet, please talk to me."

"Jimmy, I'm okay, I just need to work through some personal stuff."

"Scarlet, are you sick? Is there something I can do? Look, sweetheart, I'm coming over now; I need to see you. I need to know you're okay."

"I'm okay Jimmy, Mallory's here, can you come later?"

"Yes, of course, are you sure? I need to see you, Scarlet. Let me in on what's going on."

"Jimmy, I'm okay, just come by later and we can talk." *I think I'm ready to tell him my secret and who I really am.*

"Okay, I'll be there at six. I love you."

"Love you too, Jimmy."

"I heard him tell you he loved you last night; it sounds like you two are getting serious."

"I am serious, I love him Mal. I really do love him. I don't know what he'll think, or what he'll do. Will he run away from me? I'm so screwed! They're coming for me, and I don't think Duke can protect me this time."

"Honey, my guess is Jimmy is a stand-up guy, and he will never run from a fight, especially if it has anything to do with you. He's madly in love with you, sweetheart."

"I hope you're right. Mal. But realize, he could look at this as a giant lie. I should have told him when I realized how serious we've become. It's not fair to put him in the middle of this."

Mallory stayed for a few hours, and they talked about what happened in New York and how Scarlet ended up in Wisconsin. When she left around four, Scarlet laid down on the couch and cried until she dozed off again. Duke was there by her side, trying to lend a comforting paw.

SEVENTY-FIVE

Hampton Inn/West Bend Wisconsin

Jack used his new laptop to perform a Google search of all the places that sold flowers in the entire area. Driving around and looking gave him a great lay of the land, but obviously, it wasn't working to find Charlotte. He drew a map and started plotting florists with Jackson as ground zero. There were seven florists within a ten-mile radius of Jackson and five grocery stores with flower shops. Jack planned to call each floral shop and ask for Scarlet. He knew her new name from the article. He thought, *each of the grocery stores will likely have to be staked out, because she may go by a nickname.*

Jack began calling the florists and struck out at one after another. It became clear he needed to drive by each shop and see for himself. Jack spent the day driving from one florist to the next. After spending the entire day driving from shop to shop with no luck, Jack decided to stop by that diner in Jackson and eat some dinner. Jack pulled into Jimmy's parking lot at six PM and walked inside. As Jack passed through the front door, Jimmy looked hurried and was rushing out. Jack said hello, and Jimmy looked at him cautiously and just nodded. The place looked different at night.

He picked out a spot at the end of the bar, and the waitress brought over a menu. He ordered a bottle of red Chianti and a

Caesar salad to start, and the Osso Bucco. *Delicious sauce and excellent veal.* After eating everything on his plate, Jack noticed the owner Jimmy, walked back inside the restaurant, and told everyone there was a gas leak in the kitchen and cleared the place. Jack paid his bill, left a good tip, and drove back to the Hampton Inn.

Tomorrow he planned to drive to each grocery store in the area and stake them out. Jack only had a few more places to check-on before he would have to figure out plan B. She had to be in a flower shop somewhere around there, maybe Milwaukee.

SEVENTY-SIX

Jimmy left the restaurant at six. He passed a customer on his way out the door and thought to himself, who is this guy? He looks suspicious here by himself. *I think I saw him the other morning by himself too.*

Mallory left a few hours ago, and Scarlet and Duke were napping. Jimmy's knock on the front door woke Scarlet up. She got up off the couch and walked over to the door to let Jimmy inside. He immediately grabbed her and kissed her hard, and then held her like he never wanted to let go. *Honestly, I don't want him to let go of me.* Scarlet started crying again.

"Scarlet what's happening, what's wrong?"

"Jimmy, I have to tell you some things about me that may change everything between us. I'm so scared and sad. I'm just sick to my stomach."

"Baby, you can tell me anything. I'm in love with you. I'd do anything for you."

"Jimmy, you need to let me talk, don't interrupt me or I'll never get it all out okay?"

"Yeah, of course. What's wrong, sweetheart?"

"Jimmy, I promise you, I swear on my soul, I didn't lie to you on purpose. Believe me, please, I just couldn't tell you everything. It's, um, it's against the rules and for your own protection."

"What is it, Scarlet?"

"Jimmy, the FBI put me here in Jackson under the witness protection program. My ex-husband is a hitman." Tears flowed down her cheeks. "I accidentally saw him kill some people in New York. I swear to you, I didn't know he was a hitman. The problem was I had to testify against his boss, a mobster. His name is Tony Gambucci, and he still has a contract out on my life."

"Scarlet, that's a lot to take in. How long ago did this happen?"

"When I first got here to Wisconsin a couple of years ago."

"And there's still a contract out on you?"

"Yes, Jimmy, these guys never let it go."

"What's your real name?"

"Charlotte, Charlotte Mancini, and I was born on Long Island. Jimmy, please don't hate me. Please, I swear to you, I wanted to tell you, but I couldn't."

"I could never hate you, baby, that could never happen, I told you, I'm in love with you. So, what happened, why are you crying, did something go wrong?"

"Somehow, the New York mob found out where I am, and they're sending some guys here to kill me. The FBI wants to relocate me again, now!" Through the tears, she said, "and I don't want to leave. I love you so much, Jimmy." she squeezed his hand and wiped the tears from her cheeks with her other hand. "I love Mallory, too, and I don't want to leave this life." Jimmy pulled her tight to his chest and stroked her hair. Scarlet couldn't stop sobbing.

"Scarlet, don't worry, we'll figure something out. I don't want you to leave either. I'm not going to lose you."

"I don't know how they found me, Jimmy. I'm so careful, no Twitter, or Facebook, I don't use Instagram. Nothing, no social media at all. I don't let anyone take pictures of me. I keep an extremely low profile, and I watch for everything. Trouble always seems to find me, though."

"I might have an idea on how they found you," Jimmy said.

She pulled away quickly and challenged him. "What, *you* ratted on me?"

"No, no way, Scarlet. But my cousin Frankie, that piece of shit boyfriend probably knows someone back in Jersey and told them about you."

"But how? How did he know who I am? How would he recognize me?"

"Hell, I'm sure your picture was probably passed around all the neighborhoods in New York and New Jersey, and that dumb ass saw it. Honey, you are so beautiful. You have a face to remember. I'm fairly sure JD put two and two together and made a phone call. He probably thinks he'll be a hero for finding you and turning you in. Shit, he might even get paid for it."

"I knew something wasn't right about him. He's an asshole. I didn't trust him from the get-go. Remember, I said something to you the next morning? Oh God, what am I going to do, Jimmy? What can I do?"

The entire tone in the room suddenly changed. Jimmy's

demeanor changed; he was angry and looked determined. Duke sensed the change in Jimmy and the mood in the room. He stood and walked over to Scarlet and sat between them in a protective stance. Jimmy hugged her tight, kissed her on the forehead, stood up, and said he knows some people that might be able to stop this before it starts.

"Jimmy, please tell me you're not part of this mob thing. You're not a mobster, are you?"

"Scarlet, I'm not part of this mob thing, I know people. I know people on both sides of the law."

"What are you going to do?"

"First, I'm gonna have a little chat with JD and see what he knows and what he did."

"What will that do?"

"I don't know. But at least we'll know how Gambucci's people found you, who this asshole told, and what they told him they were going do about it."

"Be careful, Jimmy; these guys are for real. I saw John shoot my friend in the head and his innocent wife in the chest. He didn't even flinch, he didn't have any remorse whatsoever. Jimmy, they don't screw around; They're really serious people."

"So am I Scarlet. I'll be back in a little while. Stay put, lock the door, and keep Duke next to you. Baby, I won't let anything happen to you. I promise."

Jimmy left the house about seven that night. Scarlet and Duke laid on the sofa together, and she cried for the next hour, once again crying herself to sleep.

SEVENTY-SEVEN

"Frankie, I need you and JD here at the restaurant now," Jimmy demanded.

"Why?" Frankie said.

"Because I said so, get your asses here now, and you drive."

"Okay, don't bust a nut Jimmy, we'll head over now, be there in 30." Jimmy ended the call.

Jimmy dialed the next number. "Alex, this is Jimmy, I need a favor."

"Anything, bro, what's up?"

"Look, Alex, I need some information out of somebody; then I want you to put him in the hospital for a month or two."

"No problem, I'll bring my boy with me, okay?"

"Yeah, come here to the restaurant now, the front doors open."

"Done, brother."

Jimmy cleared the restaurant by telling everyone there was a gas leak in the kitchen. He sent home the kitchen and wait staff. While sitting at the bar alone, Jimmy poured himself a glass of Pappy Van Winkles 15-year-old bourbon he kept stored in his office. He waited while quietly trying to figure out what to do to help Scarlet. Frankie and JD walked in first at eight-thirty. Jimmy told JD to wait in the dining room until he was done talking to his cousin in the kitchen.

Jimmy and Frankie walked into the kitchen, and he immediately turned to her and said, "Frankie, how close are you to this JD character?"

Challenging him, she said, "Close enough, why?"

"I think he ratted on Scarlet," Jimmy said.

"What do you mean, ratted? How, why?"

"I think he made a phone call back to New York or New Jersey and told them she was here."

"Wait. What? Jimmy, who is she that she's hiding?"

"Doesn't matter, the little prick ratted on my girlfriend Frankie, and now a hitman's coming from New York to kill her."

Fear took over Frankie's face, and her voice began to tremble, "Jimmy, I—I didn't know anything about this. I swear to you on Noni. What are you going to do?"

"Alex is on his way over, and we're going to find out who he told and what he said."

"I'm down with that, Jimmy," Frankie said. Visibly afraid and her hands shaking, she said, "And I swear I didn't know anything, Jimmy, please believe me I didn't know. You know I would never do anything to cross you. I would never rat on anyone close to the family. You know that, right Jimmy?"

"I believe you, Frankie. Now go out the back door, go home, forget you ever knew this guy. I think JD's going to the hospital for a while."

Frankie quickly walked out the back door, climbed into her car, and drove home. Jimmy returned to the dining room as Alex and his friend were walking in.

Jimmy said, "Alex, how's it goin, buddy? Need a drink? I've got some 15-year-old Pappy over on the bar." Jimmy leaned in to give Alex a man hug. Alex was a Latino man born in Mexico, he stood six-five, very dark skin, and a bald head. He weighed north of three hundred pounds and play middle linebacker for most NFL football teams.

"No, man, thanks." Pointing to the exceptionally large man behind him, Alex said, "This is my cousin, Juan." Jimmy nodded and shook his hand. Juan could easily have been Alex's twin brother. They were built similarly. He was six-one, two hundred and eighty pounds of all muscle, and bald like Alex. Juan had a full beard, and large diamond studded earrings in both ears.

Jimmy then introduced everyone to JD. "Hey Alex, Juan, this is JD, my cousin Frankie's boyfriend." Everyone nodded or said hello, and then the room was quiet. Eerily quiet.

"Where's Frankie?" JD asked.

"She ran an errand for me; she'll be back in a few minutes. I need you to go with Alex and Juan for a minute. They need some help on a job they're doing for me. Can you do that?"

"Sure, anything I can do to help." *Yeah, you helped asshole, I want you buried in a shallow grave for your help.*

Alex, Juan, and JD walked out to Alex's Lincoln Navigator. Juan told JD he could sit in the front seat because his legs were so long. As soon as JD put his seat belt on, Juan put a piano wire around his neck and began to pull JD back into the leather seats.

JD started to squirm and fight it. He screamed, "What the

fuck, what are you doing, man?"

Alex told him, "Don't fight it, bro, or he'll slice your head off." JD stopped squirming and sat back in the seat as far as he could, and then stayed completely still. Jimmy walked up to the passenger side window as Alex rolled it down. Jimmy stuck his head in the window, so he was eye to eye with JD.

"JD, you little worm, who did you call back east about Scarlet?" Jimmy demanded.

Now JD had real fear in his eyes. With blood dripping from his neck, snot running from his nose, and tears rolling down his cheeks, he said, "No one, Jimmy, I didn't call no one."

"You're lying to me, should I go ahead and have Juan slice your dumb ass head off?" He nodded toward Juan, who then pulled the wire a little harder, slicing JD's neck a little more, causing more blood to drip down the front of his shirt.

"No, please, no wait…I called my cousin in Jersey. I called my cousin Dom, Dominick."

"What did you tell him?"

"That I found the hitman's ex-wife. I told him we went out together, and Frankie's cousin, you were dating her. That's it. That's all I said."

Jimmy nodded to Juan again in the back seat, and said, "you're still lying; go ahead, slit his throat." Juan pulled back a little harder while Jimmy turned to walk away.

JD yelled, "No, wait! I asked if the contract on her was still active. You know there was a hit ordered on her in New York, right?"

"And what did he say, this cousin of yours?"

"He didn't know; he said Big Tony blames her for everything, though. He said that bitch is the only reason he's in prison. So, the contract on her will likely never go away."

"How much *was* the contract for?"

"At first, I think around fifty-grand. But that was when she was supposed to testify against Big Tony a couple of years ago. Who knows now, it could be more or less."

"Seriously, fifty-grand?" Jimmy said.

"Yeah, he wanted to know if I would do her."

"What did you say?"

"I'm a lover, man, not a killer." Juan pulled the piano wire harder. "Wait, Dominick told me if it was still good, they were going to send someone from New York to Wisconsin to do her."

"You motherfucker. I should kill you myself." Blood continued to drip down the front of JD's shirt as Jimmy paced around the vehicle. Juan kept a steady grip on the wire, so JD was unable to move without it cutting deeper into his neck.

Alex finally asked Jimmy, "What do you want me to do with this piece of shit?"

"Make him disappear and send me the bill to get your Navigator detailed." He turned to JD and said, "Look, you motherfucker, you're done with my cousin, and if I ever see you again, or hear of you coming around my cousin, I'll kill you myself. You got it?"

Crying and bleeding, JD said, "Yeah, Jimmy, I'm gone. I'm sorry but wait, maybe I can stop it."

Jimmy turned and asked, "What are you talking about?"

"I could call my cousin and tell him that I made a mistake. Maybe he'll believe me and stop the hit."

"Where's your phone? Do it now and put it on speaker, so I can hear the whole conversation."

Juan released the piano wire from around JD's neck. Using his sleeve, JD wiped the snot from his nose and the tears from his eyes. JD reached into his pocket to get his cell phone. He looked up the number for his cousin Dominick and called.

Dominick answered, "What do you want, man; I'm busy."

"Dom, look man, I screwed up, it's not Mancini's old lady I saw."

"How do you know?"

"I got to talking with her and got a much better look at her face. I was high before, it ain't her Dom. I'm positive it ain't her. Can you call off the hit?"

"Too late man, Tony sent the Tucci Brothers yesterday from New York. They're driving to Wisconsin to take her out."

"Will they call me, so I can tell them it ain't her?"

"I don't know, man; they're going straight to the chick's house or work, I gave em the addresses you gave me. They'll probably kill her and then call you to pay you for the tip. She's as good as dead, whoever she is."

Jimmy was getting even angrier, listening to JD talk to his cousin.

"Can't you stop them, Dom? Isn't there anything you can do?" JD pleaded.

"I don't know how to reach the guys Tony sent. I told you Big Tony sent them, not me. I just passed on the information you gave me. Blonde, Jackson Wisconsin, whatever street you told me, Rose something. Too late JD. Look, what's it matter? It'll just be one less blonde bimbo on this earth. Who gives a shit?"

"Ok, Dom, later." Click.

As soon as JD hung up the phone, the piano wire swooped back over his head and around his neck. Juan pulled him tight against the back of the seat, causing a new slice in JD's neck. JD quickly leaned back as far as he could, and squirmed but couldn't loosen the wire from his neck. Jimmy walked around the other side of the vehicle to talk with Alex. He whispered something in Alex's ear, and then they bumped fists. Jimmy turned and back into the restaurant. Alex, Juan, and JD drove off. Jimmy thought to himself; *I doubt we'll ever see JD again.* Jimmy locked up the restaurant and drove back to Scarlet's house.

SEVENTY-EIGHT

Jimmy parked on the street in front of Scarlet's house and approached the front door. Duke barked once, and Scarlet opened the door to let him in. Once again, Jimmy put his muscular arms around Scarlet and hugged her for a long time, and then kissed her forehead. They returned to the sofa and discussed what JD said, and what to do next.

"Scarlet, I really think for now you should come live at my house."

"Jimmy, I told you they will never let me go. It won't matter where I am; they'll eventually find me. I can't just quit working and become a hermit. Besides, I have Duke; I don't know how to re-train him for a different house. I would need Michelle to teach me that, and she's undercover somewhere."

"What about the FBI, can't they protect you?"

"They said they could have some people check on me and the house occasionally, but they want to move me to California or some shit like that. Look, Jimmy, I'm going back to work tomorrow, so I don't get fired. Besides, I don't think they're going to kill me on the street."

"Yeah, work is probably the safest place you can be."

"This weekend, we'll figure something out." And that was the end of the discussion. They walked upstairs and went to bed.

It was another restless night for Scarlet. Perhaps because

she slept so much over the last two days, or that she was just nervous and scared. She laid in bed, trying to figure out how to end this madness. *I suppose I could disappear again, that would save Jimmy from all of this, but how many times can I do that? And I really love this man sleeping next to me. Perhaps I could reason with Gambucci? Maybe pay him off to leave me alone? It's doubtful that it would work. Maybe I can get Vincent to tell me where they're hiding John, and trade that information for my life. John is the one who buried Big Tony, not me.* It was nearly four AM when Scarlet finally dozed off to sleep. What should have been dreams of a life with Jimmy were nightmares of the mob's killer coming to get her while she slept.

SEVENTY-NINE

Jack spent two days checking out grocery stores in the area. He decided to start in Jackson and walk around the local Piggly Wiggly. He asked a few employees in the store if they knew Scarlet, but no one heard the name before. He stayed in each store's parking lot for a couple of hours and watched for her but never saw her coming or going. After a while, Jack moved on to Hartford and spent time at both Piggly Wiggly and Pick and Save with no luck.

The next day, he went into West Bend and checked out Meijer's, then he drove over to the Pick and Save there. No one heard of Scarlet, and he never caught sight of her either. On his way back to the hotel, he saw a grocery store, not on his list called Sendiks. Jack pulled into the parking lot and walked inside. He looked around the store and located the small flower shop. There wasn't anyone working in that area of the store. Jack walked toward the back of the store until he ran into a manager named Heather. He casually asked if Scarlet was working in the flower shop this evening.

"She's not here tonight, but I think she'll be back in the morning around 8:30. Is there something I can help you with?"

"No, just an old friend. Thank you." *Gotcha bitch!*

Jack almost couldn't contain his excitement. He'd dreamt of finding Charlotte from the first day he walked into El Reno. *Jackpot! He thought to himself.* Now that he knows where she works, his plan was simple, follow her home, sneak in at night, and make the world a better place without one more rat.

EIGHTY

South Bend, Indiana

Carmine and Gino Tucci were driving past the beautiful Notre Dame campus in South Bend, Indiana. They'd been in the car for nearly twelve hours, driving from New York City on Big Tony's orders. The brothers were contract killers used mostly to clean up messes left by others in the organization.

Carmine is the older and larger brother. He's six three, three hundred pounds, mostly muscle, dark black hair slicked back, dark eyes, and some facial hair. His nose was crooked from being broken several times from fights he usually won. Carmine was always dressed in custom made dark suits with heavily starched white shirts and usually a fancy tie with a matching pocket square in the breast pocket of his jacket. Finally, his trademark was he wore the same diamond-studded cuff links every day. The story was he took them off the first person he assassinated.

Gino, on the other hand, was only six feet tall and two hundred pounds. He had dark hair slicked back too, and a dark complexion. Gino looked like he came from the old country. He liked to wear nice slacks, polo shirts, and a sport coat to cover his shoulder holster.

Of the two brothers, Carmine was the ruthless one: he was a cold-blooded killer. Carmine loved The Godfather movies. He always said he was like Luca Brasi, the killer played by Lenny Montana. Unfortunately for Montana, Luca is swimming with the fishes.

Gino said, "Isn't that golden dome gorgeous? You know it's real gold?"

"Yeah, that's what I hear. Why? Do you want to steal it?"

"No asshole, I think it's beautiful. I Googled the history, and that's the third golden dome the priests built up there on the campus. They built the first one in like 1843. They thought it was too small."

"Just like the Catholics not happy unless it's overly gaudy," Carmine said.

"So, they rebuilt it in 1865. That one burned down like fourteen years later, and so they replaced it with the one that's there now. That makes the one up there now about a hundred and forty years old?"

"Gino, why do you know so much about this?"

"We're Catholic Carmine, and I love Notre Dame football. I always have. I've followed them my whole life, you know that. I researched the campus when I knew we were going to drive through South Bend."

"Why?"

"Dude, you know I love history. I also saw that Studebaker's were built here in the fifty's and early sixties. Think about it; Studebaker was in business for over a hundred years. How does it happen that you're building cars for over a hundred years and then poof one day you're gone?"

Carmine quickly responded, "Yeah, who gives a shit? It's like a hit, one day you're here and poof you're gone because

Carmine blew your fucking head off." Carmine began laughing at his own joke.

Gino, ignoring him, said, "ain't you interested in history at all?"

"No, not really. Why should I care?"

"Because it's interesting. Because it's our heritage, our history."

"Gino, I don't give a damn. Let's talk about how we're going to take out this bitch in Wisconsin. I'd say let's drive through to Wisconsin; it's about four or five more hours. We'll drive up to her house, knock on the door, and when she answers, we shoot her in her blonde head. Done. We're back home for dinner at Angelo's on Saturday Night eating linguine with white clam sauce."

"What if a neighbor sees us and calls the cops? Or if a neighbor gets our plates and calls the cops?"

"What *do you* want to do?"

"Let's drive to Wisconsin tomorrow; we'll watch her for a day and get her routine. We know where she lives and where she works. We can follow her and see where she goes, and then pop her when nobody's around. I'm tired, let's get a couple of hotel rooms here, and some food. I read about a place called Macri's Italian Restaurant. Coach Parseghian used to eat there all the time. It's supposed to be great food, just like the old country. We can rest up tonight and then drive to Wisconsin tomorrow."

"Sounds like a plan. That way, we can pop her on Friday or Saturday and be back home in the city on Sunday or Monday."

EIGHTY-ONE

Columbus Correctional Institution, Columbus, Wisconsin

Jose Batista Lopez (Aka the banger from down the street who tried to burn down Scarlet's garage and bomb her car) picked up the phone on the opposite side of the glass separating him from his friend Alfonzo DeLaCruz.

"Wha's a happening essay?" Jose said.

"Nutin. You, bro?"

"You know brother, jus livin the dream here in Columbo land."

"My cuz in Sinaloa protecting you on the inside?"

"Yeah, essay, I'm good. I need one more solid from you, though."

"Anything for you, bro. what choo need essay?"

"You know the crib on Rosewood?"

"Yeah, of course."

"Need you to go over there and take care of my problem down the street, dig? I need a Houdini act performed, you following me, essay?"

"Permanent?"

"Yeah, bro, make dat bitch disappear for good. And, while you at it, put that fucking dog down too."

"I got choo essay. Consider it done. Dat bitch be history."

Alfonzo hung up the phone in the visitor's room, rose from

his chair, turned, and walked out with his marching orders. *Make the blonde bitch and her dog disappear.*

EIGHTY-TWO

Scarlet's cell phone buzzed with a 414-area code and a number she didn't recognize, so she let it go to voicemail. When the phone buzzed again, indicating there was a message waiting, Scarlet immediately dialed her voicemail to listen to it.

"Ms. Maxwell, this is Kate Baxter again from the Milwaukee office of the FBI. I wanted to let you know that we received a recording from Columbus State Prison this morning. The gang member that tried to burn down your home has engaged with a fellow gang member to do you harm. Ms. Maxwell, with the New York Mob heading your way, the gangbangers heading your way, and now I'm told your ex-husband had been released from prison last week, I strongly encourage you to reconsider our offer to relocate you once again. I will report this latest development to our New York office and Special Agent Patterson. If you would like to talk, I'm available day or night for you. Please call me at 4-1-4-5-5-5-1-2-2-2 and leave a message if I don't answer. Once again, I strongly encourage you to change your mind. This is Special Agent Kate Baxter with the FBI in Milwaukee, and you can reach me day or night at 4-1-4-5-5-5-1-2-2-2."

"Are you fucking kidding me?" Scarlet looked at Jimmy and said, "Great, I already have the hitman coming to kill me from New York, and now the FBI picked up the banger down the street talking on the phone in prison. He's hiring someone else from the gang to come and kill me too. Jimmy, this is getting ridiculous.

Maybe they'll all kill each other trying to get at me. What am I going to do?"

"Look, babe, come stay at my place for a while. That will give us some time to think. Maybe they won't be able to find you, and they'll give up and go home."

"I already told you I won't do that. These guys don't give up until you're dead, they'll never stop. Besides, I don't want you caught up in this too and get yourself killed. I need to figure out a way to end this once and for all. They aren't going anywhere; they'll keep looking for me until something breaks, and they find me. Besides, what am I going to do Jimmy quit my job or try to retrain Duke to protect your house? I love my job. I need to figure something else out." *There must be something I can do.*

EIGHTY-THREE

Scarlet tossed and turned most of the night, making sleep a challenge. It was well past three AM when she finally dozed off to sleep. She laid in bed, staring up at the ceiling. Scarlet pondered all the things that have happened to her in her short life. *John killing Greg and Carol, the bomb at the safe house, the sniper at the courthouse, Bob the stalker, the car bomb, the fire, the drug deal and the gangbanger threatening to kill her, Big Tony, the trial, how that dick attorney made her out to be a drunk, and of course the contract Tony put out on her. Now John is out of prison. How did that happen?* How did she make a mess of her life?

Wednesday morning, Jimmy got up first and kissed Scarlet goodbye. He had to take his Grandmother to church.

Scarlet showered, put on jeans and a light blue silk blouse, open-toed flat shoes, and the necklace Jimmy gave her. *It was so beautiful.* She had to wear it because of all the break-ins. Scarlet didn't want anyone stealing it out of the house. She and Duke drove to work and arrived at about eight-thirty.

Jack was already in the parking lot, waiting to see when Scarlet showed up for work.

As Scarlet and Duke made their way into the store entrance, the excitement in Jack stirred. He couldn't believe how easy it was to find her. It had been over two years since he had seen her, and she still looked good. Tall and thin, blonde hair, great body, and a perfect ass. She was hot and sexy then and even better now. Jack waited for about thirty minutes and dialed the number for the store. "Good morning, connect me to the flower shop, please."

"One moment, I'll transfer you."

The phone in the back rang, "hello flower shop; this is Scarlet." There was nothing but silence.

"Hello, can I help you?" *Damn it. They're here.* Scarlet slammed the phone down on the receiver and tried to go back to work, but had a difficult time focusing.

Jimmy called around noon and asked how her day was going. She told him about the phone call earlier this morning. He said, "Stay close to Duke, I doubt they'll mess with you with him by your side."

"Jimmy, you do know they have guns, right?"

"They would have to get pretty close to shoot you, Scarlet. Duke won't let that happen; he would take them out in seconds. Just keep him by your side at all times. I love you, babe."

"Love you too, Jimmy." The line went dead.

EIGHTY-FOUR

The Tucci brothers were eating breakfast at a Bob Evans restaurant just off the Indiana toll road. "Gino, according to Google Maps, it should take us around four hours to drive to this place, Jackson, Wisconsin."

"Yeah, but I want to go see something in downtown South Bend first."

"What now?" Carmine said.

"The last bank Dillinger had a shootout at, is here. It's called the Blackstone Theater Vaudeville House. It still has all the bullet holes and shit in it. I read there are like a hundred marks where they had the shootout. It was 1934, and you'll like this, they killed a cop. You know they got away with $30,000. That was a lot of money in the '30s, especially during the great depression. Come-on that has to be pretty cool to you too, right?"

"Gino, if you don't stop with this shit, I'm going to put some bullet holes in you. Let's get outta here. We gotta job to finish."

Gino won the argument; they drove downtown to what used to be the Merchant Bank and acted like a couple of tourists while they checked out the marks on the old building. They also stopped at the Studebaker Museum for about an hour. Finally, they left South Bend at about eleven-thirty that morning.

At three o'clock that afternoon, Carmine's black Cadillac

Escalade with New York plates pulled into the parking lot at Sendiks. Carmine and Gino Tucci had made good time and driven straight from South Bend and wanted to get a jump on following Scarlet. They waited in the SUV, watching the storefront until 5 PM when she appeared with a dog and walked to her Jeep. She looked just like the picture they had from the trial.

Scarlet pulled out of the parking lot and drove toward the freeway to head south and go home. She continually looked in the rearview mirror but didn't see anyone following her. Until she exited the highway onto a roundabout at the Jackson exit. There it was, a Cadillac Escalade like John's with New York plates, behind her. She knew those plates from living and driving in New York City.

Scarlet slowed down and waited for the Escalade to catch up so she could see the plate number in her rearview mirror. There was a light blue Ford Taurus in front of the Escalade with some guy driving, making it difficult to read the license number. The Cadillac pulled up behind the Taurus, Scarlet took the roundabout and slowed to just under the speed limit the rest of the way home. As usual, she parked in the driveway and had Duke get out first. Scarlet looked down the street and saw the Taurus and the Cadillac drive past. She thought, no doubt, they'll be back.

EIGHTY-FIVE

After work Scarlet drove home and walked to the front door and opened it for Duke, she stood in the alcove and waited. "Duke pass auf." Duke ran around the house and returned and sat next to her. No bark, "Damn it!" Someone was in the house again. First, she dialed 911 and told the operator someone was inside the house and to please send a squad car right away. Then, she said to Duke, "Duke voran!" (search) Suddenly he ran around the corner to the small bathroom on the main floor. A couple of seconds later, she heard Duke barking and a man screaming in Spanish.

When she walked around the corner to the bathroom, Duke had a man pinned against the wall by the window. With a terrified look on his face, he was standing there yelling at Duke in half English and half Spanish. From his gaze, he was obviously with the gangbangers up the street. He was a short Latino man, very muscular, with tattoos all over his arms and neck, he was wearing all black right down to his black tennis shoes.

His right hand was hidden behind his back; Duke had him pushed up against the wall barking at him. The man appeared to be having trouble getting something out of his back pocket. That was when Scarlet saw him draw a gun; Scarlet yelled, "Duke attack!" The dog jumped at the man so quickly it didn't register in the man's mind what was happening.

Duke first bit down on his arm, and the gun fell to the ground, and then he dragged the man down to the bathroom floor and started biting him all over so fast the man couldn't react. Duke kept returning to his wrist and biting at it and growling. The man was screaming bloody murder, trying to pull his arm away and kicking his legs.

There was blood splattered all over the bathroom. On the floor, the toilet, the walls, and even the ceiling. Duke had blood covering his face and teeth. After a few moments, Scarlet told him to Fuss or Heel, and he returned to her side and sat down, panting heavily, and staring at the banger. The banger was lying still like he passed out, probably from all the pain. His wrist was barely hanging on his arm. Duke had chewed it nearly off. The banger opened his left eye, Duke bit the right eye, and blood was pouring from the socket. He looked up while lying on the floor in a pool of his own blood and quietly moaned.

Officer Delgado, with the Jackson police, showed up within ten minutes and called an ambulance. The banger was grotesque; Duke had bitten him hundreds of times all over his upper body and his face, and blood was pouring out of the man. The officer found his gun on the floor by the toilet, which explains the mutilation of his wrist. The officer told Scarlet it was a good thing Duke stopped him, or he might have killed her.

Scarlet walked out on the front lawn with officer Delgado as the Ambulance pulled away. He said he would drive up and down her street several times throughout the night to make sure the bangers didn't send someone else. As he was getting into his car, he turned to Scarlet and said, "watch your ass, Ms. Maxwell, these guys are crazy, and now you nearly killed one of them. They won't quit until they get revenge." *If he only knew.* Scarlet kept her secret from the police, and now regretted not telling the officer what else was happening.

The Jackson police left, and Scarlet cleaned up Duke first by putting him in the shower. Next, she got out a bucket and poured Clorox bleach and hot water into it. With a pair of rubber gloves on, she wiped up all the blood in the bathroom. *It will probably need painting.*

EIGHTY-SIX

After cleaning up the bathroom, Scarlet grabbed her cell phone and placed a call to New York City.

"This is Special Agent Patterson."

"Hi Vincent, this is Scarlet Maxwell again. Do you have a couple of minutes to talk?"

"Yes, of course, Scarlet, what can I do for you?"

"I had an intruder in my house tonight. Duke just about killed a gangbanger that was hiding in the bathroom. They won't give up Vincent. Also, earlier today, I saw a black Escalade with New York plates follow me home from work. Is there any way you can come to Wisconsin and check it out?"

"It would be far more efficient to send Agent Baxter to you. She's right there in Milwaukee. But if you feel you need me, I can catch a flight and be there tomorrow."

"I would appreciate it, Vincent. I think because you know my case and you know Duke and me and my situation with John and all, I would feel a lot better having you around for a day or two."

"Done Scarlet, I'll see you tomorrow. By the way, it sounds like Duke has been remarkably busy lately, huh?"

"Yeah, he has, thank God I have him. Bye, Vincent, see you tomorrow." The line went dead.

Next, she called Jimmy at the restaurant and asked if he would come over now. Jimmy left at once and drove the ten minutes from the restaurant to Scarlet's house.

Outside on the street, a black Escalade with New York plates was parked at the end of the block. The windows had a dark tint on them, so it was impossible to see if anyone was inside. Carmine and Gino saw the police cars pull up in front of Scarlet's house and thought they were there to hassle them. Then suddenly, an ambulance pulled up, and paramedics ran into the house. A few minutes later, the paramedics retrieved their stretcher and ran inside again. They returned with a stretcher to the ambulance and put what looked like a dark-skinned man inside.

"Carmine, what do you think happened?"

"Hard to say, Gino, but it doesn't look good. Maybe the bitch shot some poor sucker that tried to break-in."

Just then, a light blue Taurus drove down Scarlet's street, passing the Escalade and slowly driving past her house. Jack took note of the Escalade with the New York plates. *How did they know I was here?* He thought to himself. *And what the hell happened at Charlotte's house?* She was on the front lawn, talking to a cop. *Does she know I'm in town too?* Jack continued driving up the street and pulled around the corner to park and watch. Now he knew where she lived and where she worked. It was just a matter of time until he can get into her house and take her out. But first, he needed to deal with the Escalade. Who are they, and what are they doing in Wisconsin?

EIGHTY-SEVEN

Scarlet was in the bathroom, wiping down everything again with bleach when Jimmy knocked on the front door. By now, she had Duke pretty much cleaned up but needed to finish cleaning the floors and walls. She went to answer the door and let Jimmy in and explained what happened and how Duke bit the banger hundreds of times. "The asshole didn't have a chance."

Jimmy hugged her tight and kept kissing her on the head. "I'm so glad you're okay and not hurt. Scarlet, I promise you it will all work out. Duke can certainly protect you in the house. I worry about outside the house."

"I know Jimmy, I worry about me too. The banger had a gun, and he was going to kill me."

"Are you okay? Are you sure you don't want to go somewhere? Maybe a hotel for the night. Or back to my place?"

"No, Jimmy, I'm a little shaken up, but I'll be okay." Scarlet went back to the bathroom to finish cleaning up while Jimmy started making some pasta for them to eat for dinner. They sat at the kitchen table and ate the pasta and talked about what her options might be. She explained to Jimmy that she called her FBI handler in New York, and he's coming to Jackson tomorrow. Next, she shared her sighting of the Escalade following her home from work. They finished eating and sat on the couch for a while, watching television, and then went up to bed around eleven.

EIGHTY-EIGHT

Thursday morning, Jimmy got up early and drove home before he turned around and went to work. Scarlet got up, got dressed, and walked out front to see if there was an Escalade parked anywhere on the block. It appeared to be all clear, so she went back inside and fed Duke, showered, and got ready to go to work. She promised Jimmy she would stop running in the mornings for now.

On her drive into West Bend, Scarlet kept her eyes peeled for the Escalade. *So far, so good.* She pulled into the Sendiks parking lot and parked closer to the front door than usual. Duke followed Scarlet in the side door that directly led into the flower shop area behind the coolers.

Scarlet never noticed the blue Taurus parked between two cars out in front of the barbershop. Jack watched Charlotte and her dog walk into the store. He wanted to make sure she was at work so he could drive back to Jackson and check out her house. He was also looking for the Escalade but didn't see it anywhere in the parking lot.

Once he was sure Charlotte was at work, Jack pulled out onto the street and saw the Escalade come around the corner and drive directly into the Sendiks parking lot. Jack thought, *there they are, they must be following her, not me.*

Jack continued to the freeway and drove south to the Jackson exit. He kept looking in his review mirror to see if the

Escalade followed him, but they didn't. Jack pulled up to Scarlet's house, parked on the street a couple of houses away, and walked around the back. The first thing he noticed was the charred garage. Then he turned his attention to the basement windows. Jack wedged a knife into the top to release the locking mechanism. Jack crawled into the basement and stopped to take in where the furnace was located, and all the boxes stacked up, so he could navigate in the dark without making any noise. Next, Jack walked up the stairs noting the squeaks and stopped by a landing next to the back door. From this spot, he was able to look directly into the kitchen and see the living room. Jack walked around the main floor, observing the layout and noises the old floor made as he crossed the room. He wanted to memorize the floor plan, so at night he could move quietly throughout the house without any light.

Jack walked up the stairs, again noting which steps creaked and which did not. He tested the creaking steps and checked edges to make sure they didn't squeak too. At the top of the stairs, he turned a corner and saw there were three doors. Jack walked through the first door; it was Charlotte's bedroom. His excitement rose immediately. He paused to smell the room and stood with his back to the dresser facing the bed for a long time. Jack got excited, visualizing himself screwing and killing Charlotte in the bed. Jack was committing the layout of the room to memory like a professional hitman would do. The first thing he noticed was the king-sized bed placed against the back wall, she likely slept on the left side, like when they were married. He noticed there were nightstands on both sides of the bed and a lamp on each nightstand.

On the nightstand on the left was her sketchbook, and some romance novel Charlotte was probably reading. Her dresser was behind him up against the wall, and there was a door beyond that leading to a bathroom. He also saw there was a dog bed in the corner. Jack made a mental note to bring the dog a piece of meat laced with poison to distract him.

He finished walking around the house and made his way back down to the basement to shut and lock the window. Next, he strode upstairs and left out the back door, having it self-lock as he closed it behind him. Paying attention to the cars parked along Charlotte's street, he got into his rental car and drove back to Sendiks to see if the Escalade was still there.

When Jack pulled into the parking lot, he noticed the Escalade backed into a spot in the last row. Jack selected a spot to park that was down about twenty yards from the Escalade in front of Papa John's and waited.

EIGHTY-NINE

The Gulfstream landed at the West Bend Airport just past noon and pulled up to a hanger. Bob met the aircraft with a dark blue Chrysler 300, all gassed up and ready to go. Special Agent Patterson stepped off the plane and got into the Chrysler 300, and drove off toward West Bend following GPS on his mobile phone. He arrived at the Sendiks parking lot at about 12:30. As soon as Vincent pulled into the parking lot, he spotted the black Escalade with New York plates parked in the last row. Vincent parked his car next to the Escalade, got out, and drew his weapon. He walked around the back of his car, coming up on the driver's side of the Escalade. Vincent used the butt of his gun to knock on the window.

Carmine rolled the window down and said, "Can I help you, um, officer?"

"Yeah, give me your license and registration."

"Who the fuck are you?" Carmine insisted.

Vincent flashed his FBI badge and again demanded, "Give me your license and registration." Looking at Gino, he said, "You too, I want your ID."

Carmine was being obstinate and said, "What's the problem, officer?"

"The problem is you're not giving me your ID. And this is the last time I'll ask nicely. Give me your ID and the registration to the vehicle."

Carmine pulled his wallet out of his pocket and plucked out his New York driver's license. Gino handed his license to Carmine to provide to Agent Patterson. As Carmine leaned over to open the glove box, Vincent moved his finger to the trigger and pointed his gun at Carmine's head and said, "Very slowly pal. If I see a gun in that glove box, I'll shoot you right here and make a mess of the pretty interior and your brother. Before you open it, tell me now, is there a gun in the glove box?"

"No officer, there isn't a gun in the glove box and stop pointing that fucking gun at me for no reason."

Looking down quickly at his driver's license, Vincent said, "Carmine Tucci of Queens New York, I'm fairly sure I have plenty of reason to be pointing a gun at your head. Now give me your registration, very slowly."

Handing the registration to Vincent, Carmine said, "here you go, now go screw yourself."

"Hey, I'm not the one who's going to end up in prison asshole. Sit tight while I run these." Vincent took the two IDs and the registration and returned to his car. All the while keeping his gun in his right hand and ready.

In the car, he pulled out his cell phone and took pictures of all the documents, and then called his office to have a background check run. The background check came back that there were no open warrants, but Carmine and Gino were both people of interest in several homicides in New York, New Jersey, and Philadelphia, but nothing to hold them on. There was no doubt these are the hitmen Big Tony sent to kill Scarlet. Vincent got out of his car and returned to the Escalade. He put his gun back in its holster as he walked up to the driver's side window.

"What are you two doing here in Wisconsin?"

"We're just visiting a friend," Carmine said.

"Who's your friend?"

"Frankie Sabatini is her name, not that it's any business of yours. She lives around here." Vincent committed her name to memory, so he could write it down in his notebook and check on her later.

"Why are you just sitting in this parking lot?"

"We um, we were going inside to get some wine. We're sitting here talking about what else we need to get."

"All right get your wine and get out of here. I don't want to run into you two again. If I do, we're going to have a big problem." Vincent handed Carmine their licenses and the registration.

"Got it, boss. We'll find a liquor store. We're outta here." Carmine rolled up his window and slowly pulled out of the parking lot and headed toward their hotel to regroup. Carmine drove the length of the parking lot and exited out the far end entrance by the Papa John's Pizza. As they were leaving, Gino noticed the same blue Taurus in the parking lot that they were behind the day before when they followed Scarlet home. Gino pulled out his binoculars and looked at the guy sitting in the Taurus.

"Holy crap Carmine, it's John Mancini in that Taurus. No shit, I'd know him anywhere. That's him probably here to take out his old lady, too."

"Are you sure? How the hell did *he* find her?"

"I don't know man, but with the FBI on our ass, this could be great, he'll take her out, and we get credit for it back home."

"Why don't we make a call and collect on Mancini too?" Just then, Carmine pulled his cell phone out of his pocket and called back to New York. He explained what was going on and asked if they took out Mancini after Mancini takes out his old lady can they collect on both?

"Carmine, sit tight, let me reach out to Tony." The line went dead.

Jack watched Agent Patterson harass the guys in the Escalade. When Carmine rolled down his window, Jack recognized him from New York as one of the Tucci brothers. It became apparent they were here for Charlotte. He realized this when they didn't follow him earlier to her house. Now that Agent Patterson is in town, it's going to make this hit a little tricky. He's probably here to protect her from the Tucci's.

Jack had a new plan formulating in his head. He needed to take care of the Tucci's before he takes out Scarlet. He needed the FBI to get out of town. With the Tucci's gone, Patterson will leave and leave Charlotte exposed. This unfortunate turn of events is going to delay the hit a day or two.

Carmine's phone rang, and he answered, "Yeah?"

"Carmine, it's on. If they both end up out of commission, Tony said he'll pay you for both, that's a hundred grand. Just make sure they're both eliminated for good. Don't bring any heat down on the family, though. Got it?"

"Yeah, we got it." The line went dead. Carmine turned to Gino and explained how they're going to get paid a hundred grand for both kills. So, the new plan is to keep watching the old lady and wait for John to kill her, then they move in and kill Mancini. Problem solved.

Vincent called Scarlet from the parking lot and said he was outside. She roused Duke from his daily nap, and they walked out the side door to meet Vincent. As soon as she saw Vincent, she gave him a big hug. Scarlet felt immediate relief from the pressures of the last few days. Vincent explained what just happened in the parking lot and said, "I'm fairly certain they'll leave you alone for a while. Especially because they know, I know who they are, and I'm here watching you."

"Thank you so much, Vincent. I really appreciate it. And thank you for coming."

"Of course, Scarlet. I'm going to check into a hotel tonight, do you want to meet for dinner?"

"Yes, my boyfriend owns a great restaurant just up the freeway, you remember him, don't you? You ran a background check for me. Will you be okay if we meet there at seven?"

Vincent nodded and said, "Seven is perfect."

Scarlet gave Vincent the name and directions to Jimmy's. She then returned to the store to finish the flower arrangement she was working on, for delivery by the end of the week.

Jack closely watched as Charlotte hugged Special Agent Patterson. He wasn't jealous; he was pissed that she was so close to a Fed. He was probably the cop she ran to in New York after he took care of the Fletcher's.

Jack watched as the Fed got into his car and left. He followed Patterson to a Country Inn Hotel on the outskirts of West Bend. To avoid being seen, Jack drove around the back of the hotel. He noticed the same Escalade as before with New York Plates parked in the very last space in the back of the hotel. *Sometimes they make it too easy.* Jack turned around and drove to his own hotel to think through how and when he was going to get rid of the Tucci's first and then sneak into Charlotte's house and kill her.

NINETY

At five-thirty, Scarlet and Duke packed up and headed home. She called Jimmy at the restaurant to let him know Agent Patterson was in town and was going to have dinner with them at the restaurant tonight. She also insisted Jimmy sit with them for dinner. He agreed without an argument. When they arrived home, Scarlet opened the front door and told Duke, "pass auf." The dog quickly ran through the house and returned and barked twice.

"Damn it; someone was in the house again." *Could it be the damn Bangers again, are they sending someone else? It makes no sense, what the hell do they think they're going to do by coming in and snooping around?*

Scarlet walked down to the basement first to see if the window was open. It was not. Then she climbed up the stairs to her bedroom and said, "Duke spur" (track) He sat and turned to stare at her dresser and barked twice. "Really?" she said out loud. And then thought, w*hat is it with guys and underwear? Maybe I should put a big rat trap in my drawer, so when they reach in, it takes off a finger or two.*

She didn't bother reporting it to the Jackson police, or even Vincent. Scarlet walked downstairs and let Duke out in the backyard to do his business. He returned a few minutes later and was fed and received fresh water in his bowl.

Scarlet returned to her bedroom and changed into a floral dress, brushed her hair out, and put on a pair of pumps. Of course, she wore Jimmy's necklace. After getting ready to go to the diner, Scarlet went back downstairs to the basement and made sure all the windows were locked tight. Then she returned to the main floor and checked all the windows there. Everything was locked up. Scarlet walked out to her Jeep to make the short drive over to Jimmy's for dinner. Duke stayed at home to guard the domicile. *I doubt anyone will be breaking in tonight with Duke on guard.*

NINETY-ONE

Hampton Inn West Bend, WI

Jack Mason (Aka John Mancini) walked over to a local BP gas station. He purchased the Milwaukee Journal, the West Bend Daily News, and he picked up a free Penny Saver. Jack searched the ads for someone selling a handgun. He found an Ad for a *Springfield XDM 9M, like new. $700.* He called the person and said he would drive by later tonight to purchase it. Jack wrote the address down and climbed into the Taurus and drove about forty-five minutes south to a city called Waukesha. He pulled into a trailer park and located the address.

Jack knocked on the door of the trailer, and a man answered. Jack said he was interested in the Springfield he had for sale. The man's name was Barry. Barry looked like he was ex-military, or at least an ex-military wanna be. Barry wore Army fatigues, a green muscle shirt, and his butch haircut was styled like the first day of boot camp. Barry invited Jack inside. The place smelled like stale beer and cigarettes. Barry told Jack to have a seat at the table while he retrieved the gun from the safe. Barry used his handprint to open the safe and pulled out the Springfield 9mm. He first dropped the magazine and unloaded the bullet in the chamber. He turned the weapon backward and handed it to Jack by the handle. Jack looked it over carefully. He quickly field-stripped the gun to get a feel for how well Barry took care of the weapon. The smell of gun oil and Hoppes No. 9 cleaning solution filled the air. Jack could tell the gun was recently cleaned. It looked practically new.

"This gun retails for about twelve hundred dollars, why are you selling it for seven hundred?" Jack asked.

"I need the money, man. Do you want it or not? I'll throw in a couple more magazines and a case."

Jack lunged across the table and hit Barry in the face, splitting his nose and knocking him backward. Then he stepped out from his seat and stuck his shoe on Barry's neck and crushed his windpipe. He was dead within a couple of seconds. Jack then wiped down every surface he touched with a towel, and picked up the gun, case, and extra magazines and walked out of the trailer as if nothing had happened. *Damn, that felt good to kill again. I can't believe how much I miss the adrenaline rush. I can't wait to kill that bitch.*

As Jack drove back toward West Bend, he thought to himself, maybe he'd stop at that Italian diner have some of the Osso Bucco again.

Jack exited the highway and drove past Charlotte's house. Her Jeep was gone, but her dog was in the window. He also noticed that the Escalade with New York plates was parked up the street. Jack pulled into Charlotte's neighbor's driveway and turned around. He drove back to the highway and pulled off a couple of exits later.

Across from Charlotte's work was a store called Fleet Farm. Jack parked his car and walked into the Fleet Farm to buy some bullets for the gun. He picked out a fifty-round box of Winchester 9mm hollow-point bullets. Fleet Farm required him to show a driver's license to buy the ammunition. He didn't like that, but he had no choice but to use his fake ID. After paying cash for the bullets, Jack left the store and returned to his car. Next, he drove to the hotel, walked into his room, and proceeded to load fifteen bullets into each of the three magazines. Jack put one magazine in the gun and pulled the slide, so it was ready to fire. He slipped the gun in the small of his back under his belt. Then he took the other two magazines and put them in his sport coat pocket.

Jack had formulated a new plan. Catch the Tucci's off guard in their car or in their room and put one bullet in each of their heads. Then, late the same night, sneak into Charlotte's house, distract the dog with a steak, wake her up with a gun in her face, screw her once more, and then shoot her between the eyes. Once she's dead, drive to the airport the next morning, and fly back to Flag. Then he could get the million dollars sitting in the Caymans and disappear off the grid and start a new life as Keith Banes (his fake ID).

Jack drove from West Bend to Jackson and parked in Jimmy's lot. He made his way in the door and told the hostess he would like to sit at the bar. She said to pick a spot at the end of the bar by the bubbler, and she'll bring him a menu.

"The bubbler?" Jack asked.

"You're not from Wisconsin, are you? The Bubbler is the drinking fountain by the restrooms."

"Why is it called a bubbler?"

"Kohler is headquartered in Wisconsin, and they named it the bubbler a long time ago. I guess it stuck. In any case, please take a seat at the end of the bar by the restrooms."

Jack chose the last seat at the end of the bar near the bubbler. That way, he could look out the windows in several directions in case the Tucci's decided to eat there too. There wasn't anyone sitting right next to him, but others were sitting at the bar eating too. Jack ordered a tomato salad, calamari, and the baked mostaccioli with Bolognese sauce. When he finished eating, he paid his bill with cash, left a good tip and walked back to his car. Jack drove back to his hotel, laid on his bed, and thought some more about how he was going to kill Charlotte.

While lying on the bed, his mind wandered back to the day he married Charlotte. He asked Charlotte to marry him and told her he wanted to get married in San Diego near Coronado Island. Killing Charlotte now, after what she did to him, will rank right up there with one of the greatest kill shots of his career. He was hired by a Los Angeles crime boss to take out his competition in San Diego. The plan was to shoot the guy at his daughter's soccer game. The crime boss insisted the hit be in public view to embarrass his family and send a chilling message to the number two guy. Jack set-up on a grassy knoll with his Barrett M82 sniper rifle and laid in wait for hours. The mark showed up but never left his car. Jack only had a few hours before the wedding, so he quickly relocated to a spot where he could see the man sitting in the back seat watching the soccer match through the window.

Jack smiled to himself when he could vividly see the man's head literally explode from about seven hundred yards. The problem, however, was his bodyguards spotted Jack and ran after him. He had to leave his $9,000 rifle and run for his life. He lost them after about thirty minutes and then made his way to the wedding just in time. His suit was crumpled, and he was sweating profusely. Charlotte never suspected a thing. Fletcher, however, knew exactly what was going on.

NINETY-TWO

When Scarlet pulled into Jimmy's parking lot, Vincent was parking his car. She waved him over, and they walked into the restaurant together. Jimmy met them immediately at the door and led them toward a table in the back. On the way to the table, they stopped to say hello to Rachel and Mike Stanley. Scarlet thanked Rachel again for the lovely party a few weeks ago and introduced Vincent as an old friend. Scarlet introduced Rachel as the Honorable Judge Rachel Stanley. Vincent asked what court she ruled in? Rachel said she was a "Federal Judge for the seventh circuit, eastern district." They chatted for a few more minutes, and then Jimmy led them directly to their table.

Jimmy had a couple of bottles of his favorite red wine brought over to the table immediately. The bottles were opened and decanted so they could breathe. They talked about the Tucci brothers and how Vincent disposed of them today. The banger is going to the hospital for an extended stay, and John, aka Jack getting out of prison. Scarlet asked where they relocated John, and Vincent told her northern Arizona. That was all she could get out of him. Vincent also felt the Tucci's weren't going to be too much trouble anymore since he took copies of their driver's licenses and car registration. Vincent said, "The Federal Government had been trying to pin something on these two brothers for years. I don't see them sticking around too much longer."

When the subject of the bangers came up, Vincent had a

different take. He said, "they have a deep and broad organization. They'll keep sending people after you, even when you send one of them to prison, or I guess in your case, Scarlet, the hospital. I looked into this gang, and it's well known they mostly reside in the northern suburbs of Chicago. They use the house in Chicago as a sort of headquarters to feed violence in Wisconsin and Illinois." He paused and then said, "Scarlet, why don't you buy a handgun and take lessons on how to use it? It's pretty easy to get a conceal and carry license in Wisconsin."

"I don't think I could shoot someone, and I'm pretty sure I couldn't kill a person," Scarlet said.

Vincent countered with, "You may have to accept the fact that it's a real possibility, Scarlet. Especially with Duke around. He's trained to kill, and there may be a time when he will have to do that to protect you. It sounds like he nearly killed the banger when he broke into the house."

Jimmy weighed in with, "Look, honey, having a gun in the house is just another insurance policy. These bangers only understand violence."

"I think the guy that Duke mutilated will never forget. That was as violent as it gets. Pretty gruesome too!"

"Scar, we spend most nights together, I'll make sure I have my gun on me from now on. I usually keep it here, and then on me when I take money to the bank."

Scarlet longingly looked at Jimmy and said, "My hero."

"Funny babe. But this is serious."

They proceeded to order the ricotta and roasted tomato

bruschetta with pancetta as an appetizer to share, pan-fried scamorza with arugula salad, and two pesto's. Jimmy had the waitress bring an array of antipasto trays, including fresh olives, cheese, and imported salami. Vincent and Jimmy ordered the Osso Bucco and Scarlet the garlic penne pasta. As the meal arrived at the table, they devoured the food. With everything going on, Scarlet hadn't eaten much lately. She said she was famished.

"Jimmy, the food here is delicious. I feel like I'm back in New York in Little Italy," complimented Vincent.

"Thank you. I pride myself on the fact that we make just about everything from scratch. We make the pasta ourselves, and I make the sauces every day fresh. The tomatoes are fresh, the bread comes from an Italian bakery in Chicago, and all the meats are fresh. I don't freeze anything. The butter is the absolute best too. It's creamy, salty, and sweet, all at once. The best restaurants in the world have the best butter. I insist that the butter is made every day and is the best you'll ever taste."

"Well, I have to tell you; I would put this meal up against anything I've eaten in New York City."

Finally, at the end of the meal, dessert and coffee were served. Everyone ordered a slice of homemade cheesecake. Afterward, Jimmy brought over a bottle of Anisette and poured small shot glasses for everyone. Vincent said he was going to stick around another day and keep an eye on the parking lot at Sendiks to make sure the Tucci's are gone for good. He would swing by Scarlet's house on Saturday and make sure everything was okay before he boarded the plane back to New York.

They all said their goodbyes, and Scarlet gave Vincent a giant hug and thanked him over and over for making the trip to Wisconsin and shooing the Tucci brothers away.

Vincent walked to his car and drove back to the Country Inn hotel in West Bend.

Scarlet climbed into her Jeep, and Jimmy followed her home. She parked in the driveway and Jimmy on the street. They walked inside together, and let Duke out to do his duty, gave him a treat for watching the house, and then walked upstairs and crawled into bed.

NINETY-THREE

At breakfast, Carmine told Gino they should find new wheels. Gino said he saw a park and ride up the highway a few miles. They should steal a car until this thing is over in case the fed keeps looking for them. Friday morning, the Tucci's drove south on the 41/45 highway to the park and ride and stole a Ford Explorer.

"Gino, we can't let that Fed see us again. He knew us from the plates on the Escalade."

"Yeah, we can't let Mancini see us either. He's staking out that bitches house and work, so if we steal something with Wisconsin plates, they won't be able to track us."

"Yeah, good point. Look, Gino, keep your sunglasses on, and keep your head on a swivel."

They drove the Explorer back to the Sendik's parking lot and parked down by the Papa John's. They decided to leave the Escalade at the park and ride, so it appeared they left town. Carmine pulled in-between two other SUV's and kept moving the car once an hour. They knew if they stayed on Charlotte, Mancini wouldn't be far behind in his blue Taurus.

NINETY-FOUR

Scarlet woke up early and snuck out of bed before Jimmy realized it. She left a note in lipstick on the mirror in the bathroom that she and Duke were going running. With the Tucci's gone and the banger in the hospital, Scarlet felt it was safe to resume her running routine. She dressed quickly in her running clothes and tiptoed down the stairs and out the back door. The plan was a three to four-mile run this morning. She wanted to run off some of that rich food she ate last night. Scarlet was stretching in the driveway and noticed a shadow of a man sitting in light blue Ford up the street. Bangers? She started walking toward the vehicle with Duke, whoever it was started the engine, backed into a driveway, and turned the other direction away from her, and sped off. Scarlet kept repeating the license number to herself out loud so she could memorize it.

Scarlet ran about 4-miles and returned home to find Jimmy making coffee and bagels in the kitchen.

"You know it's probably dangerous for you to be running out there."

"Well, like you said, as long as Duke is with me, I should be okay. Besides, the banger's in the hospital, the hit guys from New York, are running scared. I thought it was probably okay to run this morning. Besides, I really needed to run off some of the rich food you fed be last night. You don't want me to get fat, do you?"

"I'm not worried about you getting fat. Speaking of food, are you hungry?"

"No, but I saw a car parked up the street watching the house. We walked toward it, and they took off. I got the plate number memorized." She wrote the license plate number down and planned to give it to Vincent later that day. She kissed Jimmy, put some food in Duke's bowl, refreshed his water, and then went upstairs to brush the garlic taste from the night before out of her mouth. When Scarlet finished showering, there wasn't a sound in the house. It was quiet as a church mouse. Jimmy had left, and Duke was lying in the living room looking out the window. Scarlet put on jeans, a light pink sweater, tennis shoes, and she put her hair up in a ponytail. She put Jimmy's necklace on for safekeeping.

They climbed into the Jeep and drove to work, once again parking closer to the front of the store. As they walked through the parking lot, Scarlet kept looking for cars with New York plates, a blue Ford, or Vincent. None of the above were present, so she continued into the side door by the flower shop.

Scarlet spent the morning finishing up the flowers for a wedding that was happening that evening. The bridal consultant said she would pick up the order at one o'clock sharp. At noon Vincent came inside the store and said he didn't see the Tucci's in the parking lot. Scarlet told him about the light blue Ford at the end of the block and gave him the paper with the license plate number. He said he would run it and see what comes back. Since everything seemed to quiet down, Vincent decided to head back to New York in a few hours. He wanted to hang out here for a little while longer. Scarlet told him again how much she appreciated him coming to Jackson. Vincent thanked her for the great meal.

At six, she packed up and drove back to Jackson. Vincent was already on his way back to New York. She stopped by the restaurant to drop off a key to the house. Jimmy had a party at the restaurant tonight, that wasn't supposed to end until at least midnight. Then she drove up and down her street twice before pulling into the driveway. Scarlet didn't see anyone sitting in a car on the block. They walked in the side door, "Duke pass auf." He returned with one bark. She called Mallory to see if she wanted to have dinner, but she was busy with Adam's family.

"It's just you and me tonight, Duke." Scarlet poured some food in his bowl and then proceeded to make herself a salad. She opened a new bottle of wine and sat on the couch and watched old reruns of the TV show Friends. About ten that night, Scarlet texted Jimmy that she *missed him, loved him, and was going to bed. She would see him later.* Jimmy must have been busy because he didn't respond right away. Scarlet climbed the stairs with Duke, brushed her teeth, put on a sexy nightgown, and crawled into bed.

Just past midnight, her cell phone on the nightstand lit up and began to buzz. Her first thought was it's probably a text from Jimmy, but she was too tired to look. Scarlet rolled over and went back to sleep.

It was a text from Special Agent Vincent Patterson. *"Scarlet, we suspect John rented the blue Ford. A fake ID from Arizona and a stolen credit card were both used at the car rental counter. Be careful! He may be in town looking for you too. V"*

NINETY-FIVE

Jack saw the Tucci's Escalade parked in the lot at the Country Inn Hotel when he followed Agent Patterson the day before. He decided to drive over to the hotel and take care of part one of his plan. As Jack drove around the hotel, he didn't see the Escalade anywhere. *Hmm, maybe they checked out after the fed harassed them.* Jack looked up the phone number for the hotel on his smartphone. He dialed the number and asked the front desk to ring Gino's room. When the front desk clerk rang the room, Jack hung up his phone. He now knew they were just out.

Jack backed the Taurus into a space between large vans. Making it difficult to see from the side. He waited for about an hour and a half, and the Tucci's finally showed up in a Ford Explorer. *They must have stolen it.* They walked into the hotel lobby and down the first hallway to the right. He saw the lights come on in a room, and then the light in the room next door also came on. Jack counted the number of rooms, and it was eight from the lobby. He drove around the back of the building and entered the hotel through a door that was left ajar. Jack walked to the lobby and counted eight rooms down the hall where he saw the lights come on. Jack looked both ways down the hall before drawing his gun. He then put his finger over the peephole and knocked on the door. Carmine answered.

"What the fuck are you doing here?"

Jack pointed the gun at Carmine's face and pushed him

back into the room and said, "Shut up and get inside."

Carmine backed up and raised his hands. "John, I got no beef with you. We're here to take out your ex-wife. We got orders from Big Tony himself. You know how much he hates that bitch. That's it."

"I don't give a crap. Knowing you, Carmine, you probably told Tony you saw me, and you were waiting for me to kill Charlotte so you could kill me and collect on both of us."

"No man, it ain't that way. We were going to hit her tomorrow morning. That's it, and then we were headed back to New York, I got reservations at Angelo's on Sunday night. You remember Angelo's, the best Veal Parm in the city. Besides, John, nobody knows where you are or where you been. I told you we got no beef with you."

Jack told Carmine to turn around and face the bed. He picked up a pillow from the bed and stuck the gun in it. "Well, Carmine, you won't be making that reservation Sunday night." Jack pulled the trigger twice. Carmine fell forward on the bed. Blood came pouring out of his back and began to soak the mattress. Jack used hollow-point bullets, so, the shell exploded inside of Carmine's body, hollow points shouldn't go through the body like a regular bullet. He was dead by the time he hit the bed.

One thing Jack knows about an assassin is when hired to do a job; there are specific tools of the trade you always bring along. Carmine is a professional, so Jack expected to find a silencer in Carmine's baggage. Jack searched Carmine's luggage and found his Beretta M9A3, suppressor, and ammunition packed away in a hidden compartment. He put the silencer and ammunition in his coat pocket and the gun in his waistband. The downside to Carmine's choice was the suppressor is an Aurora II. Meaning it won't work with hollow-point bullets. On the upside, it was small and noticeably light. Jack took one more look at Carmine's body on the bed, turned, and walked out the door.

Jack walked to the room next door, covered the peephole, and knocked lightly. When Gino answered the door, Jack, pointed the gun at his face and told him to get inside. Gino complied and then raised his hands above his head. Jack told him to turn around and face the bed.

"John, what are you doing here? You know your old lady lives right up the street?"

"Yeah, Gino, I know Charlotte lives here. Once I'm through disposing of you two idiots, I'm going after her."

"John, I can help you. I know where she lives and where she works. I even know the guy she's sleeping with. Look, man; I'll kill him for you. We can do this together."

"Thanks, Gino, I got all that already covered." Right then, Jack grabbed the pillow off the bed to muffle the sound of his gun. He shot Gino two times in the chest. Gino fell backward and died immediately. Jack put his gun inside his belt in the back underneath his sport coat and walked out of Gino's room, never looking back.

It was after eight o'clock at night, and Jack wanted to get this over with so he could get back to Arizona and start a new life. He stopped at the Piggly Wiggly in West Bend, to buy a steak and some rat poison. He used his knife to slit the steak in the middle and poured the poison inside. Then he re-wrapped the steak in the butcher paper it came in.

Jack drove directly to Scarlet's street and parked a block away from her house. He sat in the car and observed all the things going on in the neighborhood. He saw what looked like a Latino gang doing a drug deal. Kids were riding their bikes and skateboards up and down the street and playing in their yards. Then, at about ten o'clock, the kids all went inside. A police cruiser drove up the street, and the gangbangers all disappeared. Scarlet's street became eerily quiet.

The lights in Scarlet's living room dimmed, and the light in her bedroom came on. He waited a few more hours until just before midnight and climbed out of the car. Jack walked up the street to Scarlet's house and into the backyard. He located the window that he had broken into earlier in the week. Jack removed the screen and used his knife to unlock the window again. Then he crawled inside with the steak in hand. It was total darkness in the basement. Jack memorized the number of steps to the bottom of the stairs. Scarlet must have moved a box because Jack tripped on something as he began to walk to the bottom of the stairs. A moment later, the basement light came on. Jack stepped behind the furnace to hide.

NINETY-SIX

Jimmy left the restaurant just before midnight and drove directly to Scarlet's house. He parked his Range Rover on the street in front of the house and walked to the front door. He used the key Scarlet dropped off earlier to get inside.

Duke heard Jimmy come through the front door. He got up and looked out the window and recognized Jimmy's SUV, so he went and laid back down. It took a long time for Duke to get used to Jimmy and the odd hours he would come and go. Eventually, he became comfortable with the affection he showed Scarlet, and the attention he paid to Duke.

Jimmy walked through the living room and into the kitchen. Because he spent the entire night working at the party, he never had an opportunity to eat dinner. Jimmy put the pasta he brought with him into the microwave for a couple of minutes and then sat at the kitchen table to eat. Before he had a chance to take his first bite, he heard a noise in the basement.

Jimmy pushed back from the table and got up slowly. He quietly walked to the landing at the top of the basement stairs and listened for any sound. He stood quietly for a moment but didn't hear anything. He turned the light on and slowly walked down the stairs. When Jimmy reached the bottom step, he looked around the basement and didn't see anyone. He did, however, notice the window was open again. Jimmy walked toward the window to close it, and before he got there, out of the corner of his eye, he saw the gun pointing at him. Jimmy turned, and before he could say anything or react, he felt a burning sensation in his chest. His legs suddenly gave out, and he dropped to the cold concrete floor.

Jack stepped over Jimmy's body, unwrapped the steak, and tossed the butcher paper on the floor. He slowly walked over to the stairs that led up to the kitchen. Jimmy had turned on all the lights, making it much easier to move through the house. When Jack reached the top of the stairs, he stopped to listen for the dog. He didn't hear any sound at all. Jack walked over to the pasta and took a bite. *Shame I had to kill him, that's a damn good meat sauce.*

Duke heard the very distinct sound of a silencer. He rose and walked quickly and quietly to the hallway. He stood outside of Scarlet's room as if he were guarding the door. Duke patiently stood, staring at the top of the stairs.

With the steak in his hand, Jack slowly walked up the stairs, remembering which steps creaked and which didn't. He took the steps very slowly, sometimes walking on the edge, or just skipping steps altogether. Jack walked up the stairs in almost total silence. When he reached the top, he turned the corner and took a couple of steps into the hallway when he came face to face with Duke.

There was just enough light in the hall from the reflection of light coming from downstairs, and a nightlight to see Duke's eyes and his teeth. The only sound you could hear was the guttural noise of Duke growling. Jack threw the steak down in front of him and raised his hands. He whispered, "take the steak boy." Duke didn't move; he just continued to stare and growl.

Jack heard Scarlet's phone buzz, and she stirred some. He didn't move; he stood there staring at the dog with both hands raised in the air. Duke then barked twice and continued to growl, never taking his eyes off Jack.

Scarlet heard Duke bark and jumped out of bed. She quickly turned on the light and peeked around the doorway before stepping into the hall. Astonished at first, she saw John, with his hands in the air and Duke staring and growling at him.

"Get the dog out of my way, or I'll shoot him," Duke growled louder.

"Don't do it, John! He's a trained guard dog, he'll chew off your hand before you get your gun out of your pants."

"Call him off, Charlotte. I'm not kidding. I'll kill him, and then I'll shoot you in the head."

"John, what are you doing here? *I already knew the answer to that question.*

"You ratted me out to the FBI. I spent two years in prison, you bitch. Why did you screw me over, why didn't you just talk to me? We had a good life."

"Are you kidding me? I saw you kill our friends in cold blood." *You're a heartless bastard.*

"Oh, screw you, Charlotte. Fletcher was a rat; he was skimming off Tony. The piece of shit got what he deserved; the world's a better place without him. Why do you care anyway?"

"They were our friends John. Why did you kill Carol in cold blood? I saw you shoot them with no remorse. You just walked in and killed our friends. Didn't it bother you that you killed people we had dinner with, and went to their house for parties?"

"First of all, Carol married the wrong guy and was just in the wrong place at the wrong time. And no, it doesn't bother me. I was paid to remove the scum from the earth. I make the world a better place to live in."

"You're a sick bastard, John!"

"Look, Charlotte, where did you think all the money came from? Did you really believe I made enough money in the computer business to afford our lifestyle? Do you have any clue what it costs to live in New York City?"

"How would I know how much money you made? You managed all the finances. Also, it was never about money. I loved you. Who are you anyway?"

"The same guy you married and screwed over. You were clueless back when we were together, and you're clueless now. You think you're safe here, hiding in plain sight, you know the Tucci's were here to kill you, and I took care of them because I didn't want anyone else to have the pleasure of killing you. I wanted to do it myself."

"John, I'm telling you, don't pull a gun near Duke, he'll attack you." Duke began to growl louder; sensing Scarlet was afraid.

"You know Charlotte, you still look good in that sexy nightgown. I'd still do you."

"Fuck you, John. You weren't that good in bed when I was

married to you."

At that moment, John reached behind his back for his gun. Scarlet yelled again, "Don't do it!" As soon as he brought his arm around where Duke could see the gun in his hand, the dog leaped four feet right on top of John and bit down on his wrist. John dropped the gun, and Duke continued to bite at his wrist and arm. John was yelling and screaming to get Duke off him.

. "Duke, hier." Duke let go of his wrist and walked over by Scarlet and stood. He didn't sit; he was still on guard showing his teeth and growling. Blood was dripping from Duke's mouth. John's wrist was a bloody mess. He was holding onto his wrist as the blood squirted between his fingers. Duke must have severed something. John's gun was lying on the ground next to him. "I told you not to pull a gun on him. He's trained to kill," Scarlet said.

John started to get up and reach for his gun while yelling, "I'm going to fucking kill you, Charlotte! You're dead, you hear me, you're dead just like that boyfriend downstairs! I shot that asshole, and now I'm going to shoot you and that dog! You're dead, you bitch!"

Rage bubbled up in Scarlet's gut. Something snapped inside of her. Her anger rose to a point she couldn't control any longer. Mallory once said, when your shit can's full, your shit can's full, and that was it, her shit can was full, Scarlet heard enough. She looked down at the bloody dog and calmly said, "Duke, kill!"

Duke jumped on John so fast he didn't even realize what

Scarlet's Secret 353

was happening. The dog leaped in the air, landing on John, and taking him to the ground. Duke went right for the throat and bit down so hard blood was squirting all over. A large piece of john's throat was now missing. Within seconds John was dead. Duke then stepped off to the side and stood over him like a prizefighter in a knockout fight panting.

Scarlet quickly ran back into the bedroom, put on a pair of jeans, and threw on a sweatshirt. Looking down at her phone, she saw the message from Vincent. Scarlet ran downstairs and didn't see Jimmy but saw the food on the table and quickly realized the light was on by the basement stairs. She ran down the stairs two at a time and found Jimmy lying on the floor in a pool of his own blood. She could see his chest struggling to rise and fall. She said out loud, "Thank God, you're alive. Jimmy, I'm calling for help now. You're going to be okay, keep breathing baby." His breathing was strained but steady. Scarlet dialed 911 and pled with the operator to send an ambulance. "Someone's been shot, and my dog killed an intruder."

Within minutes, the police arrived. Scarlet ran up to the front door and let them in. They called the dispatcher and made sure the ambulance was on its way. Moments later, the EMT's showed up and started working on Jimmy. They stabilized him and took him to the hospital. The bullet went through him, so there was blood dripping from two holes in his body — one in front and one in back where it exited. The police wouldn't let Scarlet go to the hospital with Jimmy, because of the dead body on the second floor.

Scarlet used her cell phone and called Vincent and

explained what happened. She shared what John told her about the Tucci's and then explained what Duke had done. Then she told him how Jimmy was shot by John when he broke into the basement. Vincent asked if he could speak with the police officer. They talked for a few moments, and the police officer told her she could leave and go to the Emergency Room. He said they would return tomorrow to take her statement. "Agent Patterson will take care of everything else."

Scarlet quickly put Duke in the shower and cleaned him up before taking him to the Jeep and driving to the hospital. She stayed in the waiting room until Mallory and Adam arrived about a half-hour later.

NINETY-SEVEN

Jimmy was in surgery for about an hour and a half.

Fortunately, the bullet only nicked his lung and went through Jimmy's body and didn't cause any significant damage. He'll be in a sling for a couple of weeks while he heals. Scarlet could see him when he finally made it to the recovery room. Jimmy will have to stay for a day or two in the hospital for observation and make sure there isn't any infection. Then he'll be released to recover at home.

Mallory and Adam followed Scarlet back to the house. When they arrived, there was a white panel van parked outside in front. It said, "Crime Scene Clean-up" on the side. She pulled into the driveway, and a man on the porch approached her car. Before she let Duke out of the car, she immediately said, "Can I help you? How did you get in my house? What are you doing here?"

He handed her a card, and the key, and said, "Agent Baxter with the FBI provided us with keys to enter and said to come here and clean the site right away. Ma'am, you can't even tell anything happened in that hallway upstairs or the basement. We took care of everything."

"Really? Thank you." They dragged all their equipment out of the house, packed it in their van, and drove off.

Mallory and Adam only stayed a few minutes because Scarlet wanted to get back to the hospital. She fed Duke, refreshed his water, and then went upstairs to shower and brush her teeth. By the time she arrived back at the hospital, Jimmy's Grandmother and an entourage of other friends and relatives were in the room visiting. Jimmy was sitting up, eating Jello, and loving all the attention.

Scarlet left the hospital after visiting hours ended at ten. She drove home and went right up to bed. It had been a very long couple of days. It was Midnight when Duke went to the window and barked. Scarlet rose from her bed and looked out to see a dozen police cars, vans, and a SWAT truck in front of the house. There were agents with vests and jackets that said DEA, ATF, POLICE, and FBI. They had automatic weapons drawn and pointed toward the house the bangers were using for drug deals. Scarlet watched as the agents ran in and out of the house. After about 30 minutes, officers were leading the bangers to the van in cuffs. They all had their heads down, and many of them were in their underwear. Some girls too, they came out with blankets covering their naked bodies. There must have been thirty agents involved in the raid.

NINETY-EIGHT

While all the chaos was going on, and the bangers were being perp-walked to the van, two agents approached Scarlet's house. A few moments later, the doorbell rang. She and Duke walked downstairs and opened the door.

"Hi, Scarlet?"

"Yes, hi, how do you know who I am?"

"I'm Special Agent Kate Baxter from the Milwaukee office of the FBI." She displayed her credentials. "We talked on the phone a couple of times. Let me introduce Fiona Johnston with the ATF." She nodded. "Special Agent Patterson requested that I come by and inform you that while we're raiding this drug house, another team is raiding a house in Chicago that is connected to these drug dealers. We're seizing both houses and all their cars and property. He wanted you to know along with the help of her Honor, Rachel Stanley; we were able to acquire warrants for these raids. These guys won't be out of prison for a long time. Her honor had assured us they will be held without bail. So, Agent Patterson wanted you to know you're now safe from the bangers down the street. They shouldn't be bothering you any longer."

"Thank you, that's amazing. Do you know how long this had been in the works?"

"I'm sorry ma'am, I'm not privy to all the details, Agent Patterson coordinated this operation from New York with the judge, local police Chicago PD, ATF, and the DEA. I'm here strictly to supervise the operation from the FBI perspective. I can tell you we found narcotics, explosives, illegal guns, and a pile of money in there. I don't see any way they see the light of day for a long time."

"Please let Vincent know how much I appreciate his effort too."

"I will ma'am, and I understand your New York problem took care of itself, and your ex-husband has been taken care of as well. Agent Patterson asked that I check in on you from time to time if that would be okay with you?"

"Yes, of course, and thank you. I look forward to getting to know you, and thanks for the clean-up crew, Agent Baxter."

"No problem, ma'am, and please call me Kate. That was Agent Patterson too, I just made the phone call and provided the keys. Have a good night, ma'am." They turned and walked away back toward the crack house.

As soon as Agent Baxter got out of site, Scarlet's phone buzzed again, and this time it was Vincent calling. "Hello Vincent, you are amazing. Thank you, thank you so much."

"It's my pleasure, Scarlet. I wanted you to know we confirmed the Tucci Brothers were killed last night too. We assume John did it since he told you he did. They were professionally hit in their hotel rooms in West Bend."

"Vincent, how did you pull off this raid?"

"Well, after I met Rachel at Jimmy's restaurant the other night, I went to see her the next morning. I told her about you being one of our witnesses from the Gambucci trial. Because it was such a high-profile federal case, and she is a Federal Judge, we can share that information. I told her what I was trying to do, and all about the operation, and asked if she would be willing to issue the arrest warrants and search warrants. She agreed and told me to make sure it was designated a federal operation. In other words, she wanted me to charge them all with federal crimes so she could ensure they appear in her courtroom, and they never get bail. She promised me they will also do every day of a maximum sentence for illegal drugs, weapons, and explosives. Also, since you were a witness in a federal RICO trial, we're charging them with witness tampering for harassing you."

"That's amazing. I'll be sure to thank Rachel the next time I see her. Since she now knows my secret."

"You should Scarlet because we could never have pulled this off so quickly without her. She also ordered Big Tony into solitary confinement. I can promise you this, he won't be ordering any more hits for a while. Rachel is very fond of you. And, she considers Jimmy, a dear friend. I just thought you should know that."

"Vincent, I'm so grateful to you and Rachel, and of course, Michelle. Do you think I'm safe now? Can I stay?"

"We believe so Scarlet, but just in case I'm going to have Agent Baxter check in on you from time to time."

"I appreciate that, and thank you for the crime scene, clean-up crew."

"Of course, and Scarlet, Michelle says she's enormously proud of you and Duke. I spoke with her a few minutes ago. She's still undercover for at least another few months."

"If you talk to her again, tell her we miss her. And thank you again."

"Bye, Scarlet." The line went dead.

NINETY-NINE

The next day Jimmy was released from the hospital into Scarlet's care. The back of her Jeep quickly filled up with plants, flowers, and stuffed animals. It was clear Jimmy knew a lot of people around town. When they arrived at her house, Duke greeted them with a wagging tail and a big smile. At least it looked like a smile.

Scarlet told Jimmy about how Vincent reached out to Rachel and was able to get warrants to raid the banger's house. He said they wouldn't get bail, and all their property had been seized. So, she should be safe from the gangbangers. They talked about John and how Duke killed him. Scarlet said, "it was seconds; it really was scary fast." Finally, she shared the story of how John killed the Tucci brothers, and Big Tony went into solitary confinement compliments of her honor, Rachel Stanley.

"I'm quite sure I'm safe from the mob, the bangers, and my ex-husband. So, now what are we going to do for fun?"

Jimmy said, "I have an idea."

ONE HUNDRED

Three months later, Paola Italy

They arrived at the Lamezia Terme, Calabria's airport early Monday morning. It was a long flight for Jimmy, Noni, and Scarlet. They did fly first class on the long legs of the trip. They flew from Milwaukee to New York to Rome and finally Rome to Calabria. A car service picked them up at the airport drove the hour it takes to get to Noni's sister's home. The roads were narrow, the mountains were beautiful, and the sea was incredibly blue, it was stunning.

They pulled up to a set of iron gates, and Pasqua, Noni's sister, greeted them. Pasqua's home is a villa on the hillside overlooking the west coast of Calabria. There were several olive and fruit trees; As Jimmy said, Scarlet couldn't believe it. Jimmy told her the villa was made of stone from the old buildings of Calabria. A large patio led to the main entrance to the villa. The main floor was made up of a living room, separate dining and kitchen area, and a large bathroom. There were beautiful stone steps that led to the second floor. Upstairs there were two large bedrooms and two additional smaller guest bedrooms who share the fourth bathroom. The large terrace faces the sea from the master bedroom. The views are mainly mountain with sea views only from the terrace.

When they arrived, they were greeted by a spread of cheeses, bread, olives, and meats laid out on the dining room table. Of course, there was plenty of wine as well — m*y kind of people.* They sat around the table, eating, and drinking and talking about life in Italy.

Jimmy was so excited to show Scarlet everything in Paola. He wanted to go to the Fontana dei Sette Canali, Piazza del Popolo, and the Santuario di San Francesco. They spent the first three days in Paola, and then they took the train up to Rome.

In Rome, Jimmy booked a room at a hotel called Palazzo Naiadi. It was in the center of the city. They were able to walk to the Colosseum, the Pantheon, Trevi Fountain, and Via Veneto. The ceilings were high; the décor was perfect; the hotel itself was both art and history coming together. An amazing place and Jimmy knew everything about it.

Jimmy spoke beautiful Italian, so getting around was not an issue. On the third day in Rome, Scarlet started to get that uneasy feeling like someone was following her again. She mentioned it to Jimmy, but he dismissed it. He kept saying, "nobody knows we're here, and nobody knows who you are. They keep looking at you because you're so beautiful. That's how it is in Italy. Italians love beautiful women." It didn't stop her from thinking she was being watched.

Scarlet kept looking around everywhere they went, but there were so many people it was too hard to tell if they were being followed.

To add insult to injury, Scarlet felt so naked without Duke next to her. On Saturday afternoon, they took the train back to Paola. They arrived at nine PM, and Scarlet was tired and decided to turn in early.

Scarlet woke up and looked at the clock on the nightstand. It was two AM, and Jimmy didn't stir at all. The surroundings were unfamiliar, and Scarlet had to shake off the sleep. She rolled over and quietly climbed out of bed. Scarlet's mouth was parched, and she decided to go downstairs to the kitchen for a glass of water. Scarlet slipped on a robe and walked down the stone stairs toward the kitchen. As she approached, she could see the lights were on, and people were talking. Scarlet recognized Pasqua and Noni's voices, they were speaking in Italian. A third voice, however, a man's voice, she didn't recognize. Scarlet didn't speak Italian, so she had no idea what they were saying until she heard the one word she did understand. Scarlet froze, a chill ran down her spine, and she began to shake all over. That word was "Gambucci."

The End

Acknowledgments

Michelle, for always being there when I need you. Your input was invaluable. Your insights, suggestions, and help with story development made this book a reality. There is no way I could have finished this book without you. I love you.

Jonathan Nick, thanks for taking the time to read the book, and giving me feedback. You have no idea how much I appreciate it.

Jessica Nick, thank you for your edits and for providing insight into Scarlet and her friends from a millennial point of view.

Jennifer Clement, what can I say? But thank you, thank you, thank you. Your ideas, inputs, and insights were invaluable to me. Your editing was the difference between a good book and a great book. Your story suggestions were invaluable. Thank you!

Jack Chillemi, your incredible knowledge of writing and story development was much appreciated.

Kurt Koenig, thank you for taking the time to edit and help me once again. You're the best!

Drew Wright, you were one of the first to offer advice and encouragement. Thank you for that. It takes an Army.

Doug Dare, thanks for reading and commenting. It was much appreciated.

Nancy Yach, your early insights, and story edits were very helpful in getting to where we ended up. Thanks for taking the time.

ALSO, BY MICHAEL NICK

The Key to the C-Suite
Adapt or Fail
ROI Selling
Why Johnny Can't Sell

If you have any comments, please email me at michaelnick34@gmail.com. I will respond to all inquiries.

Coming in 2021 Part II

Scarlet meets Ernesto Gambucci, Big Tony's Father, in Italy, and he puts demands on her to call off the hit on her life. Once she returns to America, the Sinaloa Cartel didn't like the outcome when Vincent shut them down. Scarlet is kidnapped and taken to Mexico. She is up for sale to a Saudi Prince. Read what happens next with Michelle, Vincent, Jimmy, Scarlet, and of course, Duke.

Printed in Great Britain
by Amazon